"You offered for me so I would not be forced to marry Lord Denbigh?"

"Yes." Brandt's expression was watchful and she had no idea what he was thinking.

"I still do not understand why. You cannot possibly want to marry me! Is it because of last night? I told you that did not matter."

"No, it is not because of last night."

"But why? I still do not understand why. I don't even think you like me! And I am an heiress! You do not want an heiress!"

A slight smile touched his mouth. "I've no intention of touching a penny of your money. And you are quite wrong about the other," he said softly.

A feeling of pure panic washed over Chloe. She had no idea why, but the thought of having him want to marry her scared her. He was not at all the sort of man she wanted. Nor did she want him to...like her. Not like that.

D0608948

Ann Elizabeth Cree is married and lives in Boise, Idaho, with her family. She has worked as a nutritionist and an accountant. Her favourite form of daydreaming has always been weaving romantic stories in her head. With the encouragement of a friend, she started putting those stories on to paper. In addition to writing and caring for two lively boys, two cats and two dogs, she enjoys gardening, playing the piano and, of course, reading.

The Viscount's Bride features characters you will have met in *The Duke's Mistress*.

Recent titles by the same author:

THE MARRIAGE TRUCE
MY LADY'S PRISONER
THE DUKE'S MISTRESS

THE VISCOUNT'S BRIDE

Ann Elizabeth Cree

First published in Great Britain 2003
Harlequin Mills & Boon Limited,
Eton House, 18-24 Paradise Road, Richmond, Surrey TW9 1SR

© Annemarie Hasnain 2003

ISBN 0 263 83948 6

Set in Times Roman 10½ on 12 pt.
04-0204-83583

Printed and bound in Spain
by Litografía Rosés S.A., Barcelona

THE VISCOUNT'S BRIDE

Chapter One

Chloe glanced at the clock on the mantelpiece and jumped up from the chair. She should have met the others in the drawing room five minutes ago. Her attention had strayed from the article concerning the scarcity of grain in Europe to an article about Madame de Staël's death and she had found it so interesting she forgot to watch the clock.

'Does Justin know you hide away in his study to read his journals?'

She whirled around, heat rising to her cheeks. Brandt, Viscount Salcombe, stood in the doorway of the study, an amused smile at his mouth. She stifled a groan. Of all the people to find her, why must it be him? 'I am not hiding away. I had something I...I needed to read.'

'From the *Gentleman's Magazine*? Could it not wait until after the assembly or did you hope to bring up one of the topics during the evening?'

Since that was exactly what she intended, her flush only increased. 'How ridiculous!' Why must he always plague her? And make her feel so young and silly? 'Is it not time to leave for the assembly?' she asked pointedly.

'Yes, which is why Belle sent me to find you. It was

fortunate Mrs Keith noticed you were here as Belle failed to inform me that you might be in the study reading Justin's journals.'

'There is no need to mention that.' What if Belle or worse, her husband, the Duke of Westmore, questioned why she had developed such an interest in agriculture?

'Very well, I will keep your secret on one condition.'

'What is that?' she asked cautiously.

'That you agree to stand up with me tonight.'

Stand up with him? 'I…'

His mouth curved. 'Or I will mention to my cousin or Belle your interest in farming.'

He would probably do so just to annoy her. 'Very well,' she said ungraciously.

'Then I suggest you put it back in its place. Unless you plan to bring it with you.'

'You may tell Belle that I will join you in the drawing room very shortly.' She was behaving childishly, not at all as a proper young lady should towards someone she disliked, but she did not seem to be able to treat him with the cool politeness she desired. That he seemed to find her a source of amusement only irked her more.

She set the journal on the pile of magazines on the desk. She prayed Brandt would keep his word and say nothing. What if Belle or Justin should guess that she intended to marry Sir Preston? They would need to know some time, but she preferred that to be after Sir Preston had…

'By now, Belle will undoubtedly think I've abducted you.'

She marched to the door and cast him a cold look as she passed him into the hall. Her mood was not improved as she climbed into the carriage and seated herself next to Belle, only to find Brandt seated next to Justin and across from her. Her time at Falconcliff visiting Belle, who was now the Duchess of Westmore, had been marred by this man's arrival yesterday.

The month and a half she had been in Devon had been idyllic. For the first time in ages, she had felt a sense of freedom; her guardian, Arthur, the Earl of Ralston, and his plans to marry her to the highest bidder far away. She had been recovering from a severe bout of influenza when she first arrived but the sea air and her increasingly longer walks had helped recover her strength. As had her happiness at being with Belle, Belle's husband, Justin, and baby Julian, now nearly six months old. Their neighbours had welcomed her. And she had decided to fall in love with Sir Preston Kentworth, whom she was certain was beginning to return her regard.

Everything was perfect. Until yesterday.

She cast a dark look at Brandt as he talked easily with Justin and Belle. He was Justin's cousin and certainly there was a resemblance. Both were tall, broad-shouldered, dark-haired men possessing an arrogant confidence. Justin, with his cool reserve, was considered the more handsome, but she knew from the London gossip that many women considered Brandt, with his disarming charm, equally attractive. His father's scandalous death two years ago only added to his desirability. His lack of wealth did not seem to deter them one whit as there were rumours he was well on his way to recovering the fortune his father had lost.

He would undoubtedly charm all of the ladies in the neighbourhood just as he had charmed the London women during the Season. She only hoped he would not leave a trail of broken hearts behind him since he was unlikely to stay in a village as slow as Weyham for very long. At least she was immune to him. She supposed he was handsome, but she did not like overly handsome men. And he was too tall as well. She preferred men who did not hover over her, making her feel helpless as if they might overpower her. Another point in Sir Preston's favour, for she could actually have a conversation with him without straining her neck.

Chloe glanced out of the carraige window and saw they had arrived at the assembly rooms. An assortment of carriages already stood outside the square building.

The rooms had been built half a century ago when Weyham had been a modestly popular seaside resort. Only a few visitors frequented its pleasant beaches now, but the weekly assemblies continued to be popular, often attracting guests from the neighbouring towns.

Inside the small entry hall, Belle allowed the men to go on ahead. She halted and turned to Chloe. 'I know you do not particularly like Brandt,' she said in a low voice, 'but please try not to allow your feelings to show so clearly on your face.'

'I am sorry. It was just that he always teases me so. Was it really so obvious?'

Belle smiled rather ruefully. 'Yes, I fear so. At one point you were fixing him with a most fierce look.'

'Oh, dear.' She knew Belle's fondness for the cousin Justin considered a brother. 'I promise I will try to be very civil. I am to stand up with him tonight.' She hoped that would make Belle feel better.

'I will not ask how that came about.'

She should probably not mention blackmail. She gave Belle a vague smile. 'I suppose we should join the others. But do not worry.'

'I know you have a kind heart, but I hope you will consider extending it to Brandt. He is really not so terrible. And he will not be leaving very soon.'

How disappointing. 'I will.' She followed Belle in, intending to put Brandt completely from her mind. They were joined by Mrs Heyburn, the local squire's wife. Chloe only half-listened to the conversation as she looked around the room, hoping to find Sir Preston. She finally spotted him standing with a group of men in one corner.

She excused herself from Belle and Mrs Heyburn and started across the room, then hesitated as the men burst into loud laughter, most probably over one of the Squire's boisterous hunting jokes. It was one thing to approach Sir Preston when he was alone, but quite another when he was with friends. It was just that he needed rather a lot of encouragement. He was shy about dancing and did not seem comfortable asking anyone to stand up with him.

Before she decided what to do, Lydia Sutton bounded up to her. 'Chloe! Why did you not tell me Lord Salcombe was coming!'

'I did not know until last night, when he arrived unexpectedly,' Chloe said without much enthusiasm. The last thing she wanted to do was discuss him.

'He is so dashing. And a rake, is he not? My friend, Harriet—she is Lady Harriet Pumphries, the Marquis of Lawton's daughter—wrote he was nearly called out by Lord Bixby for trifling with his wife.'

'It was only a rumour as Lord Bixby does not seem to care who flirts with his wife. If anything, Lady Bixby was flirting with him. Or attempting to,' she said, distracted by the sight of Sir Preston leaving the ballroom. She hoped he was not going to the card room.

'Chloe! How could you say such a thing!'

Lydia's squeal of enjoyable horror brought Chloe back to the conversation. 'I should not have repeated such gossip. I pray you will not say a thing to anyone.'

'Of course I will not.' Lydia fanned herself as she looked about the room. 'Do you know if he plans to dance at all?'

'I really cannot say. He did not dance very often in London.' Or engage in any of the scandalous behaviours his reputation warranted. Instead, he had been rather aloof, which only added to his overall attraction.

'I hope he will.' Lydia's attention had strayed again. 'I see Mrs Clifton is wearing her new London gown. How I wish I could persuade Mama to take us to town for some new gowns. But she says there is nothing in London that we cannot procure from Madame Dupré. And there is Emily. Really! One would think she would realise how atrocious lemon is for her complexion. But then she never knows how to go on.'

Chloe glanced in Emily Coltrane's direction. She stood in one corner of the room, her broad face wearing its habitual scowl as if she wished to warn everyone away. Lydia was right, her yellow gown only emphasized her sallow skin and mousy hair. Despite Emily's evident and puzzling dislike for her, Chloe could not help but feel sorry for her.

Lydia shut her fan. 'Lord Salcombe is dancing with Lady Haversham. He dances very well, does he not?'

Chloe glanced in his direction just as he held out his hand to Marguerite, Lady Haversham, who was the wife of their nearby neighbour. She smiled at something he said and Chloe looked away. She really must escape from Lydia, not only to find Sir Preston, but because she did not want to spend the evening discussing Brandt. 'I suppose so. Lydia—' she began, but before she could say more Gilbert Rushton sauntered up.

He grinned. 'Good evening, Lady Chloe, Lydia. I saw you over here looking out at the crowd and then chatting madly and wondered who was the subject of such animated speculation.'

'We were merely commenting on how well Lord Salcombe dances,' Lydia said.

Mr Rushton glanced at the dancers. 'He does indeed. Certainly Weyham is much enlivened by his presence. Should I add to the speculations concerning Lord Salcombe?'

'I must…' Chloe began. She was beginning to think she would never escape.

'I never pay the least attention to gossip,' Lydia said primly.

'But this concerns all of us.' Mr Rushton paused for effect. 'There are rumours he is Waverly's mysterious benefactor.'

'How splendid!' Lydia said.

Chloe's stomach lurched, all thoughts of Sir Preston gone. 'That is impossible!'

He cocked an eyebrow. 'Why?'

'Because…' Because she could not fathom where he would find the funds. But more than that, he was the last person she wanted in the old stone house she had fallen in love with the first time she saw it. As forlorn as it was, with its overgrown gardens and crumbling stone walls, the house still maintained an air of solid dignity. Its old neglected chapel with a tiny walled garden was the most romantic thing imaginable, along with rumours of secret passages that led from the house to the chapel and even to the sea below. She had been delighted when, shortly after her arrival in Devon, workmen began repairs to the roof and walls. The identity of the buyer remained unknown, although conjecture as to whom he might be ran rampant in the village. 'It is not the sort of house he would like at all. I am certain you are wrong.'

'You appear quite adamant that he should not live there.'

'I am certain it is not that! Chloe just does not want to know that we have guessed. But do not worry, we will not say a thing!' Lydia beamed at her.

'I do not know anything at all.' What if Lydia decided to repeat the rumours and mentioned Chloe? 'I really must find Belle.'

'But you are coming to my house tomorrow, are you not? Remember, we are to practise the dances for the Haversham ball. Sir Preston will be there and Tom and Emily Coltrane as well as Mr Rushton,' Lydia added, looking hard at Mr Rushton.

'I fully intend to be there. But for now I must keep my appointment at the card tables,' Mr Rushton said. He executed a neat bow and sauntered off.

'So, you will be there, will you not, Chloe? Do you not recall that you promised to show Sir Preston the waltz?'

'Oh, yes.' How could she possibly forget when she spent as much time as possible reading about farming so that she might impress Sir Preston with her newly acquired knowledge? In fact, she planned to take the opportunity tomorrow to discuss a new breed of sheep she had read about. 'I must go.' She started to edge away.

'Do you think Lord Salcombe would come?'

'Lord Salcombe?' She stopped and stared at Lydia. 'Most certainly not. I am sure he would find such entertainments too dull.'

'But he might not. We could ask him. Or perhaps you could ask him since you are related and you must know him very well.'

'I really do not know him well at all. And we are only related through marriage and hardly even that.' For Belle was only her sister-in-law through her first marriage to Chloe's half-brother, Lucien, although she thought of Belle as her sister.

'But will you ask him?'

'Perhaps,' Chloe said vaguely. The image of him among the young people of the neighbourhood practising dances boggled her mind. And most certainly she did not want him watching her with his sardonic gleam while she attempted to discuss sheep with Sir Preston. 'I really must go.'

She was thankful that, at that moment, Henry Ashton appeared to solicit Lydia's hand for the next dance. After promising she would most certainly be in the Sutton drawing room tomorrow, Chloe finally made her escape.

Sir Preston still had not reappeared. He was probably in the card room. She had just reached the edge of the assembly room when she heard her name. She turned and found Lady Kentworth, Sir Preston's mother, at her side. Her heavy face creased in a smile. 'My dear Lady Chloe! How delightful it is to see you. How charming you look? Is that a new gown? You had it made up in London, I have no doubt. There is nothing quite as stylish here in Weyham.'

'Yes, it is from London.' She managed a smile. Lady Kentworth's effusiveness always overwhelmed her. Although she was all that was friendly, something about her small eyes and thin mouth made Chloe cautious. But perhaps it was only a natural desire on her part to avoid offending a potential mother-in-law.

'Have you seen my son? I believe he is in the card room. I do hope he can be persuaded to dance at least one of the dances. Perhaps with you, since you and he have become such particular friends.' She did not give Chloe a chance to reply and chatted on for a few more minutes in her loud voice before finally declaring that she thought she might play a hand of cards. Somehow, Chloe found herself entering the card room with Lady Kentworth, who insisted she must greet Sir Preston. Chloe wanted to cringe. She only hoped Lady Kentworth would say nothing about a dance.

The card room was small and stuffy, the tables crowded together, and her embarrassment increased as Lady Kentworth marched her across the room. Several people glanced up as they passed, including Lady Haversham, whose look of sympathy rendered Chloe even more mortified. Then she wanted to run when they stopped by Sir Preston's table. Two other men sat with him. And one of them was Brandt.

But it was too late. Lady Kentworth was already speaking. 'Ah, Preston, here is Lady Chloe.'

The men looked up. Heat stained her cheeks when Brandt's gaze fell on her. 'Lady Chloe. Have you come to join us? Or did you wish to remind me of our dance?'

The dance? She had completely forgotten about it. 'I merely came to…to watch the games. I must be going.'

'Perhaps Lady Chloe might like to play a hand. Sir Preston has been instructing her, you know,' Lady Kentworth announced.

'No, I really must go.'

Sir Preston turned around to look at her. His pleasant, square face lit with a smile. He stood. 'No need to hurry off. Be glad to have you play a hand. Blanton, here, has to do his duty on the dance floor.'

Blanton rose and bowed in her direction. 'My wife won't give me a moment of peace until I do the pretty with her.' He pulled the chair out. 'The chair is now yours.'

He walked off. Chloe restrained herself from following. 'I do not think…'

Mr Rushton smiled at her. 'No need to be shy, Lady Chloe. Kentworth claims you are a most promising pupil.'

'Most certainly is,' Sir Preston said kindly. 'Promise we won't ride roughshod over you.'

'But…'

'See, you have no need to worry,' Lady Kentworth said. 'Sit down, Lady Chloe.' She gestured to the chair, her tone brooking no argument. Chloe sat in the vacated seat to Brandt's right. Lady Kentworth beamed. 'Very good. I see Sylvie Compton in the corner. I promised I would play a game with her.' She bustled away.

Chloe hardly knew where to look. 'I really do not wish to play.'

'Afraid you'll be badly trounced?' Brandt inquired with a wicked gleam.

'Of course not,' she snapped and then remembered she was supposed to be a novice. 'That is, I expect to be badly trounced.' That did not sound any better and the open amusement in his face only flustered her more.

'Whist, then. Salcombe can partner you,' Mr Rushton offered. 'Even up the odds.'

Brandt? She glanced at him. He returned her regard, his expression bland. 'Lady Chloe would undoubtedly prefer someone else.'

He didn't need to make it so obvious he didn't want her. She lifted her chin. 'I rather thought Sir Preston could be my partner.'

Sir Preston looked startled. 'Er, honoured, of course, but may not be the best partner. Salcombe is more skilled.'

Now, she understood. They thought she played so poorly that she would need Brandt to make up for her skills. 'I am certain we will do fine.'

She would have to be completely blind not to miss the look that passed between the three men. 'Er, no doubt,' Sir Preston said.

But they could hardly be blamed. Until a month ago,

she had rarely played card games except with her most intimate friends. And even then, she refused to play for stakes. She had not intended to play in Devon at all, but at an assembly a month ago, Sir Preston had noticed her watching one of the games. Assuming her reluctance to play was due to her lack of ability, he offered to instruct her. He had been so kind she could not refuse, nor had she the heart to correct his impression. It was then, as she watched his blunt, kindly face while he explained the rules of commerce, she decided he was exactly the sort of husband she wanted. After that, as he continued to instruct her, his pleasure in her progress had only increased her conviction he was the man she wanted to marry. However, her happiness was marred by knowing she was deceiving him. Worse, she found feigning ignorance increasingly difficult and keeping the competitiveness she so hated in herself at bay.

'Then that is settled.' Brandt picked up the deck. 'Whist? Or do you wish something else?'

'Whist, if you please.'

He shoved the cards towards Sir Preston. 'Since Sir Preston is seated to my left, he will shuffle the cards and then you will cut them,' he told her.

She bit back the urge to tell him she knew that perfectly well. She cut the cards and then Brandt dealt the hand and turned up the trump. The game began.

It did not take more than a few plays to realise the three men were indulging her, Brandt most of all. When he did not play a card she suspected he had in his hand and let her win a trick, she suddenly was tired of her pretence. On her next play, she won the trick. As she did the next one, Rushton started and glanced at Brandt, his brow raised. And when she took the next trick as well, she could almost feel the atmosphere change. The single-minded concentration she had not felt for an age took over and she forgot everything but wanting to win. She would prove to Brandt she was not the silly chit he thought her.

They played three rounds and, in the end, she and Sir Preston triumphed. She looked at Brandt, taking no pains to hide the elation she felt. 'We have five points.'

There was silence. She realised the three men were staring at her. 'Indeed you do,' Brandt finally said. She could not read his expression at all.

'Good God!' Rushton exclaimed. 'Appears your lessons paid off after all, Kentworth.'

'Brilliant!' Marguerite exclaimed from behind her. 'No one ever beats Brandt at whist. Or most other games for that matter.' Startled, Chloe saw Marguerite and several others had gathered around them. She wanted to sink in her chair, but she forced herself to look at Sir Preston who appeared stunned.

'Splendid, Lady Chloe,' Sir Preston said. 'Never thought…well, had no idea last time we played.'

'Must have you give me a few pointers, Kentworth,' Squire Heyburn boomed. 'Another round, Salcombe? A match between you and Lady Chloe. I, for one, will place my money on Lady Chloe. What else have you been teaching her, Kentworth? Piquet?'

'I do not think…' Chloe began.

'Come, Lady Chloe,' Mr Rushton said. 'Just one more hand. Such skill should not be allowed to languish.'

'Although I always find there is a great deal of luck in cards. And some are much more lucky,' Emily Coltrane said with the cool, disapproving stare she always bestowed on Chloe.

Everyone turned to look at Emily whose neck coloured to a dull red. Her brother, Thomas, gave a disgusted snort. 'Hold your tongue, Em.'

'Ah, but it depends on whether you know how to take advantage of the opportunity presented to you,' Brandt drawled.

'Most certainly Lady Chloe does,' the Squire boomed. 'Come, now, one more game.'

Come, Chloe, just one more game. Suddenly, she was back in the dark, dank study at Braddon Hall, her half-brother, Lucien, smiling at her in his charming way, his voice cajoling, as he urged her to play another hand against one of his half-drunk friends. Refusal was impossible, for then the dazzling smile would disappear from his face, replaced by a cold sneer that frightened her. And so she would play again and again until he sent her back to her bedchamber where she would tumble into bed, only to fall into a sleep filled with nightmarish images.

'Chloe?' Marguerite's worried voice jerked her out of her trance. Chloe rose, her sense of victory completely vanished. She wanted only to escape. 'I would rather not. At least not now. I am certain Emily is quite right. It was only luck.'

'There is one way to find out,' Mr Rushton said. 'Be glad to partner you this time.'

'No, I cannot!'

Everyone stared at her, the astonishment on their faces at her outburst making her feel even more wretched.

Brandt stood. 'Another time, perhaps. Lady Chloe has promised me a dance.' He turned to her. 'I will escort you back to the ballroom.' He held out his arm.

She took it, hardly knowing what she was doing. Marguerite smiled, although her face still held concern. 'A splendid idea. I've no doubt Chloe would much rather dance than spend the evening in a stuffy card room.'

'Of course, of course,' Squire Heyburn said. 'Can play again some other time.'

Chloe nodded and managed a smile. Brandt led her to the ballroom where a country dance was in progress. He released her arm and looked down at her.

'Where did you learn to play cards like that?'

She started. 'Sir Preston taught me.' Even to her own ears, she sounded as if she were lying.

'Apparently his skills as an instructor far exceed his skills as a player. I've never seen anyone make such progress in so short a time.'

'I was merely lucky tonight.'

'Of course.'

She suspected he did not believe her at all. 'I…I have no doubt if I play again I will lose quite badly.'

'You underestimate your ability. You are uncommonly talented.'

'If I am, then it is a talent I would prefer not to have!' she burst out, then wished she had bitten her tongue at his startled expression.

'It is nothing to be ashamed of,' he finally said. 'I doubt you are planning to exploit your talents at the gaming tables.'

Her head spun for a moment and she felt almost sick. 'No,' she said faintly.

He stared at her. 'I did not mean to overset you.'

'I…I am not overset.'

'You look as if you are about to swoon.'

'I am not.'

'You are. Forget the dance. You need to sit down.' Before she could protest, he tucked her arm more firmly through his and guided her through the chaperons clustered along the edge of the room and to a small anteroom off the ballroom. Two very elderly ladies, one of whom appeared to be napping, occupied the two chairs near the mantelpiece, but several vacant chairs lined the adjacent wall. He led her to one of them. 'Sit down. I will send Belle to you and then fetch you a lemonade.'

She looked up at his rather grim face. 'There is nothing wrong. I…I suddenly felt very warm.'

'Then there is even more reason for you to sit. And if I discover you have moved, I will have no compunction in carrying you to a chair.'

She gasped. 'I beg…' But he had already stridden off.

Belle appeared a few minutes later, her face worried. 'Chloe, what is wrong? Brandt said you almost swooned in the ballroom.'

'I really did not. He is exaggerating.'

Belle took the chair next to her, her concerned gaze going over Chloe's face. 'What happened?' she asked gently.

'Noth…' she began and then stopped. 'Oh, Belle, I did the most dreadful thing. I played a game of whist with Sir Preston and Mr Rushton and Brandt. Sir Preston was my partner and…and we won.'

Belle was silent a moment. 'That does not sound so dreadful.'

'It was because I have been pretending I knew nothing about cards and Sir Preston has been instructing me and I never meant anyone to find out. I had not meant to play but Sir Preston invited me and Lady Kentworth insisted that I should so I finally agreed. I could see that Brandt…that is, all of them felt very sorry for me and intended to give me a few hands, which made me angry. Instead of pretending, I…I wanted to prove to them I was not as stupid as they thought after all. And then I was very sorry I had done so. Everyone was astounded and wanted me to play again and I wanted only to escape.'

She took a breath. 'After we were back in the ballroom, Brandt asked where I had learned to play cards like that and I told him that Sir Preston had taught me and I could see he did not believe me. He said I was talented and I told him I did not want such a talent and he said that he doubted I would use it at the gaming tables.' She fixed her eyes on Belle's face. 'And tonight, I felt such a desire to win. Just as I did before. I never wanted to feel that way again. Or have everyone stare at me with such astonished expressions and then wager on whether I could win another game.'

'But it wasn't like before,' Belle said gently. 'Lucien was not there to coerce you into one more game and use you for his own means. You were not surrounded by drunken rakes, but by friends who only wished you well.'

'They would not wish me so well if they knew how I have deceived them. And how wicked I have been.'

'Chloe.' Belle took her hand. 'You were never wicked. You were very young, only thirteen, hardly more than a child. It was Lucien who was wicked—using you in such a way, taking advantage of your innocence.'

'But I felt what I was doing was wrong—I should have told Papa,' she whispered. Oh, how many times had she thought or said that? Lucien had been forbidden to come to the house, but he came none the less when Papa was away on one of his frequent journeys. Mama could not bear to turn him away and if Chloe whispered a word, Papa would be furious with Mama. So she had said nothing. Mama, often in bed with one of her headaches, had never guessed that Chloe was downstairs with Lucien and his friends.

'But Lucien convinced you he would make it much worse for you if you did. And for Maria. How could you fight against that?' Belle squeezed Chloe's hand and then looked up. 'Brandt is coming with your lemonade. You must put it aside—it is all in the past. Lucien is gone and he cannot hurt you or any of us now.'

'Yes.' Except she very much feared that, after tonight, she would not be able to put her past behind her as she had worked so hard to achieve.

Chapter Two

Brandt stood near the breakfast room window holding his newest cousin in his arms. 'Tree,' he said, pointing to an example on the other side of the glass. He had no idea what sort of conversation one made with a five-month old human, although the young Marquis of Wroth did not seem at all dismayed by his efforts. He made a gurgling sound and Brandt looked down to find the child's solemn unwavering gaze on his face. Was he about to cry? Brandt cleared his throat. 'I fear your mama has left you in very inexperienced hands. She should be back shortly. I hope.'

The small mouth suddenly moved. Brandt braced himself for a scream. To his astonishment, he realised his tiny cousin was actually smiling at him. He found his own mouth tentatively curving in response as he stared down at the babe. He gently touched the soft cheek and young Julian gurgled again. A small finger came up to grasp his. Unexpected warmth flowed through Brandt and he suddenly knew exactly why his cousin was so thoroughly in his son's thrall. Certainly he had seen Julian before at his christening when he had been the child's godfather, but he had resisted doing more than briefly hold the babe, fearing he would harm such a small and helpless life. Somehow his cousin's happiness had made him feel left out, but now he was beginning to regret he had stayed away so long.

He heard footsteps. He lifted his head. Expecting Belle, he was startled to see Chloe instead. She looked equally taken aback. Her gaze fell to Julian and her eyes widened in astonishment.

'The Duchess decided I should play nursemaid while she went to confer with Mrs Keith.'

'I see.' Her expression was controlled as it always was around him. She wore a gown of creamy muslin tied with a green sash. Her dark auburn hair was tamed into a knot at the back of her head, but a few tendrils framed her face. She looked fresh and pretty. And completely untouchable. He had no idea why a girl whose smile could hold so much warmth managed, at the same time, to neatly keep any potential suitors at bay. That she disliked him he was well aware of, and, to some extent, he could not blame her, but that she would spurn the advances of other eligible young men puzzled him.

As did her behaviour last night at the card table. Any fool could see she was no novice. Then why go through the pretence of having Kentworth instruct her? Even more puzzling was how horrified she had looked right after she had won, and even more so after he had taken her from the card room. She had appeared much better after he returned with the lemonade, and Belle had said nothing more than that Chloe had become overheated and that, after her illness, she was still inclined to fatigue. Nothing had been said about cards, so perhaps her reaction had been only in his imagination after all.

Julian struggled in his arms. He looked down and saw the babe was reaching towards Chloe. 'I think he wants you.' He cast a doubtful look at her gown. 'If you want him.'

'Of course.' She stepped closer to him, held out her arms and took the infant. The babe snuggled against her and then turned his head to look back at Brandt. He offered Brandt another tentative smile. Chloe glanced down at the child, her expression softening, and then back up at Brandt. 'He likes you.'

'I would hope so since we are related.'

'I doubt that is the only reason.'

'And what other reason might there be?'

'I…' She looked flustered. 'You are…are kind.'

'Ah. A compliment from your lips. I shall treasure it.'

Colour flooded her cheeks. 'There is no need to be so sardonic.' Her face closed again and she looked quickly down at the child.

He bit back a curse. He had no idea why he was so boorish around her. 'I beg your pardon.' He picked up the silver pot from the table. 'Will you take tea or coffee? Or chocolate.'

'I always take tea.' She looked flustered again. 'You do not need to pour me anything.'

'But you are occupied, so it is the least I can do.' He poured the tea into one of the china cups. 'Sit down. How much sugar?'

Still looking taken aback, she sat in the nearest chair. Julian promptly picked up a spoon. 'Two, if you please.' She watched Brandt spoon the sugar into the cup. Almost as soon as he set the tea in front of her Julian reached for it. Chloe pulled the child back just before he grasped his object. The spoon fell from his hand and he started to cry.

Brandt stared at him, completely at sea. 'Should I find Belle?'

'No. Pick up the spoon.' She stood and started to gently bounce the child, speaking to him in soft tones.

Brandt retrieved the spoon from under the chair. He held

it out to Julian, who had stopped crying. Instead of taking
the spoon, he sniffed and held out his arms to Brandt.

'He wants you again,' Chloe said.

'I've no idea why. He would do much better to stay
with you. What if he starts to cry again?'

Julian wriggled and reached towards Brandt. He made
a little sound of protest. Chloe smiled at the child and then
looked back at Brandt. 'He will probably start to ˙cry if
you do not take him. Here…' she held Julian out '…you
were doing very well when I came in.'

Once again he found himself holding a chubby, pink-
cheeked bundle who fixed him with a dazzling smile. It
occurred to Brandt that he could not recall the last time
someone had smiled at him with such pure, joyous pleasure at merely being in his presence. He smiled back at
the babe with the oddest sensation he would never be the
same again.

'See, there was nothing to be afraid of.'

He looked up at Chloe and found her watching him.
Even more amazing, she actually smiled at him. For the
second time in the space of a minute, he nearly reeled.
'No. He is…is charming.' That seemed completely inad-
equate.

'He is.' She was still smiling, the warm smile he'd only
seen once or twice, the smile that lit up her face and rendered her incredibly lovely.

He felt as if he'd been punched in the stomach. Her
smile faded as she took in his expression. Julian started to
wriggle and make happy, impatient noises. When Brandt
tore his gaze from Chloe he saw why. Justin and Belle had
just entered the room.

The Duke of Westmore stopped. 'You look amazingly
domestic. I feared I might find you cowering in the corner
when Belle told me she had left Julian with you.'

'Fortunately Chloe came shortly after Belle departed and rescued me.'

'He really did not need to be rescued,' Chloe said.

He glanced at her, surprised at her defence of him, but her expression had reverted back to the same guarded one she always wore.

Julian squealed again and held his arms out towards his father. Justin's dark face broke into a smile as he took his son. He planted a brief kiss on the child's head and then looked at his wife. She met his eyes, a little smile on her face. For a moment, the three of them existed in a timeless bond that excluded the rest of the world.

Longing shot through Brandt, swift and hard. He forced his eyes away only to meet Chloe's. Their gazes locked and for an instant he saw the same yearning reflected in her face and he knew she read his mind as clearly as he read hers. She quickly looked away.

He pulled his gaze away as well, disconcerted by the connection between them. He wanted to escape. 'Now that you no longer need my services as nursemaid, I will take my leave. Carlton has the final papers ready for me to sign.'

'Then it is not yet too late for you to change your mind,' Justin said.

'I've no intention of doing so at this point.' He grinned at Belle. 'I fear you will find me underfoot more often than you might want.'

She smiled back at him. 'I doubt that. I am only a little angry you have not been to visit more often. I feared Julian would consider you a stranger.'

He glanced down at the child who had so suddenly stolen his heart. 'You no longer need to fear that,' he said softly.

He took his leave, only nodding to Chloe. For once he

felt no desire to tease her. In fact, avoiding her as much as possible seemed the best tactic.

He was nearly at the solicitor's office before he recalled that while he had been procuring a lemonade for Chloe last night, he had been approached by Miss Sutton. She had invited him to attend an afternoon of dancing lessons at her house. She hoped he might consider it even if Chloe had expressed the opinion that he would find it dull, which had been enough to secure his immediate acceptance. Particularly when he had heard Chloe would attend. He had looked forward to proving that he was not nearly the jaded sophisticate she seemed to see him as. Now, the prospect had lost some of its appeal.

This morning had merely been an aberration. Undoubtedly, she would be back to regarding him with the same disapproval as always and he would treat her in the same teasing fashion as if nothing had happened.

In the future, he would avoid any situations in which he found himself alone with her with only a baby as a chaperon.

Chloe sat back down at the breakfast table, her thoughts in turmoil. Whatever had happened? For a moment, when her gaze locked with Brandt's, she had known exactly what he was thinking, but more than that, exactly what he was feeling; she had glimpsed a vulnerable side to him that rendered him completely human. But she had already been thrown off when he had reluctantly taken Julian, the arrogant, cool peer suddenly stripped away by the mere thought of holding a baby. When his face had softened as he looked down at the child and then looked up at her and pronounced him charming, her antagonism had melted away.

'Chloe?'

She realised she had been staring at her toast. 'I…I fear I was wool-gathering.'

'I can see that. Are you still worried about last night? Or did Brandt say something to distress you?'

'He said nothing. He was worried about holding Julian.'

Belle smiled. 'Men do that. I have never seen Brandt look quite so dismayed as when I told him to hold Julian while I spoke to Mrs Keith. He tried to protest, but I told him it was time he became better acquainted with his god-son. I imagine he was overjoyed when you arrived, although I was quite surprised to find him still holding Julian. I would have thought he would wish to hand him over to you straight away.'

'He did, but Julian made it very clear he wanted Brandt again. I told him if he did not take him, Julian would cry.'

Belle laughed. 'Very good.' She poured herself another cup of coffee and eyed Chloe. 'It does not sound as if you were at daggers drawn then.'

'For once we were not.'

'Good. I rather hope you might become friends of a sort.'

'I doubt that. We do not rub along well together.'

'Are you certain? I rather think it is mostly on your side. I still have no idea why you hold him in such dislike.'

'He is too arrogant, I suppose. He is just the sort of man I do not like very well.' Chloe looked down at her teacup.

'That is unfortunate, for I rather think he likes you,' Belle said gently.

Chloe's head jerked up. 'I doubt that. He teases me mercilessly and seems to delight in annoying me as much as possible.'

'I rather expect he does so to get your attention. Otherwise you tend to snub him.'

Heat stained Chloe's cheeks. She could not deny the accusation as much as she wanted to. It was not in her nature to deliberately hurt someone, but she had excused her rudeness to Brandt because she doubted he had any feelings to hurt. 'I suppose I still cannot forgive him for how he treated you in the beginning. To think that you could possibly be involved in Lucien's plot to destroy Justin.' She would never forget how cold he was to Belle, the first time Chloe had met him at a musicale. She had detested him on the spot for that alone.

'But that's in the past. And certainly you disliked Justin equally, but you do not seem to bear any ill will towards him now. If anything, he set out to hurt me whereas Brandt was merely attempting to protect his cousin. Just as you were attempting to protect me.'

'I know.' Certainly her feelings were irrational. When Justin had returned to England a year ago he had every reason to believe that Belle had been an accomplice in Lucien's plot to destroy Justin's father by killing Justin in a duel. Instead Lucien had been wounded and Justin had been exiled to the continent. Intent on revenge, he had set out to make Belle his mistress. So, if anything, Chloe should detest Justin, but how could she when he so obviously loved Belle and now Julian? And when he made her so welcome when he could very well detest her as Lucien's half-sister?

'There is another reason I hope you might come to like Brandt.' Belle paused. 'He is soon to become our neighbour.'

With a sinking heart, Chloe knew Mr Rushton had been right. 'He's bought Waverly.'

'How did you know that?'

'Mr Rushton said something about it last night.' She bit her lip. 'Why did you not tell me?'

'He asked us not to say anything as there was some dispute over the title that needed to be resolved and he did not want more rumours to complicate the matter. He will complete the purchase of Waverly today.'

'But I cannot imagine why he would want it! It is old and neglected and has no modern conveniences. Why can he not live at Salcombe House?'

'He does not like Salcombe House,' Belle said gently.

'But how can he possibly have the funds to do so?' she blurted out and was instantly ashamed when she saw Belle's quietly reproving expression. 'Oh, Belle, I am so sorry. I should not have said such a rude thing. It is none of my affair at all.'

'No, it is not, but I've no doubt others will ask the same thing. He sold most of his unentailed properties in order to pay off his father's debts and make the necessary improvements to his estate. He invested whatever was left and I assume it is from those monies he is purchasing Waverly.'

'He must want it very much. I suppose I do not understand why.'

Belle looked steadily at Chloe. 'I imagine it is because he fell in love with the house the first time he saw it. Just as you did.'

Brandt paused for a moment outside the gate to the Suttons' pleasant brick house. What the devil was he doing? He had no desire to participate in the sort of entertainment he envisioned; a gaggle of young ladies and their admirers going through the steps of the newest dances. Just the sort of rustic entertainment he would expect from an unsophisticated village such as Weyham. The sort of entertainment he had never had the opportunity to enjoy. His mother's constant illnesses and his father's rigid morality and cold disregard for most of his neighbours had not encouraged mixing with the local gentry. After his mother's death, when Brandt finally went out into society, he fell in with the most wild, rakish crowd possible. Not until his father was found dead in one of London's most notorious brothels did he come to his senses. By then, he was too disillusioned to enjoy such simple pleasures as an afternoon of practising dances.

Which was why he had no idea why he was standing here now.

'Planning to go in, Salcombe?'

Gilbert Rushton's voice startled him. He turned. 'I am still debating.'

'A bit too late for that. Miss Sutton is leaning out of the window. Bad *ton* if you were to walk away now.' He grinned at Brandt. 'Don't worry, only a couple of hours at the most.'

Miss Sutton was indeed waving at them from a first-floor window. He followed Rushton up the path. 'So, Miss Sutton talked you into this as well?'

'Precisely. However, when I discovered Lady Chloe would be here, I didn't need much persuading.'

'Lady Chloe?'

'She's a deuced pretty gal, clever, and an heiress to boot. Some men might resent a gal who could best them at the table, but not me. Always like a bit of spirit and brains. Besides, one never knows when a way with the cards might prove profitable.'

Brandt was unaccountably annoyed. 'I doubt Lady Chloe wishes to exploit her talent for profit.'

By now they had reached the front door. Rushton glanced at him. 'Not intruding on your territory, am I?'

'Not at all. I've no interest in Lady Chloe. That is, beyond that of a relation.'

'Then no objections if I pursue an acquaintance with her?'

Oh, he objected all right. He hardly wanted her to fall under the charm of a loose screw like Gilbert Rushton. 'No, unless you trifle with her.'

'Intentions are strictly honourable.'

That hardly reassured him. But the pink-cheeked house-keeper had opened the door and after taking their coats and hats and Rushton's cane, ushered them into the sunny, crowded drawing room. The furniture had been pushed aside to clear a space for the dancing. Half a dozen young people were already clustered around the piano. Chloe, however, sat on a small sofa with Sir Preston. She glanced up, her expression astonished, and then looked quickly away. Brandt quelled his desire to march over and say something to fluster her.

Mrs Sutton greeted them with a pleasant smile. 'Good day, Gilbert. How delightful to see you, Lord Salcombe. We cannot tell you how splendid it is to have you among us. We so feared Waverly would be pulled down and—' She stopped at his expression. 'Oh, dear! I fear I have said something when I should not...'

He had not quite been able to keep the surprise from his face. 'Not at all. I have just signed the final papers today so I no longer wish the matter kept private.'

The anxiety left her face. 'How delightful!'

'So the rumours were true! Congratulations!' Rushton said.

Everyone else gathered around to offer their congratulations and pleasure at the restorations taking place. Everyone except for Chloe, who hung back, her expression closed. Brandt was annoyed. She might not be delighted, but she could at least offer a token word.

Lydia finally turned to Chloe. 'See! I knew Lord Sal-

combe would come today. He assured me he would not
find this at all dull as you said he would.'

'I see,' Chloe said faintly. She did not look at him.

Lydia was all smiles. 'Shall we begin? Harriet will play.
We will first perform a country dance so Sir Preston might
see how it is properly done. Then he can try it.'

Sir Preston tugged at his cravat. 'Er, certainly.'

'Do not worry. We can take it very slowly,' Chloe told
him. She gave him a reassuring smile.

'But do you not think it will be too confusing if we are
all dancing at once?' Emily said. She stood near the pianoforte, observing the company with her usual disdainful
gaze. Her eye fell on Brandt. 'I think it would be best if
Lady Chloe and Lord Salcombe demonstrate the steps first
since they have been in London the most recently. I dare
say they are the most expert.'

Chloe looked taken aback. 'I do not know if that makes
me very expert at all.'

'And I rarely dance,' Brandt said. He crossed his arms,
his mood surly. He had no intention of forcing himself on
Chloe.

'But I was,' Rushton said. 'I should be happy to partner
Lady Chloe.' He sent her a smile that set Brandt's teeth
on edge.

'Then Lydia may partner Lord Salcombe,' Emily said.

Lydia, who had looked increasingly annoyed at Emily's
interruption, suddenly brightened. 'That is a splendid idea.
Two couples will make it much more easy to observe.'

'Here, here. Now that we've settled that, let's get on
with it,' Tom Coltrane said. He stood near the pianoforte
with Henry Ashton, attempting to affect a look of bored
amusement.

They took their places in the middle of the room and
Harriet launched into an uneven country dance. Brandt,

who had danced at numerous balls with the most haughty members of the *ton* in attendance, suddenly found himself attacked by an unexpected bout of self-consciousness because he was on display in front of a mere handful of people. Harriet's choppy rhythm and the fact she tended to repeat passages whenever she hit a wrong note made keeping time nearly impossible. Rushton's low-voiced flirtation with Chloe threw Brandt off further. And when he handed off Lydia and found himself reaching for Rushton's hand, he had no idea whether to laugh or curse.

'Sorry,' Rushton said. 'Lydia, where are you? Salcombe, here, you take Lady Chloe.'

The others were beginning to titter. She stared at him and he saw her mouth begin to quiver. 'Chloe?' he asked. 'Are you all right?'

'Y…yes.' She bit her lip and then a laugh escaped her. She stopped and Lydia careened into her. 'Oh, dear… P…please do not say anything more.' She clapped her hand over her mouth and he saw she was laughing.

He grinned. The rest of the company was now laughing except for Lydia. 'Oh, do stop!' she cried. 'It was not that dreadful!'

'But it was!' Tom held his sides. 'Is that what they do in London? Had some idea those *ton* balls were a bit stodgy! Seems I was wrong!'

Even Sir Preston was grinning. 'Could have shown you that myself.'

Lydia marched over to the pianoforte. 'Harriet! Could you not have tried?'

Harriet jumped up. 'I told you I hate to play for dances!' She looked as if she were about to burst into tears.

'Never mind, Harriet,' Emily said briskly. 'Dances are always difficult. You can stand up with Tom, and I will play this time.' She gave her brother, who was still wiping his eyes, a meaningful look.

'Er, yes.' Tom held his arm out to Harriet. She beamed at him as they took their places along with the others.

This time everything went smoothly. When it was over, Emily stood. 'I know you play most delightfully, Lady Chloe. Perhaps you can play this time and I will show Sir Preston the proper steps.'

Brandt glanced at Chloe in time to see a peculiar look cross her face. She glanced at Sir Preston and finally said, 'I fear I am like Harriet and cannot play for dances.'

'Oh, I doubt that,' Emily said. The smile she bestowed upon Chloe was hardly sincere.

'Do play, Chloe!' Lydia said.

Chloe walked to the instrument and sat down, but it was obvious she was not pleased. Emily took Sir Preston's hand and then went through the steps in her no-nonsense fashion. When the dance began, it was apparent Emily's instructions had been adequate; Sir Preston only mis-stepped once.

After that, Mrs Sutton bustled in, followed by the house-keeper who carried a tray of refreshment. Despite the cheerful chatter of everyone else, Chloe seemed subdued and distracted. Brandt, intending to keep his distance, in-stead found he wanted to inquire what was wrong. Before he could extricate himself from Lydia, Gilbert Rushton took the place next to Chloe on the sofa. He said some-thing to her, and she gave him a slight smile that set Brandt's back up.

'Do you plan to make your home at Waverly, Lord Sal-combe?' Lydia was asking him.

'Yes, I am, Miss Sutton.'

'But you will keep a house in town, will you not? I

imagine you must find Weyham very dull after the delights of town.'

'Not at all. We rarely have entertainments such as this in London.'

'But you will be going to London often.'

'Do you wish to see me gone from the neighbourhood so soon, Miss Sutton?'

She coloured. 'Oh, no! I merely thought that you would wish to go there often.'

'Actually, I don't intend to spend much time at all in London except when necessary. Waverly will keep me occupied.'

She looked disappointed for some reason. Miss Coltrane, who seemed to have appointed herself in charge of the entertainment, stood. 'We can practice the waltz. However, this time Lord Salcombe and Lady Chloe must first demonstrate.'

Brandt looked over at Chloe and waited for the inevitable reason why she could not stand up with him. She met his sardonic gaze and lifted her chin. 'I would be glad to do so if Lord Salcombe does not object.'

'I do not object, as long as you don't, Lady Chloe.'

'I thought that was what I just said.' She came to his side.

'So, what has made you decide you would care to stand up with me after all?' he murmured.

'If you must know, I still owe you a dance. I merely wished to repay my debt.'

He'd nearly forgotten about that. 'Ah, although performing the waltz in someone's drawing room was hardly what I had in mind.'

Miss Coltrane played a few notes and then peered around the music at them. 'I believe the gentleman is to take the lady's hand and then put his hand at her waist.'

'If you don't know the waltz, Salcombe, I can take your place,' Rushton said.

Brandt started. 'Should we proceed, Lady Chloe?' He held up his hand.

She placed her hand in his. While he put his other hand on the small of her back. Miss Coltrane began the music. After a moment of hesitation, Chloe followed his lead easily. He forgot he was in a small drawing room with an assortment of onlookers—he was only aware of the pleasurable feel of her slender back, the delicate touch of her hand in his, the face so sweetly upturned towards him, her mouth soft and inviting. A vision of crushing those lips beneath his made him catch his breath.

He heard her own intake of breath and her eyes widened as if she guessed his desire. The music came to an abrupt halt and he jerked his gaze away. What the hell was he doing, practically making love to her in the middle of the afternoon in a country drawing room? He dropped his hands and gave a slight bow. 'Thank you for the dance, Lady Chloe.'

She curtsied. 'Thank you, Lord Salcombe.' She did not quite look at him.

There was silence and then Rushton applauded. 'Splendid! A worthy performance that quite makes up for the less than spectacular beginning.'

Chloe turned to Sir Preston. 'Do you wish to try, Sir Preston? I should be quite happy to show you the steps. Miss Coltrane did such a splendid job of playing I am certain she would be glad to play again.'

'Oh, most certainly,' Miss Coltrane said with a cool smile.

This time she played the waltz as if it were a requiem. However, Brandt was distracted from speculating why by Chloe's efforts to teach Sir Preston the finer points of waltzing. The sight of her guiding Sir Preston's hand in the appropriate position and the warm colour in her cheeks made him wish he were in need of instruction. The only gratification was that Sir Preston didn't appear to be nearly as affected by Chloe's efforts as Brandt was by watching them. The baronet's sole concentration centred on executing the steps correctly.

When Sir Preston finally danced without a misstep, she smiled at him in such a way that Brandt was pierced with jealousy.

Mrs Sutton insisted on playing so that everyone might dance. After another country dance and a cotillion, Miss Coltrane announced it was time for her to leave.

The others followed suit and the party broke up. Brandt took his leave of Mrs Sutton and she smiled up at him. 'How delighted we were to have you today! I hope you will not find our little corner of England too dull. We have the assemblies and sometimes there is a dinner party, but I dare say they are nothing compared to the splendid entertainments of London. Except for Lady Haversham's summer ball. I imagine you will be here for that?'

At that moment he heard Rushton say, 'Perhaps I could escort you home, Lady Chloe.'

Brandt realised Mrs Sutton was waiting for his reply so he pulled his attention back away from Chloe, irritated that he could be so easily distracted. 'Yes, I will be here.'

Mrs Sutton beamed. 'Splendid. It is always the most elaborate affair…'

He finally managed to escape, but once outside he saw no sign of Chloe. Rushton was conversing with Tom Coltrane, so at least Chloe had possessed the sense to refuse his offer. Of course, what she did was none of his concern. He'd best remind himself of that.

* * *

Chloe walked slowly up the lane, feeling curiously disgruntled. She had no idea whether today could be counted as a success or not. Certainly she had spent some time sitting with Sir Preston before the others arrived. But once Emily and Tom came, the conversation turned to racing, a topic Chloe knew little about. Brandt's unexpected arrival had only thrown the afternoon off even more, particularly when Lydia made the remark about him not finding the entertainment dull. Chloe had wanted to sink.

As the afternoon progressed, she realised that, for some reason, Emily was determined to keep her away from Sir Preston. At least Chloe had managed to thwart Emily in the end when she showed Sir Preston the waltz. For some reason, however, it had felt rather flat after waltzing with Brandt. Of course, Brandt was very experienced and had undoubtedly danced dozens of waltzes so naturally it would be more interesting. But that did not explain why, when Brandt took her hand and then rested the other on her back, a peculiar tingle raced through her. And why, when Sir Preston did the same thing, she felt nothing at all. Or why the look in Brandt's eyes when they finished made her heart skip a beat.

The only reason she had agreed to waltz with him was because of her promise last night. And because he had looked at her in that knowing way as if he was just waiting for her to cry off. She had wanted to prove him wrong.

Which was idiotic. As was thinking about him when she should be thinking of Sir Preston instead. He was the sort of safe, trustworthy man she wished to marry. A man she would be comfortable with. A man who did not overpower her, treat her as if she were incapable of thinking for herself. Not the way her father had. Or the way Lucien had. Or the way Arthur still did.

A cool, confident, overbearing man such as Brandt would be no different.

She heard her name. She turned to see Emily hurrying after her. She bit back a groan. Emily was the last person she wanted to see at this moment.

She caught up to Chloe. 'You certainly waltzed very well with Lord Salcombe. How kind of you to take the time to show Sir Preston the steps, although I doubt your expert instruction will have quite the same results for him as his expert instruction in cards has had for you. Particularly after last night.'

'I was merely lucky last night. As you pointed out.'

'I don't suggest it was luck for you. In fact, I think you are quite talented. But such talents run in your family, do they not?'

She was no doubt referring to Lucien. Chloe felt as if she had been struck, but she managed to keep her voice calm. 'Such talents seem to run in most people's families.'

'Perhaps. Lord Salcombe did not seem at all dismayed that he was bested by a mere female.'

'The game was not between Lord Salcombe and me. Sir Preston and Mr Rushton also played.'

'Poor Sir Preston. Anyone could see that you carried the game. I would imagine that must have been very humiliating.'

'I hardly think of Sir Preston as "poor"! He played very well and sometimes it is merely a matter of which cards are drawn. I should be happy to have him for a partner any time.'

Emily gave a little laugh. 'How quickly you come to his defence. One would almost think you have a *tendre* for him.'

Her manner indicated no woman in her right mind would ever consider such a thing. 'I can imagine any number of women developing a *tendre* for Sir Preston,' Chloe said.

'So you do! I would think you would prefer a man such as Lord Salcombe to someone as dull as Sir Preston.'

'I never said I had a *tendre* for Sir Preston.' Chloe's cheeks heated. 'I do not consider him dull, at any rate. I have no idea why you think I would prefer Lord Salcombe.'

'He is more sophisticated and has more address and I cannot imagine him thinking only of his land. Or his horses and dogs, and shooting. One must have something in common with the object of one's affection after all. I do not suppose you are interested in farming and dogs and sheep?'

'Of course I am.' She was beginning to resent this line of questioning very much. 'Not that it is any of your concern.'

Emily gave her a superior smile. 'Poor Sir Preston. Does he suspect? No, of course not. He is too thick.'

Chloe wanted to hit her. 'I do not have a *tendre* for anyone. If you must know, I have no intention of falling in love. I like Sir Preston because he is kind.' Thank goodness, they had reached the path Chloe needed to take to reach Falconcliff. 'I must go this way. I pray you will not repeat such speculations to anyone. They are quite untrue.'

'Oh, I shan't say a thing,' Emily said breezily. 'But I think you would do better to set your sights on Lord Salcombe. Good day, Lady Chloe.' She walked away, her head high.

Chloe stared after her. Oh, heavens! What if Emily said something? She would die of humiliation if anyone else thought she was setting her cap at Sir Preston.

Particularly Brandt. She could only imagine his amusement. No, she did not want anyone to know until she and Sir Preston were betrothed.

If, indeed, that happened.

Chloe's disgruntled feeling only increased when she entered her bedchamber and found a letter on her dressing table from Arthur. She tore off her gloves and picked up the missive. He never wrote unless he wished to admonish her for spending all of her pin-money. In her present mood, she looked forward to his certain lecture even less than usual.

Her first impulse was to put the letter off until later. On the other hand, she might as well open it and put it out of her mind. She broke the seal and spread open the paper. 'Oh, no,' she whispered. Surely, she had misread what he wrote.

But another read of his neat, precise handwriting left no doubt. *The Marquis of Denbigh and his sister, Lady Barbara, have most graciously invited us to a house party at Denbigh Hall. I will arrive at Falconcliff ten days after Lady Haversham's ball, but rather than going to Dutton Cottage we will leave directly for Denbigh Hall the following day.*

Not Lord Denbigh, who reminded her of a large frog with his great bulk, bulging eyes and clammy hands! She had met him this past Season and had hardly thought of him at all when he was first presented to her, except that he was the sort of man she disliked for he reminded her of Lucien's acquaintances. She had been puzzled as to why his widowed sister, the sophisticated Lady Barbara Grant, took an interest in her, inviting Chloe to the theatre, seeking her out at assemblies, taking her for drives in her stylish barouche. Chloe began to notice that Lord Denbigh was almost always present as well. She tried to avoid him; the expression in his eyes when he looked at her made her uneasy. But one evening, when she and Mama were invited to Lady Barbara's home for dinner, Lady Barbara left Chloe and Denbigh alone in the small garden behind the Denbigh town house. He suddenly declared that she was the sweetest creature alive and had pulled her into his arms and kissed her with his wet, thick mouth. His breath and odour had nearly made her gag and only when she had started to retch did he draw back. He had called for Lady Barbara.

Lady Barbara accepted his explanation that Chloe had suddenly taken ill while strolling in the garden. Maria had fussed over her, insisting she must stay in bed the next day. Horrified and ashamed, Chloe could not tell her mother about the kiss. Just as she had not told her mother about an earlier, even more brutal kiss. Chloe ended up ill anyway, for the day after that, she developed a fever and her body ached everywhere. After several weeks, she had still remained weak. The physician finally suggested that the air of London might be responsible and that the fresh air of the seaside would undoubtedly prove beneficial. By then she was eager to escape London and the fact that Belle had invited her to Falconcliff for an indeterminate amount of time pleased her even more. Thus her Season had ended, and, with it, she had thought, the attentions of Lord Denbigh, too.

What was she to do? The thought of facing Lord Denbigh again filled her with panic. If only Sir Preston would make her an offer! She turned from the window, still clutching the letter. If they were betrothed, then surely she would not be expected to go to house parties at Denbigh Hall or anywhere else. She could stay at Falconcliff until the marriage and then after that she would be here in Devon for ever.

She sat down on the bed. Certainly Sir Preston had been all that was kind and attentive, but he was not particularly polished in matters concerning females. He rather reminded her of Serena's betrothed, Charles Hampton. Serena, who was her dearest friend, had written that she had been forced to bring her Charles up to the mark.

How had she done it? Chloe rose and rummaged through the small wooden box where she stored her letters until she found Serena's letter.

I will own I was forced to take matters into my own hands, for I fear Charles would never come up to scratch if I did not. You would probably be shocked at my boldness, for I know how proper you like to be! During last night's assembly I asked him to escort me to the garden under the pretext that the room was far too warm. There was a nicely secluded bench and we sat. Then I told him I was rather cold and moved very close to him. I then smiled at him, but instead of looking away I held his gaze. In a most bold fashion! And then he kissed me, very nicely I must add, and after that he felt most obliged to make me an offer, which I modestly accepted.

The kissing aspect made her feel slightly ill, but if she married Sir Preston there would need to be kisses—as well as other more intimate contacts she shied away from thinking of. Perhaps one grew used to such things after a while.

Certainly Belle had, if the dreamy look in Belle's eyes when Justin regarded her in a particular way was any indication. But then she was in love with Justin and he was in love with her, so that undoubtedly made the difference. At such times, Chloe was uncomfortable, almost as if she had intruded on their privacy, but at least she had not felt repulsed by their mutual desire. Unlike the revulsion she experienced when Denbigh looked at her. Or when Lucien's acquaintances had stared at her so long ago.

Which was another reason, she felt safe with Sir Preston. He never looked at her in such a repugnant way. At least, she cared very much for Sir Preston, so perhaps she would not mind his kisses. And she wanted children, soft, rounded babies who would grow into lovable children, which meant she must learn not to mind such intimacies.

Could she possibly force Sir Preston's hand? She cringed at the thought, but she could see no other way to approach him before she was forced to leave with Arthur.

Arthur would arrive in less than a fortnight. She must think of something before then.

Chapter Three

Brandt looked down at the child who sat on his knee and wondered how he had managed to end up again with another human under the age of one. This time he held Lady Emma Peyton, the youngest daughter of Lord and Lady Haversham. Her wide blue eyes were fixed on him and when he tentatively smiled at her, her little rosebud mouth curved in an irresistible smile. No doubt she'd charm every man in sight in a few years. She had already charmed him.

'So we will have the picnic at Waverly two days after the ball,' Marguerite said. She sat across from him on one of the sofas in her drawing room.

He pulled his gaze away from Lady Emma. 'As long as it does not rain. The drawing room is still covered with plaster dust.'

'In that case we will just move the picnic here.'

Emma wriggled a little and he obligingly bounced her. She giggled.

'I think it is time you set up your own nursery,' Marguerite said.

'Why, when I can play uncle to your children and Belle's?'

'That is not quite the same as having children of your

own. What do you think, Giles? I think he would make a splendid papa.'

'Undoubtedly.' Giles grinned at Brandt from his position near the mantelpiece. 'You'd best be careful when she gets an idea into her head. You'll end up with a passel of urchins in no time.'

'But he'll need a wife first,' Marguerite said. She eyed Brandt. 'Is there not some woman who interests you? Someone respectable, that is.'

'I fear all the respectable, interesting women are either married or...' he glanced at Emma '...far too young.'

Marguerite rolled her eyes. 'Really, Brandt, can you not be serious for a moment? You cannot tell me there is no one who has caught your attention.'

He had visions of methodically looking at each eligible woman and tallying up her good and bad points. The thought was not appealing. 'So how does one go about, er...searching for the right wife?'

'Much like choosing a horse,' Giles said. 'The right breeding, fine lines, the right amount of spirit, and preferably an easy keeper.'

'You are not helping the matter. Brandt needs a wife, not a horse.' She rose and held her arms out to Emma, who had started to fuss. She pressed the baby close to her and planted a kiss on the soft cheek before looking up. 'Waverly needs to be filled with children, which means you must find someone who suits you. Someone you like.'

'At this point, I can hardly afford a new horse, much less a wife.'

'Certainly they cost as much to keep,' Giles added. 'You will need to find an heiress.'

Marguerite stared at her husband as if he'd said something brilliant. 'Of course. Chloe. She would be perfect!

She adores children and she adores Waverly! You could not find someone who would suit you more!'

Had Marguerite gone mad? 'I think you'd better suggest someone else. She would rather see one of us pole-axed before she'd accompany me to the altar.'

He realised Giles was watching them, a grin tugging at his lips. 'Well?' Brandt asked. 'What is it?'

'I am trying to imagine a marriage between you and Chloe. Rather like a Shakespeare comedy, I would think. Perhaps *The Taming of the Shrew* or *Much Ado about Nothing.*'

For some reason, Brandt was irritated. 'Since it is not likely to happen, I would save your imaginings.'

Giles only looked more amused. 'Why not? I doubt you'd be bored.'

'No. Only worried I'd wake up with a dagger at my throat.'

'You are both impossible!' Marguerite said with a look of disgust. 'Perhaps if you would cease to tease her in such an appalling fashion she would cease to be so cross with you,' she told Brandt and rose. 'I must return Emma to Nurse and then see to it the guest chambers have been properly readied. Our first guests will arrive today. As much as I look forward to the ball I am always relieved when it is over. Thank goodness it's the day after next.' She marched to the door and turned. 'If you do not consider Chloe, then I will be forced to find someone for you at the ball,' she challenged him as she left the room.

Giles laughed. 'Chloe is not that dangerous. In fact, she is quite kind and generous. Today she has taken Caroline and Will for a picnic. I do not know many young ladies who would be willing to spend so much time with two children who are not her relations. They adore her. You could do worse.'

'She is an heiress, that's true, although I've no intention of marrying anyone who brings more than a few thousand pounds to the marriage.'

'No?'

'No. In fact, I am not in the market for a wife.'

'You are now.' He laughed at Brandt's expression. 'If Marguerite has anything to say about it.'

Brandt rode along the path that ran across the top of the cliff towards Waverly. Below him lay the sparkling water of the sea. He paid scant heed to the scenery. Instead he was thinking of children. His children. At Waverly.

He must be mad. Surely he had not been so bewitched by first Julian and then Emma that he wanted to set up a nursery as soon as possible. If he had ever considered children, they had always appeared vague and faceless.

They were not faceless now. They had round cheeks and chubby little hands. And smiles that tugged at his heart. Despite the sense of rightness he felt at Waverly, it seemed lacking somehow, as if there was something else he wanted. Now he knew. The same things Justin and Giles had: warm, loving families.

Unlike his own family, with the mother who never smiled and the cold, stern father who angered at the least provocation. He could hardly remember a time when his mother was not an invalid and, although she never raised her voice, never openly wept, he had no doubt of her deep unhappiness. And his father had hardly been a father at all. If not for Justin's family, he would not have experienced any sort of warmth at all.

He had stayed with them often. The Duchess bestowed upon him the same love and warmth she bestowed upon her own son. She always listened when he talked, and had not been above getting down on her knees and playing games with them. The Duke, although more reserved, had been no less kind. Despite their welcome, Brandt could not forget they were not his own family or that, eventually, he would be summoned home.

Brandt had envied Justin. He still did.

Even if he wanted a wife, he could not afford one. Certainly he had started to recover some of the fortune his father had squandered, but he'd spent much of it on the repairs and improvements his father had neglected on the land and tenant cottages that belonged to Salcombe House. Some he had gambled on a venture that at the moment seemed fruitless. And now he had Waverly, the house he had wanted from the moment he had first laid eyes upon it.

He refused to marry for money. Or for mere convenience. Or to produce the heir his great-aunt, Lady Farrows, mentioned in every letter. He would not bring children into the world unless he married a woman who would adore them as much as Marguerite adored her children or Belle adored Julian.

A woman such as Chloe.

He wanted to curse Marguerite for even putting that notion into his head. Chloe was not for him. She was too untouched; too naïve; too good.

And he shared his father's blood. He'd set out to prove his difference when he'd run wild in London. Prove that he was not cold and passionless, prove he could sample all the pleasures of the flesh the capital had to offer. Pleasures his father had condemned.

But the irony was he had turned out to be like his father after all.

Brandt reached the ramshackle stables and then dismounted and handed his horse over to a groom. Instead of

making for the house he veered off towards the path that
took him to the edge of the cliff. Movement caught his
eye on the beach below him. He had no difficulty identi-
fying the children on the rocks as Lord Will Haversham
and his sister, Lady Caroline. Or the woman whose head
was bare and whose hair glinted red and gold in the sun.

He muttered a curse. By his calculations the tide would
be coming in shortly. He hoped she had the sense to clamber from the rocks before that happened. He headed for
the uneven stone steps that would take him to the beach.

'Look, Chloe!' William called. Chloe lifted her skirts
and carefully stepped across the rocks to where William
peered into a pool. She crouched down to look. 'What do
you see?'

'A starfish! Is he not splendid?'

'He is.' She smiled at his enthusiasm. He was six and
full of energy and spirits.

'I wish I could bring him home.'

'He would not survive very long away from the sea. He
will be much happier here with his friends.'

William eyed her. 'What friends? I don't see any other
starfish.'

'I'm sure he has friends close by.' She had no idea if
starfish were particularly social. They didn't seem as if
they would be.

She looked over at Will, and her heart swelled. She
adored him as well as his more serious older sister, Caroline, and now, of course, little Emma. Lydia could not
understand why she wanted to do dull things such as taking
them on picnics or exploring tide pools or riding ponies to
the fishing stream near the village. But then Lydia had
grown up with an older brother and a younger sister and
despite their little quarrels, no one could doubt the true

affection between them. Lydia had had a neighbourhood of playmates as well. Chloe had never had playmates and Lucien had been worse than no brother at all. With Will and Caroline she could participate in all the things she had missed as a child.

'Chloe!' Caroline appeared at her side. 'I think we should go back. The tide is starting to come in.'

'You are right. Come, Will, we need to leave.'

'I want to stay. A little bit longer.' He wriggled further on his stomach.

'No, William,' Caroline said. 'We must make our way to the beach. We don't want to be caught on the rocks.'

'We won't be. Look, now there's a crab!'

'William!'

'If the tide does come in, we can escape by going through the sea cave. Then we'll end up at Waverly in the garden.'

Caroline shuddered. 'Ugh. It is too dark and slimy and smells like fish.'

'And I hate dark, cold places,' Chloe added. Will had dragged them over to the dark opening behind the rocks. The water swirling inside echoed in a sombre way that gave her the chills. Despite Will's assurance that the passage led away from the water and up the cliff she had horrible visions of being trapped while the water rose. And even if she did like climbing about in caves, she had no desire to end up in Waverly's garden. Not any more, at least. 'We can have the apricot tarts now.'

The mention of apricot tarts had the desired effect. Will stood up and scrambled over the rocks with amazing alacrity. He paused on the last rock. 'First one to the hamper gets three tarts!' He jumped down and dashed across the sand.

Caroline made a face. 'I would like to see him race in skirts.'

'I know. It doesn't seem fair, does it? Even for activities such as this women must wear skirts and shifts.' Of course, most ladies would never think of clambering around on rocks in bare feet as she was doing now.

Caroline hopped off the last rock and Chloe followed. Then the young girl turned to Chloe. 'The next person to the hamper gets two tarts!' She started to run and Chloe dashed after her.

Running on sand was no easy feat and they were giggling before they had gone no more than a few yards. They stopped, breathless and laughing. Chloe glanced towards William and the laughter faded. She wanted to groan instead. Why ever was Brandt here?

But he was. He stood with Will, watching them. 'Lord Salcombe is here!' Caroline's voice expressed delight. She began to walk towards him at a much more dignified pace.

Chloe trailed behind her, suddenly self-conscious of her faded gown with its wet, dirty skirts, the hair that had come out of its pins, and her bare, dirty feet. She probably looked like an overgrown street urchin. She pulled up her bonnet, which dangled down her back by its ribbons, and set it on her head.

William dashed towards her. 'Look, Chloe! Uncle Brandt is here! I told him we were having apricot tarts and he could have one!' He caught her hand, dragging her towards Brandt.

Brandt's eyes were on her and for a moment he did not reply. Then he seemed to start. 'Only if Lady Chloe agrees, and if there are enough.'

'I am certain there are,' she said, feeling even more awkward.

William had thrown himself down beside the hamper. 'Come and sit down,' he said, grinning up at them.

'Only after the ladies sit,' Brandt said.

'Oh!' William promptly rose. 'You need to sit down,' he told Chloe and Caroline.

They took their places and Will sat back down. Brandt settled his own long frame next to Will while Chloe opened the hamper and distributed the first round of tarts. She made certain her hand did not contact Brandt's strong, lean one when he took the pastry from her.

She sat back on the cloth, grateful Brandt lounged next to Will and the hamper provided a barrier between them. At least she did not need to think of conversation. Will chattered between mouthfuls of tart, excited to tell Brandt about starfish, tide pools and sea creatures. Chloe's name seemed to come into the conversation far too often for her liking. More than once she found Brandt's gaze on her, which only increased her discomfort.

'And Chloe doesn't mind getting her skirts wet! She even goes without shoes! Show him, Chloe!'

Chloe started. 'Show him what?'

'Your feet! They are bare!'

'I would rather not do that.'

'But why not?'

Brandt glanced down at him and his mouth twitched. 'Because it is not considered proper for ladies to show gentlemen their bare feet.'

'Oh.' Will digested that for a moment. 'Are you a gentleman?'

'Of course he is!' Caroline said. She gave her younger brother a reproving stare. 'He is a peer.'

Brandt looked over at Chloe and grinned with a boyishness she had never seen. 'I am not certain Chloe considers those terms necessarily synonymous.'

'I...I have never thought about it.' She found herself smiling back at him. His grin slowly faded and he stared at her with an awareness that brought heat to her cheeks and made her heart pound. She looked away. 'Does anyone want another tart?' Her voice sounded odd.

'I do!' William exclaimed.

Caroline did as well. Chloe was grateful for the excuse to bring out more of the delicious tarts and direct the conversation in another direction. After eating two more tarts, William grabbed Brandt's hand and urged him to wade with him.

He stood in a lazy, graceful movement. 'Actually, I had come to warn you about the tide. But I see I did not need to.'

'We come here all the time. Chloe knows all about the tides,' Will said.

'I am glad to hear that. I would not want any deaths on my property.'

'This is your property?' Chloe asked.

'Yes. I negotiated it as part of the estate. Do not worry, you are quite welcome to come here any time you want.'

'I see.' So he now was master of her favourite cove as well. She turned away, again with that little twinge of resentment and started to pack the linens back in the hamper.

'Come, Uncle Brandt! I want to show you where we found the starfish.'

'Do we have time?' Brandt asked her.

'A little time.' At least if he was occupied she could put her stockings and half-boots on without Brandt around. Not that he would watch, but she would rather not have an audience.

'Then I had best remove my boots,' he said. To her dismay, he sat down on a nearby rock. Cheeks pink, she looked away and busied herself putting the picnic dishes back in the hamper. He finally rose and left with William and Chloe found her stockings and boots and hastily put them on. She tried to pin her hair back up and finally Caroline offered to help.

As Chloe finished tidying up, William and Brandt remained standing in the waves. William was holding Brandt's hand. He turned and saw her and then said something to William. They then started back towards Caroline and Chloe.

Chloe wiped the sand from William's feet and then helped him put on his stockings and shoes. She tried to ignore that Brandt sat on the rock next to them and was engaged in the same task.

Brandt rose. 'Do you need me to carry the hamper back?'

Chloe shook her head. 'No. Marguerite said she would send a servant for it after we returned.'

'I will be glad to offer my escort back to the Hall, in any case.'

'That is not necessary,' she said sharply, then tried to sound more agreeable. 'But if you want to that would be very kind.' Now she merely sounded idiotic.

Which he must have thought as well from his quizzical expression. He said nothing, however.

They made their way up the stone steps that led from the beach to the top of the cliff. William continued to chatter about their excursion and even Caroline, who was normally reserved when in the company of more than one or two people, participated as well. Chloe followed along, feeling rather resentful, which was ridiculous. After all, William and Caroline had every right to like whomever they pleased. It was just…she felt rather left out. She had enjoyed being their special friend and now it seemed Brandt was just as special.

She had no idea why feeling special was so important, except that since Belle married she had felt a little lost. She knew Belle loved her no less, but now her husband and her baby were of first concern to her. She belonged to them and they belonged to her.

Chloe felt as if she did not belong to anyone.

By the time they reached the steps of Haversham Hall, she was still feeling sorry for herself. She followed them into the entrance hall, and Caroline turned to her. 'Will you stay for a while with us, Chloe?'

At least she hadn't asked Brandt if he would stay. Then chided herself for being so childish. 'No. I am too dirty to even enter the drawing room. But thank you.' She gave Caroline a swift hug, careful not to soil Caroline's gown and then shook William's hand.

'I will take you back to Falconcliff,' Brandt said.

'I walked. I would not want to inconvenience you if you rode.'

'I walked as well.'

'So you found them, Brandt,' Marguerite said as she came down the stairs. 'Now you can escort Chloe to Falconcliff.'

'Which is what I told her.'

Marguerite reached the bottom and came forward to take Chloe's hand. 'Thank you so much, dear Chloe.' She looked over to Brandt. 'The children adore her.'

'I've no doubt of that,' he said.

'She needs several of her own, do you not think?'

Chloe's face grew warm.

'If that is what she wants,' he said politely.

'Of course she will need a suitable husband first,' Marguerite persisted. She cast Chloe a mischievous look. 'That will be my next project.'

'I…' Why must Marguerite tease her about this now, when she was terrified she would end up with a most unsuitable husband? And in front of Brandt, of all people? 'I…I do not want a husband.' That was not what she meant to say either. 'I should return to Falconcliff.'

Marguerite made a wry face. 'I did not mean to put you to the blush. Sometimes my tongue runs away with me. I won't do anything you don't wish, but I would love to see you settled with your own children.' She glanced at Brandt. 'Just as I hope to see Brandt wed with a family of his own.'

To Chloe's surprise, a hint of colour tinged his cheek. 'Chloe is right. We had best go before you decide to post the banns.'

'I would not be that presumptuous!' For some reason Marguerite looked quite pleased with herself.

For the first time, Chloe was actually relieved to leave Marguerite. She could scarcely look at Brandt as they started down the path that cut through the Haversham estate to the back garden of Falconcliff. He did not seem inclined to talk either, which proved to be more unnerving than his teasing.

She finally stole a look at his face. He appeared to be concentrating very hard on the path. A lock of dark hair fell over his forehead and he looked rather boyish despite the set expression he wore. He cast a quick look at her. 'Don't let Marguerite's words trouble you. She habitually concerns herself in other people's affairs, particularly when it comes to marriage.'

'It is just rather awkward to have such things brought up in front of someone else.'

A slight smile touched his mouth. 'I agree. Particularly when it is quite apparent she intended to start her matchmaking in the middle of her hallway.'

A frown wrinkled Chloe's brow. 'Did she? With whom?' She had been so confused she had hardly known what Marguerite was talking about.

'With you and me.'

Chloe stared at him blankly. 'I beg your pardon.'

They had reached the stone gate that marked the beginning of Falconcliff's garden. He allowed her to pass him and then fell into step next to her on the walk that led to the house. 'She has already informed me she thinks that you and I would make a suitable match.'

Chloe's mouth fell open. 'Oh, dear,' was all she could say.

'Don't worry. You're in no danger. I am quite aware you would rather spend your life in Newgate than wed me.' This time he looked rather amused.

'That is not true!' Hearing him put the matter so bluntly made her cringe.

'Wouldn't you?'

'No, of course not!' What if he thought she was angling for an offer? 'I…I do not really want to marry anyone.'

He didn't blink at that. 'And why not? You seem fond of children. I would imagine you'd want your own some day.'

'I am very happy being an aunt,' she said stiffly. 'One must be married in order to have children of one's own. Or at least one should be.'

'That is preferable.' His mouth twitched. 'So what has caused you to hold marriage in such aversion? Most young ladies seem eager to acquire that status as quickly as possible.'

Well, she was not most young ladies and she found his amusement irritating. 'If you must know, I do not like the idea of a husband.'

'Why not?'

'I think in general they are too much trouble.'

To her satisfaction, he actually looked taken aback. 'Why do you say that?'

'They always wish you to do as they ask, frequently without consulting anyone's tastes; they wish everyone to be quiet when they want to be quiet and to make conversation when they wish to, and in general consider a wife there for only their convenience.'

'That is hardly a romantic view of marriage.'

'I am not very romantic. If I had to be married, I would prefer a comfortable marriage. In fact, I think being in love would be a great inconvenience and certainly clouds one's judgement. And I most certainly do not think it guarantees happiness!'

'But we have, under our noses, two couples who defy that theory.'

'But Belle and Justin made each other most unhappy until they resolved their differences. I would never want to go through that! And although Giles and Marguerite are very happy now, I dare say it is because they are so comfortable with each other. Marguerite told me that when she first met Giles, he seemed to dislike her and when she realised she had fallen in love with him, she despaired for months until he offered for her. The most odd thing was he confessed he had thought she did not like him. I cannot think of anything that would be more inconvenient. I would prefer to be comfortable right away and forgo all the stupid misunderstandings.'

'I will own that, on the whole, I tend to agree with you.'

She should have been pleased that he did; instead, she felt irrationally disappointed he did not try to argue with her. 'Why are you not married? You seem very fond of children yourself.'

He kept his eyes on the path. 'Even if I were so inclined, I am hardly in a position to take a wife.'

'But why not?' Then could have clapped her hands over her mouth as she recalled her earlier conversation with Belle.

This time he turned to look at her. He read her expression perfectly. 'Precisely.'

'I cannot think it would matter if someone cared for you!'

'And you are not a romantic?'

'Not at all! I merely meant that if someone cared for you it would not matter that you are not…that is…' she stumbled, but he said nothing and just watched her with that impenetrable look. 'Wealthy.'

'Most women expect a certain amount of comfort when they marry. I doubt if living in an old house on the Devon coast far from London appeals to many women.'

It appealed to Chloe, but she could hardly tell him that. 'Surely some women would not mind. Waverly will be perfectly lovely when it is finished.'

'By the time I am done with the repairs necessary to make it tolerably livable, I will have little money left to keep a wife in any sort of style. I no longer have a house in London so there would be no frequent visits to town.'

'Not every woman wishes to visit London. But you do have your other estate, do you not?'

A cool smile touched his mouth. 'Yes, unfortunately. If it were not entailed I would sell it in an instant.'

'Why?'

He glanced at her. 'Are you always this curious? If you must know, it is because I detest Salcombe House and all it represents.'

'I…I did not know. I am sorry,' she said. She had no idea what he was talking about.

'Don't be.' He kept his eye on the road. 'I do not intend to marry for money either. No heiresses.'

Was he trying to hint her away? As if she would ever fall in love with him! Irked, she said, 'What if you fell in love with an heiress?'

'I do not intend to do so.'

'What if you cannot help yourself? And she returns your affections?'

'That is unlikely to happen.'

'What is unlikely to happen? That an heiress will fall in love with you or you cannot help falling in love with her?'

'Both.' He stopped and looked down with her, the glint in his eye dangerous. 'If you persist in this line of questioning, I might start to think you are in love with me yourself.'

'I beg your pardon?' She backed away, heat flooding her cheeks.

His smile was sardonic. 'That is what I thought. Perhaps we could discuss something more pleasurable. Such as the weather.'

They continued on in an uncomfortable silence until they reached the terrace. He halted. 'I will see you tomorrow.'

'Tomorrow? But are you not dining with us?'

'Actually, no. I am to dine with Gilbert Rushton and Sir Preston Kentworth at the Inn.'

'With Sir Preston?' The name slipped from her lips before she could stop it.

'Do you have an objection to my dining with Sir Preston?'

'Oh, no, he is most kind.'

He was looking at her rather strangely. She should escape before she made things worse. 'I had best change.

Thank you.' She dashed through the French doors before
he could say anything. Or before she said anything else
stupid.

Sir Preston Kentworth rose from the table. 'Must be off.'
He nodded to Brandt. 'Glad to have you in the neighbourhood, Salcombe. Night, Rushton.' He ambled away.
Brandt liked him; he had a blunt, pleasant manner that was
refreshing after the languid boredom affected by many of
his London acquaintances.

Rushton leaned back. 'Wonder if he yet realises he is
the object of affection of not only one, but two members
of the fairer sex.'

'Kentworth?' Brandt asked, startled.

Rushton grinned. 'Hard to believe, but then who knows
what inspires passion in a lady's heart? Causing quite a
bit of speculation over which of the damsels will land their
catch. Considered booking a wager on it, but didn't want
the wrath of certain persons to fall on my head.'

'It is probably best in these cases.'

'Don't suppose you are interested in knowing the identity of the two rivals?'

'Not particularly.' Local gossip held no more interest
for him than London gossip had.

'Ah, but in this case you might be intrigued to know.'
Rushton leaned forward a gleam in his eye.

'Then you'd best tell me.' Even as he said the words,
he was hit with a disquieting premonition.

'Emily Coltrane is one.' Rushton paused for effect. 'And
Lady Chloe is the other.'

Brandt kept his expression bland. 'How do you know
that?'

'Tom Coltrane. Says his sister's nose has been quite out
of joint since Lady Chloe's arrival. Emily noticed straight
away that Lady Chloe meant to set her cap at poor Kent-

worth. She's claimed all along that the card lessons were a ploy on Lady Chloe's part to gain Kentworth's attention. Seems Emily was right.'

He should have guessed. The signs were there; the look on her face at the dancing lessons, the way she blushed when he mentioned he would see Kentworth. 'Does Kentworth return her sentiments?'

Rushton shrugged. 'Hard to tell. Kentworth's a bit of a slow top in these matters. His mama's all for it, however. Been spreading subtle hints around the neighbourhood that she may soon have an intimate connection with Westmore's family.'

Hell. That harpy who had dragged Chloe into the card game? 'Does my cousin have wind of this?'

'Don't think so. Lady Kentworth is clever enough to keep it from the Duke until she has Lady Chloe in her net. Thought I should warn you so you might drop a word with the Duchess. Don't want to underestimate Lady Kentworth when she sets her mind on something. I wouldn't want to see Lady Chloe hurt. Or Kentworth, for that matter. From what I've heard of her guardian, don't think he'd welcome a country baronet into the family.'

Rushton was right. For all he appeared to be a loose screw, he was much more perceptive than Brandt had ever given him credit for, and he had no doubt Rushton was quite familiar with the local gossip. Although Justin and his family were warmly welcomed into the small tight-knit village, the local gentry still maintained a certain respectful distance and he doubted all the gossip reached Justin's ears.

Brandt finished his brandy. 'No, Ralston would not.' He eyed Rushton. 'You were wise to not book any wagers. You'd have not only Westmore to deal with; you would have me as well.'

'I rather thought so.' Rushton held up his hands. 'No need to look so grim. I promise Lady Chloe's reputation is safe in my hands. Just wanted to warn you.' He grinned. 'Besides, with Kentworth out of the running, thought I might have a chance in that direction myself.'

'I wouldn't wager on that either.' Brandt rose. 'I must take my leave as well.'

'I'll walk out with you.' The other man stood.

Rushton was silent until they reached Brandt's curricle. 'Don't want you to think I meant to spread gossip.' His countenance was sober. 'But Lady Kentworth has a reputation for interfering. Managed to compromise her own daughter into marriage a few years back—very nasty business—just wouldn't want the same thing happening to Lady Chloe.'

'No.' Neither would he. He would do everything in his power to prevent it, including keeping Chloe in his sights if Kentworth or Lady Kentworth were anywhere in her vicinity. But why had she been so adamant about her aversion to marriage if she had a *tendre* for Sir Preston? Or did she consider marriage to Sir Preston comfortable?

He did not intend to give her a chance to find out.

Brandt spoke to Belle the next morning after breakfast. He found her in the garden, Julian on her lap. She looked up and smiled, and then her expression sobered. 'I suspect you have something rather serious to say.'

'Yes. Rushton informed me that there are rumours circulating that Chloe is setting her cap at Sir Preston.'

'Oh, dear. I had hoped that no one would really notice or at least say anything. It is dreadful enough when one has a *tendre* for someone; then to have rumours spread about it is very humiliating. Particularly when one hopes to keep it secret.'

He started. 'You know Chloe has a *tendre* for Sir Preston?' For some reason having Belle confirm it only made him more angry. 'Then why the devil haven't you put a stop to it?'

'I cannot dictate how Chloe feels. As far as developing a *tendre* for someone, I would much prefer it be a decent, kind man such as Sir Preston than a charming fortune-hunter.'

'Are you saying you would welcome a match between them? Does Justin know of this?'

For some reason she looked as if she wanted to laugh. 'Yes, Justin does know, and his reaction was the same as yours. Once I convinced him that forbidding Chloe to have anything to do with Sir Preston would only make him even more romantic in her eyes, besides bewildering Sir Preston, he agreed we would say nothing. Of course, they are quite unsuited to each other. Poor Chloe, she knows nothing of farming and has been desperately reading all of Justin's *Gentleman's Magazines* in hopes of being able to converse with Sir Preston on topics he's interested in.'

Brandt wanted to grind his teeth. And curse. Belle's words were reasonable, but the thought of Chloe finding Sir Preston romantic only served to make his mood even surlier. 'Then perhaps you are not aware that Lady Kentworth has been hinting around that she expects a more intimate connection with your family. And that she forced her own daughter into a compromising marriage.'

'No, I did not know that.' She frowned a little. 'Do you know this for a fact?'

'Only what Gilbert Rushton told me.'

'Certainly Lady Kentworth has made it quite obvious she favours Chloe and fawns over her in a most deliberate manner. Oh, dear, I will speak to Justin, of course, but since Chloe will only be here for another week, I hate to create a stir. We will make certain she is well chaperoned and busy with other things so she will not have much time to think of Sir Preston.' She gave him a reassuring smile. 'I have no doubt everything will be fine. It is kind of you to worry about her.'

He felt rather idiotic since Belle seemed to have matters well in hand. 'I consider her a relation so, of course, I am concerned.' Now he sounded stiff.

'Of course.' Her eyes twinkled. 'I do hope you won't say anything to Chloe about this. I fear it will only antagonise her and then you will be at daggers drawn again. I should hate to see that.'

'I won't say anything.' Which did not mean he wouldn't keep an eye on her. At least he and Belle were in agreement on one point; she and Kentworth were not suited. He was a relation of sorts, so he had a certain responsibility for Chloe, and that responsibility entailed keeping her safe from her damnable romantic notions.

Chloe smiled down at Julian. 'I suppose we must take you back to Nurse.' She had just spent an agreeable hour with him in the garden. They had picked flowers, squealed at butterflies and watched the water spray from the fountain in the small pond. She rose and he wriggled until she turned him so he could more easily see where they were going. 'You are getting heavier,' she told him. 'Soon I won't be able to carry you so effortlessly.' He grinned at her and her heart melted. He smelled so sweet and felt so soft. Before Julian, she had never paid much attention to babies, but she had fallen instantly and irrevocably in love with him.

She wandered up the steps and entered the drawing room through the terrace door. Busy watching Julian, she did not notice the man standing there, until he spoke.

'Good day, Chloe. I see your clothing is in disarray as usual.'

She froze. 'Arthur? What are you doing here?'

Her guardian, Arthur, the Earl of Ralston, fixed her with his usual disapproving gaze. He was of medium height with light brown hair, and a bony face which always looked as if he were about to give someone a scold, most particularly when he focused his gaze on her. 'I see your manners have not improved either.' He clasped his hands behind his back. 'I decided there was no reason to delay the journey to Denbigh Hall as Lord Denbigh and Lady Barbara are most anxious to see you.'

'You cannot do that! I am to be here for another week, and there is Lady Haversham's ball tomorrow!'

'I did not intend to leave today. We will leave two days after the ball.' He cast a dismissive glance at Julian, who had become uncharacteristically silent. 'As soon as you return that child to its nurse, I would like to speak to you.'

That child? How dare he speak of Julian in such a way? 'I am certain you meant to say as soon as I return Lord Wroth to his nurse, you would like to speak to me.' She stalked past him and with no little satisfaction saw his brow snap down even further. In the hall, however, she felt less pleased with her little victory. She could never hold her tongue around him and put on the meek face he liked in young ladies. Instead, she always managed to make things worse.

She had started across the hall when Belle appeared, her expression one of dismay. 'Chloe, I fear Arthur has arrived. He wishes to speak to you straight away. He is putting up at the inn and arrived late last night, so we had no idea he was coming, or I would have suggested you stay away longer.'

Chloe handed Julian to his mother and made a face. 'I

have seen him. I came through the terrace doors and he has already chided me on my unimproved manners and disarrayed clothing.'

'Oh, dear.' Belle gave her a sympathetic look. 'Well, I suppose you must have your interview with him. At least you will have it over with.'

Chloe returned to the drawing room. Arthur stood near the window, hands clasped behind his back. He turned and moved towards her. 'Sit down, if you please.'

She took the chair he indicated and folded her hands in her lap. She vowed to hold back any unruly words that sprang to her lips.

He stood in front of her, a position that always made her feel like a chastised school girl. 'I hope that when you are married, your husband will be able to curb your tongue. As well as see that you dress properly.'

'Well, I do not have a husband yet,' she said brightly.

A wintry smile crossed his face. 'I trust you will before the summer is over.'

'Really? I cannot imagine why you would think that.' Had he somehow heard about Sir Preston?

'I intend to accept Lord Denbigh's offer.'

Her stomach lurched, and all thoughts of meekness fled. She jumped up. 'No! He…he is too old!'

'Nonsense. In fact, a man of his age will be able to guide you properly, which you most certainly need.'

'I will not accept him.'

'You will. Why else do you think we are going to Denbigh Hall?'

'So, I do not have any choice in the matter?'

He stared at her. 'You have had choices the last two Seasons, but you refused all of them. I've no doubt there are men who would be willing to overlook your advanced age, but I would prefer to see you betrothed before you are one and twenty.'

'I do not like him,' she said quietly.

His thin mouth tightened. 'What does that have to do with anything? You are young, and foolish if you think such emotions play a role in choosing a suitable mate. His bloodlines are impeccable. He is from one of England's oldest families. He is wealthy enough that no one could think he is marrying you for your dowry.'

'Love has nothing to do with it! I find him repulsive. He reminds me of a…a frog! In fact, I would rather marry a frog!'

Arthur stared at her and then his mouth tightened. 'You are disrespectful and childish. There is no reason why you should not accept him. I trust that after you reflect on the advantages of such a match you will come to your senses.'

'I won't. You cannot make me marry him.'

'No, but if you do not, I fear I will be forced to cut off your allowance. And your mother's as well.'

'You are despicable!'

His face contorted with such fury that she feared he would strike her. Without thinking, she turned and dashed into the hallway. She started for the staircase and then changed her mind.

If she went upstairs now, Arthur would undoubtedly find her. She whirled around. The next thing she knew she had crashed into a hard masculine chest. Strong arms steadied her and she was pressed into a coat smelling of outdoors and horses. Then she was released. She glanced swiftly up and found herself looking into Brandt's startled face.

Drat! Of all the people she must dash into! 'I beg your pardon,' she said stiffly. From the condition of his clothing, she knew he had been at Waverly. His coat was wrinkled and dusty; his breeches in no better condition. He looked rather like a ruffian. A very dangerous and very attractive ruffian. The unexpected thought flustered her completely.

His mouth curved. 'I will own you're the last woman I expected to throw herself into my arms.'

'I was hardly throwing myself into your arms.' She pulled away from him, still flustered. 'If you will excuse me, I...I must go.'

'Where are you going in such a hurry? It is nearly time to dress for dinner.'

'Nowhere. Outside, if you must know. I pray you will move.'

He stared at her; his expression changed to one of concern. 'What has happened?'

'Nothing. Nothing at all.'

'Then why do you look so agitated?'

'I...I don't.'

'Your face is far too expressive. You look as if the devil is on your heels.'

'Chloe!' Arthur's voice cut through the air. 'I have not finished with you.'

'I see. Not quite the devil, but close,' Brandt murmured.

'I must go,' she said desperately.

'Good day, Salcombe.' Arthur eyed Brandt with a look of distaste. Most likely disgusted by Brandt's dusty clothing. Arthur probably could not conceive how any gentlemen would ever be seen in such a condition.

'Good day, Ralston.' Brandt merely looked amused. 'Are you staying in Devon? Or did you merely stop by to have a word with Chloe?'

'Quite the contrary. I am to escort Lady Chloe,' he said with heavy emphasis on 'lady', 'to a house party.'

'Not today, I trust.'

'Naturally not. We will leave two days after Lord and

Lady Haversham's ball. However, I am certain you will wish to dress for dinner so we must not detain you. Chloe, come with me.'

'No.'

'I have not finished with you.'

Brandt shifted towards her. 'Apparently she has finished with you. And, as you pointed out, it is time to dress for dinner.'

His defence steadied her enough for her to say, 'And did you not point out my clothing is in disarray?'

'Yes, but…'

'Then I will see you at dinner, Cousin Arthur.' She gave Brandt a brief smile. 'Thank you.' She turned and started up the stairs before Arthur could detain her.

Once in her chamber, she shut the door and leaned against it for a moment. Her stomach began to churn again. Lord Denbigh. Even his name made her shudder. She had no choice; unless she brought Sir Preston up to scratch tomorrow, she would either be forced to marry Lord Denbigh or Mama would scarcely have a farthing to her name. Her latest letter from Mama had been full of news of purchases of lace and ribbons and two gowns; one a lilac crepe; the other a pale yellow cambric she could not do without. There had been a very small loss at whist as well. She so hated to ask Arthur for funds, for he would scold her terribly and threaten to cut off all her allowance entirely, so if Chloe had a very small sum…

And now if Chloe refused Denbigh, there would be nothing for her mother at all, which was why she *must* marry Sir Preston. Once she was married, Arthur would no longer control her fortune. True, it would then be in Sir Preston's hands, but she somehow doubted he would begrudge her the amounts she sent to Mama.

Chloe moved from the door. She really had no choice.

Just as her friend Serena had done with her man, Chloe must encourage Sir Preston to make her an offer.

Her only chance would be tomorrow night. At the Havershams' ball.

Chapter Four

'Chloe? Are you ready?' Chloe jumped when she heard Belle's voice. She nearly knocked her fan off the dressing table and caught it just in time. She snatched up the French shawl from her bed and draped it around her shoulders. She certainly did not want Belle to see her bodice; not until they were at the ball at any rate.

She turned and plastered a shaky smile to her face. 'Yes. I did not realise it was time to leave.'

'The carriages are below.' Belle stepped into the room, lovely and elegant in rose silk, diamonds at her throat and ears. Her smile was warm when she saw Chloe. 'Oh, Chloe! How beautiful you look and so grown up! I sometimes forget you are no longer a child until times such as this and I realise you are a young woman.'

'And nearly on the shelf according to Arthur.'

Belle made a face. 'He is ridiculous. You must put him from your mind. Do not worry, I will not allow him to ride roughshod over you. Come, let us go downstairs.' She paused and looked at Chloe's face. 'Are you all right?'

'Perhaps I am a trifle nervous.'

'Surely not after facing the patronesses of Almack's! Anyone who can win praise from Lady Jersey for her ''pleasing manners'' should not feel the least apprehensive about a country ball.'

She tried to return Belle's smile and followed her from the room. She could hardly tell Belle she had made up her mind to kiss Sir Preston. Or more to the point, to encourage him to kiss her. If a kiss had worked for Serena, then perhaps it would work with Sir Preston as well. If not, she might be desperate enough to propose to him.

Justin, Brandt, and Arthur waited for them in the drawing room. They stood near the mantelpiece in well-fitting dark coats and satin knee breeches. Although not as tall as the other two, even Arthur was not unattractive in his evening clothes.

Her gaze fell on Brandt. Tonight he was the elegant London lord, just as he had been this past Season. For some odd reason, she could not help but notice how well his corbeau coat fitted his broad shoulders or how his knee breeches and silk stockings emphasized his strong, muscular legs. Or that despite his civilized appearance he suddenly looked as male and dangerous as he had when she had crashed into him in the hall yesterday.

He looked up and his gaze met hers. Awareness shot through her and from the expression that leapt to his eyes, she knew he had felt the same jolt. She tore her gaze away, completely confused.

She felt no less confused when she found him at her side as they stepped out of the front door into the pleasant evening. 'You are to ride in my carriage,' he said.

'I am?' She looked up at him and wished she were a few inches taller. Or he was shorter. Although he was not the tallest man of her acquaintance, he was tall enough that she had to look up to him.

'Belle will ride with us as well so you will be adequately

chaperoned.' His eyes were laughing at her again, no trace of the earlier moment in his face. 'I thought you would prefer my company to Lord Ralston's, but perhaps I was mistaken.'

Usually she would prefer anyone's company to that of Arthur, but tonight she was not so sure as she glanced up at his face. Again she felt that disconcerting awareness of him.

She realised he was waiting for an answer. 'Of course.'

'Of course what? You would prefer my company?'

'Yes, I suppose so.'

'You only suppose? I look forward to the day when you have a definite preference for my company. Over Ralston's, that is.'

He was teasing her again. However, she was too distracted to even think of a response. He helped her and then Belle into the carriage. But as it rattled down the drive, worries about Sir Preston overtook any reaction she might have to Brandt. She would need to lure Sir Preston to somewhere private. What did one do next? She had no idea how to go about encouraging a man to kiss her. She would move closer to him as Serena had done, but what if that did not accomplish what she wanted? Should she—?

'Chloe, Brandt has just asked whether you are looking forward to the ball.' Belle's voice cut into her thoughts.

Chloe blinked. 'The ball?'

'The ball we are about to attend. Or perhaps it has slipped your mind,' Brandt said.

'I...no.'

He still watched her with that disconcerting intensity. 'Then do you look forward to it?'

'I...yes.' Thank goodness, they were already entering the arches of the drive in front of Haversham Hall. Brandt alighted and then helped them down. Justin took Belle's arm and Chloe found herself on Brandt's. Arthur trailed behind them up the marble steps to the entrance. The footman admitted them and another stepped forward to take her shawl. She reluctantly turned, and Brandt's gaze fell to her bodice. Her cheeks flamed at his blatant astonishment. She pulled her gaze away, telling herself that he had no business staring at her bosom in such a bold way. Even if it had expanded.

Thank goodness, Belle did not seem to notice anything amiss or Justin. Or Arthur, for which she was profoundly grateful.

Once they entered the ballroom, now lavishly decorated with fresh greenery, pots of plants and bouquets of flowers, her attention turned to finding Sir Preston. She spotted Emily straight away, looking like an overblown white rose in lace and flounces, and then she saw Sir Preston.

He looked quite splendid in his dark blue evening coat and black silk breeches. Yes, she could quite see herself on his arm in the future. Perhaps he was not the tallest man in the room or the most handsome, but he had a certain distinction that she found—

'Chloe, Brandt has just asked you to stand up with him for the first set.' Belle's gently amused voice broke into her thoughts.

'I…that would be very nice.' She found his gaze on her, but with a certain watchfulness she had noted in his eyes the past few days, particularly when they were in company. For some reason, it made her uneasy.

'Good.' He held out his arm. 'Shall we proceed then?'

'But the ball has not yet begun.'

'No, but I thought we could take a turn around the room.' His voice was still polite, but there was a certain note that told her he would not allow her to refuse.

She certainly did not want a scene. Rather resentful at his insistence, she rested her gloved hand on his arm. She would much rather seek out Sir Preston, but perhaps she should not make her move too soon. The ball would last for hours so there would be plenty of time.

Chloe was not so certain two hours later. She had not been able to even get near Sir Preston. He seemed to either be with a group of gentlemen or gone from the ballroom. Once she saw him talking to Emily and his mother. Then Emily had left and Chloe had started across the room. She was nearly there when Brandt appeared at her side. He had insisted she needed a lemonade and by the time she convinced him she did not, Sir Preston had vanished. She could barely conceal her impatience with Brandt. He had been in her way so much this evening, she would have accused him of following her if it weren't for the fact he would probably laugh at her. She could think of no reason why he would want to do so anyway.

She stood in one corner and looked around the room and then her heart skipped a beat. Sir Preston stood near the wall by a potted plant. For once, he was alone. She started forward, only to have Lydia grab her arm. At the same time, Brandt suddenly appeared.

'Chloe,' Lydia began and then her eyes widened when she saw Brandt. 'Good evening, Lord Salcombe.'

Chloe bit back a groan.

'Good evening, Miss Sutton.' He glanced at Chloe. 'And Chloe, of course.' His expression was rather mocking.

'I do not want to be rude, but I am feeling rather warm. So if you will excuse me I believe I will go to the garden.'

He held her gaze, a slight smile at his mouth. 'Did you not promise me this dance?'

'I do not remember doing so.' She was too frustrated to be polite. 'Besides, I do not care to dance now.' She glanced at Lydia who was staring at her, undoubtedly taken aback by Chloe's rudeness. 'However, I am quite certain Miss Sutton would like to stand up with you.'

'Oh! No…I…I…' Lydia stammered, turning pink. She managed to recover. 'I…I would be most honoured to stand up with Lord Salcombe.'

For a dreadful moment she thought he would refuse. He did not. 'I would be honoured as well, if you will favour me with the next dance, Miss Sutton.'

'That will work out quite well, then.' Chloe gave him a cold smile and marched off. Sir Preston was much where she had last seen him. His face creased in a smile as he watched her approach. 'Lady Chloe, haven't yet spoken to you. Seems you are always occupied. Hope you are enjoying the ball.'

'Oh, yes.' Her hands suddenly felt clammy and her stomach had started to churn. 'I…I am. And you? Are you not dancing at all? Even after the lesson?'

He grimaced. 'Fear it will take more than one or two lessons. Decided I didn't want to risk any lady's feet tonight.' He glanced out at the floor. 'Looks to be a waltz. You should be dancing.'

A waltz? She had hardly noticed. She spotted Brandt and Lydia straight away. Brandt had just placed his hand at Lydia's back and Lydia looked as if she had just swallowed a cream pot. Thank goodness, she had managed to evade waltzing with him, Chloe thought. She dragged her attention back to Sir Preston. 'Actually, I feel rather overheated. Do you think it is hot in here?' It was not exactly a falsehood, for she was becoming quite hot.

'Rather.' He looked concerned. 'Should I fetch the Duchess? You do look a trifle peaked.'

'Oh, no! I was rather thinking of a change of air. Perhaps I could walk to the gard—' Then she remembered she had just told Brandt that was where she wanted to go. 'Conservatory. I do not suppose you would care to accompany me?'

He hesitated. 'Most certainly. Wouldn't do for you to go alone.' He held out his arm and Chloe laid her hand on the sleeve of his coat.

She could not complain he was overly forward or flirtatious, which was fine with her. She led him from the ballroom and down the picture gallery, which connected the ballroom to the conservatory on the other side of the house. At least it should be private, which was what she needed for her plan.

No one else was there, thank goodness. A lamp was lit near the entrance, but the rest of the glass room was in shadows. The sweet scent of jasmine mingled with gardenias drifted up. Her partner shifted uncomfortably and sneezed. 'Beg pardon. Flowers make me sneeze.'

Hardly a promising start. 'We can sit on a bench,' Chloe said. She walked towards a wrought-iron seat on the other side of the room. He followed her. She sat down and patted the place next to her. 'You can sit here.'

He took the other side of the bench. Chloe frowned. Sitting this far apart would not do. She rubbed her arms. 'I fear I am getting rather cold.'

Sir Preston's gaze went to her low neckline for a second before he averted his eyes. 'Best return to the ballroom then.'

'Oh, no! I wanted to enjoy the flowers for a few minutes longer. Perhaps if I sit closer to you.' She shifted so her thigh just touched his.

He jumped. 'Er…' He looked at her face and she gave him her most demure smile. He swallowed. 'I…I do not suppose you would care to kiss me,' she blurted out and then wished she could vanish when she saw his startled expression.

As if mesmerised, he swayed towards her. His kiss was brief, and hardly enough to tell her whether she liked it or not. He drew away as if the kiss had startled him. 'Beg pardon. Not at all the thing to do.'

'I did not mind. I...I wondered if you could do it again. Longer, perhaps.'

He swallowed even harder. 'Anything to oblige.' He leaned towards her and his mouth came down on hers. This time he prolonged the contact, his lips moving over hers. It was not all unpleasant, particularly when compared to Denbigh's kiss. She would undoubtedly get used to it in time.

She tentatively kissed him back. A low sound issued from his throat and suddenly his tongue slipped into her mouth. She jumped. He pulled away, his expression stunned and then apologetic. 'Sorry. Suddenly carried away. If we go on...be obligated to offer you marriage. Not that I would mind. Have been thinking it's time to do the pretty. My mother would like it. Would be honoured if you—'

'I hardly think you've compromised Lady Chloe with one kiss.'

They both jumped at the sardonic voice that seemed to come out of nowhere. Chloe prayed she would disappear. Sir Preston half-rose. 'The devil take you, Salcombe! What do you mean by stealing up on a man like that! Having a private conversation!'

Brandt stepped out of the shadows. He folded his arms and regarded them with a stony expression. 'Lady Chloe is obligated to me for the next dance. I came to collect her.'

She had no idea whether she wanted to kill him or die of humiliation. Or do both.

'Er, had no idea.' Kentworth glanced at her. He looked confused. 'Lady Chloe was warm and wanted to cool down. So we walked here.'

'I see.' Brandt's hard gaze fell on Chloe and it took all of her will power to not look away. 'I am loath to tell you, my dear, but a kiss is hardly the way to cool down.'

She lifted her chin. 'Really.'

Kentworth took a step towards Brandt. 'Now see here. Won't have you insulting Lady Chloe. Will do my duty by her.'

'Why? I don't intend to tell anyone of this incident, and I trust you are gentleman enough not to do so.' There was a hint of steel in Brandt's voice that could almost be a threat.

Kentworth's hands curled. 'Calling my honour into question, Salcombe?' He sounded equally menacing.

They couldn't possibly be planning to fight, could they? That was not what she wanted. Brandt was deadly at fencing—she had watched him once with Justin. She suspected he was equally adept at handling a pistol. Sir Preston wouldn't stand a chance against him. She could not have him wounded or worse on her account! Not after she was the one who lured him to the conservatory. She jumped up. 'Stop this! No one is questioning anyone's honour!' She glared at Brandt. 'And none of this is your affair anyway!'

His eyes glinted. 'It most certainly is. You are now part of my cousin's family which makes you part of mine. Therefore, you are under my protection as well as my cousin's.'

'I most certainly am not!'

'Must say he is right, Lady Chloe,' Kentworth said, suddenly joining the enemy's side. 'Feel the same way about my relations and their, er…relations. Has every right to object to my, er…embracing you. Should never have done so. Still willing to offer you my hand.'

The thought apparently gave him no pleasure. Whatever was she thinking of? Trapping poor Sir Preston into a marriage he obviously didn't want only to save herself? With sickening clarity, she saw how selfish, childish and, yes, even wicked her plan had been. She could not have Sir Preston taking the blame for her actions. 'That won't be necessary, particularly since I threw myself at you. There is no reason for you to sacrifice yourself on my account. So, if you will pardon me, I believe I will return to the ballroom.' She turned on her heel and walked as quickly as possible from the conservatory.

But the humiliation hardly ended there. Emily stood outside the conservatory. She stared at Chloe, her expression contemptuous. 'How dare you attempt to trap him into marriage, you wicked creature! I swear if you have hurt him I will make you very, very sorry!' Her mouth trembled as if she were about to cry.

The truth hit Chloe with blinding force. 'You are in love with Sir Preston,' she said, stricken. 'I am so sorry. I did not mean to hurt him, or you.' She dashed away, unable to bear any more, and ran into the nearest room off the passageway.

The room was some sort of study lit only by the moonlight shining through the tall windows. There was a desk and two wing chairs and shelves on one side lined with books. She threw herself into one of the chairs and curled her legs under her.

How could she have been so utterly stupid? And forward? She had behaved like the worst trollop, wearing a low *décolletage*, padding her bodice, luring him to the conservatory, begging him to kiss her. She had never dreamed anyone would follow them there. Instead, two persons had witnessed that humiliating scene.

How long had they been there? Had they heard everything? That hardly mattered now, since she had already proclaimed that she had thrown herself at Kentworth. Brandt had looked at her with such icy contempt, she had no doubt she had made herself despicable in his eyes. And poor Emily! No wonder she had been so cold to Chloe. Why ever had she been so stupid as to not suspect Emily was in love with Sir Preston? If she hadn't been so selfish she would have seen that Emily was exactly the sort of wife Sir Preston needed. Not some silly creature who could scarcely tell one end of a sheep from the other.

She stifled a groan, and then froze when she heard footsteps and voices outside the study door. To her relief, they passed the room. She heard nothing for several minutes more. She supposed she should return to the ballroom before she was missed, but the thought of meeting Sir Preston or Brandt or Emily made her shudder. She was about to uncurl her legs from beneath her, when she heard more footsteps. She froze again, hardly daring to breathe. Surely no one would come into this dark study!

She was wrong. Her heart pounded when the person moved into the room. She folded herself more tightly into the chair. The footsteps stopped.

'Chloe,' Brandt said softly from somewhere behind her.

She fought down her panic. Perhaps if she did not answer he would go away. He came around the side of the chair and looked down at her.

'Please leave.' To her chagrin, her voice wobbled.

'Are you in love with him?'

'I beg your pardon?'

'Sir Preston. Are you in love with him?'

'I…' She should tell him it was none of his affair, but instead she said, 'I…I wanted to be. And he is the nicest man I know. I am very fond of him.'

'Is that why you wanted him to kiss you? Because you are fond of him?' His voice was harsh.

Her cheeks heated. 'I do not know,' she whispered.

'You do not know why you wanted him to kiss you? Do you know now?'

She jumped up, her humiliation turned to anger. 'Yes, I do know! I cannot see that it is any of your affair. I know you must think I am foolish and an utter wanton and undoubtedly hold me in contempt. But please do not make it worse by questioning me in such an odious fashion!'

'I don't hold you in contempt.'

'Don't you? I pray you will let me pass.'

'No.' He caught her arm and pulled her around to face him. Her eyes had adjusted to the dim light and she could see his grim expression. 'Did you like his kiss?'

She stared at him, completely taken aback. The cool, amused lord she knew had vanished. 'It…it was quite nice.'

'Quite nice?' He gave a short laugh. 'Is that all? Then allow me to give you something to compare it to.'

Before she could even think, he had pulled her hard against him. He tilted her chin with one hand and then his mouth found hers.

His kiss was nothing like Sir Preston's. Or Lord Denbigh's wet, repulsive kiss. Or the brutal, violation of her mouth so long ago. Her body seemed to meld with his; his warm, firm mouth moving over hers made her legs tremble so she was forced to cling to him. Her lips parted under his seductive pressure.

He released her so abruptly she stumbled.

'Hell,' he said.

She backed away from him. 'Oh, dear.'

'Yes.' He ran a hand through his hair. 'Damn it, Chloe, I did not mean to do that.' He wore the same pole-axed expression as Sir Preston had earlier.

'Didn't you? I...I pray you will not feel obligated to offer me marriage. After all, a kiss hardly obligates one,' she said brightly.

His expression darkened. 'No.'

She backed away. 'I...I should return to the ballroom.' The thought of facing Sir Preston and Emily was not as daunting as standing in this darkened room, the air heavy with a peculiar tension.

'Chloe, wait.' He lifted his hand towards her. 'Allow me to escort you.'

'No. You have done enough.' She turned and dashed from the room before she could humiliate herself further.

Brandt stood in the study, feeling as if he'd been punched in the stomach. What the devil had happened? No, he knew exactly what had happened. He'd allowed his baser instincts to crash through all his carefully constructed control and he had kissed Chloe. Not just any kiss. He'd kissed her with all the fierceness of a passionate lover, nearly ravishing her mouth until some semblance of rational thought had broken through. No wonder she'd fled from him.

All because of the searing, angry jealousy that had possessed him when he found her asking Kentworth to kiss her. He'd wanted to make her forget Kentworth's kiss, erase any *tendre* she had for the man.

Instead, he'd frightened her, which was undoubtedly for the best. Perhaps next time she asked for a kiss she would realise that not all men were as honourable as Sir Preston.

This hardly banished his remorse. He had only confirmed her worst opinion of his character. It shouldn't matter to him. She was far above his touch in every respect. Years ago, before he discovered what he really was, he might have allowed himself to fall in love with an innocent such as Chloe, but it was far too late for him now.

Chapter Five

Chloe rose, too nervous to sit, and went to look out of the drawing room window at the tidy garden behind the Coltranes' house. Like the rest of the house, the garden was carefully tended with a profusion of flowers and shrubs. Even on this overcast day, it looked green and inviting.

She twisted her hands together and hoped Emily would see her. After a restless sleep, she had decided she could at least try to make things right for Sir Preston and Emily. She had mustered all of her courage to come; Emily had witnessed her humiliation and, after Emily's words to her last night, she held no doubts that Emily detested her. At least she could explain and try to make amends.

Her stomach knotted even more when she heard footsteps. She turned, half-expecting to see the housekeeper, but instead Emily appeared. She wore a faded dress of yellow muslin but, despite its age, the style suited her. Her hair was pulled back in a simple chignon. Even with the smudge of mud on her cheek, she looked much more attractive than she usually did. Almost pretty, in fact.

She looked warily at Chloe. 'Mrs Potter said you wished to see me.'

'Yes.' Chloe took a deep breath. 'I wished to apologise to you.'

Surprise flashed in Emily's eyes. 'Why? I would think you would wish an apology from me for calling you a wicked creature.'

Chloe flinched, but did not look away. 'No, because you were right. It was very wicked of me to try and…force Sir Preston into marriage with me. I did not realise it until last night.'

'Are you in love with him?'

The same question Brandt has asked her, but Emily had a right to know. 'No. I thought I might be, but it was only because I wished to be. He is kind and decent and I can quite see how any woman would wish to marry him, but you are much more suited to him.'

Emily flushed. 'He does not notice me, so it hardly matters.' She twisted her hands together, a nervous gesture Chloe had never thought to see from her. 'I thought about many things as well last night. I only want him to be happy. If you would make him happy, then he must have you.'

'I do not think I would make him happy. At any rate, he does not care for me in that regard. I learned that last night as well.'

'But you were sitting alone with him. Quite close, in fact. Until Lord Salcombe showed up, that is. Then they argued and I was certain they were about to fight a duel over you.'

Thank goodness Emily had not seen the kiss. Chloe gave a little laugh. 'It was the most ridiculous thing. Lord Salcombe was angry because we were alone together. He blamed Sir Preston. When Lord Salcombe started to take me to task, Sir Preston accused him of insulting me and then I stepped in and told Lord Salcombe it was entirely my fault. Then they were both angry with me.'

'I see.' Emily did not look quite convinced, but at least she did not seem inclined to argue.

'So will you let me help you?'

'Help me do what?'

'Make Sir Preston notice you.'

Emily made a little gesture. 'Oh, no. I…I do not think that is possible. Besides—' she lifted her chin '—I have no intention of making a fool of myself over a man who does not care for me.'

Chloe sighed. 'It cannot be any worse than what I did. Besides, he does notice you. He has said the most complimentary things about you. I know he greatly admires your seat and light hands and your knowledge of farming.'

Emily coloured. 'But those are accomplishments that even Tom has. He does not notice me as a…a female. I know I am not pretty or graceful. And I hate most of my gowns. I always feel so ridiculous in lace and flounces.'

'Lace and flounces are not suited to everyone. I think you would do much better in simpler styles. The gown you are wearing today is very becoming.'

'This?' She made a face. 'But it is so old.'

'But the style is very nice for you. As is the colour. And I like your hair dressed in that particular fashion as well.'

Emily flushed, looking strangely unlike her usual forward self. 'Do you?' She looked at Chloe. 'Oh, how I wish I was as pretty as you are! You do not know how jealous I have been of you!'

'But I have red hair and freckles. I have always wanted to have a complexion such as yours. And your height. I am so tired of being short and ineffective!'

'Ineffective? I would never say that!' Emily looked

more like her blunt self again. 'Do you really wish to help me?'

'Yes. I do not have much time. I am to leave with Lord Ralston in two days, but we can at least find some gowns that would be becoming and dress your hair. I thought if you have some time today we could begin. Then you will be ready for next week's assembly.'

'I still cannot imagine why you would want to help me. I have not been nice to you at all.'

'I have not been nice to you either. Or Sir Preston.' Chloe smiled a little. 'At the very least I can try to help both of you find some happiness.'

Chloe cut through the shrubbery near Falconcliff and then found the path along the cliff above the sea. She had spent several hours with Emily going through her gowns, finally choosing one in peach moiré that suited Emily's creamy complexion. Mrs Coltrane had helped, and they both agreed all the trim except two rows of flat ribbon should be removed. After that, despite Emily's caustic comments, they arranged her hair in several ways and finally decided on a style that softened her rather broad face. Emily had stared at herself in the looking glass. 'I look almost...pretty,' she finally said.

Mrs Coltrane hugged her. 'Oh, my dear child, you look lovely. If only you had listened to me before, but you are so stubborn! I hope you will from now on!'

Emily rolled her eyes. 'Mama!'

At least that had been gratifying. Chloe bit back a sigh. She was dawdling because she dreaded returning to Falconcliff and the knowledge she was to leave soon. She should be spending as much time as possible with Julian, but it would only emphasise the reality of her leaving. She had decided last night that she would marry Lord Denbigh.

What choice did she have? If she rebelled this time, there would only be another man. She could ask Belle and Justin for assistance, but they had already done so much for both her and Mama. If Arthur did as he threatened, then Belle and Justin would be forced to help not only her but her mother as well. They would be burdens until Chloe found someone else to marry.

Engrossed in her thoughts, she did not hear the horse until it seemed to be upon her. She whirled around. Her heart leapt to her throat when she saw the bay horse and its rider. Her first impulse was to run but she could not do that. She had done enough running last night. She waited, trying to quell the nerves in her stomach as Brandt drew to a halt. His expression was hard to read as he looked down at her. 'I want to speak to you for a moment.'

'Oh.' She tried not to think of how he had kissed her, but it proved impossible with him looking at her like that.

He dismounted in a graceful easy movement and caught the reins. 'I will walk back to the house with you.'

She nodded and started to walk. He fell into step beside her. 'I wish to apologise for my behaviour last night. I did not behave as a gentleman. First I insulted you and then forced my attentions upon you.' He did not look at her.

'I...I did not behave as a lady. I suppose you meant to teach me a lesson.'

He swung around to stare at her, two spots of colour in his cheeks. 'I was wrong,' he said flatly. 'I should not have presumed to do any such thing. My actions were all that were despicable.'

'I cannot blame you for thinking I was no better than a...a callous flirt. I should thank you for saving Sir Preston from a miserable fate.'

'You wish to thank me?' He gave a short laugh. 'I am

attempting to beg your forgiveness for my damnable actions. Not accuse you.'

She looked at him steadily. 'You are not guilty. I know how wicked I was.'

'Wicked? You?' He halted and faced her. 'You are the least wicked person I know. If you thought that was what I meant last night, then I must doubly beg your pardon.'

There was nothing of the flirt about him now. He was deadly serious, the intensity of his expression made her catch her breath. She looked away. 'Then I will accept your apology.'

'Thank you.'

They walked the rest of the way to the drive in an uncomfortable silence. She almost wished he would tease her; anything would be better than this sense that unspoken words hung between them. She was relieved when they neared the side of the drive where he would need to turn to go to the stables. 'Thank you for walking me home.' Her voice sounded much too high and breathless and she forced herself to look at him.

'Yes.' He hesitated a little. 'I hope we can be friends.'

'Friends? Oh, yes. That would be nice.' What a completely inane thing to say. She rushed on. 'I hope you will enjoy living in Devon. I will own I was quite jealous when Belle told me you had bought Waverly. I always thought of it as my house. So ridiculous.' Whatever had possessed her to say such a stupid thing?

An odd expression crossed his face. 'It is not at all ridiculous.' He hesitated. 'You are welcome to visit, you know.'

'Perhaps.' She felt rather sad. It was unlikely she ever would. She had no idea what her life would be when she was married to Lord Denbigh. She gave him a bright smile and held out her hand. 'Goodbye, Lord…Brandt.'

He took it. 'This isn't quite goodbye, is it? We will see each other before you leave. There is the picnic tomorrow. Marguerite has persuaded me to have it near the old chapel at Waverly. I would be more than pleased to show you the house as well then.'

The almost boyishly eager expression on his face made her want to weep. Perhaps if they had met under different circumstances, they could be friends. There would not be a moment like this again when for once, they were in perfect accord. Tonight, they would meet at dinner and she would have her defences firmly in place. He would revert back to the impenetrable, cool lord. She smiled anyway. 'I would like that.'

'Chloe.' He hesitated as if he were about to say something else and then dropped her hand.

She turned and had started up the wide shallow steps when the door opened. Lady Kentworth marched out, head high, her lips set in a thin, angry line. Her furious gaze fell on Chloe. She came down the first step, forcing Chloe back. 'You! You may think that because you are an Earl's daughter you are too high and mighty for the likes of us! I shall make you very, very sorry for the brazen way you trifled with my son!' She sailed past Chloe, who stood stricken against the pillar.

She finally moved and stepped into the cool entrance hall and saw Arthur standing in the door of Justin's study. As if drawn by a magnet, his gaze fell on her.

'I would like to see you now,' he said coldly.

'I must change.'

'Now.'

The look on his face did not bode well. Without a doubt she knew last night's débâcle had come to his ears. To complete her humiliation, Justin now emerged from the study. At the same moment, Belle came down the stairs.

'Chloe, there you are, thank goodness. We have been worried.' She glanced at Arthur and then back at Chloe. 'But first you must go upstairs and change. And rest.'

Arthur came up to Chloe's side. 'I intend to speak to her now.'

Belle lifted her chin. 'She needs to rest.'

Arthur's lip tightened. 'I intend to find out exactly why that creature seems to think Sir Preston has compromised Chloe, before she starts to spread her lies about the neighbourhood.'

'Arthur! Not now. You are distressing Chloe,' Belle said.

'Indeed. She will be even more distressed when her reputation is ruined.' He turned a cold gaze on Chloe. 'So, my dear Chloe, perhaps you will tell me whether Sir Preston compromised you last night or not.'

Chloe wanted to sink. 'He did not…that is, I…'

'Chloe was not compromised.' Brandt's voice broke into her disjointed speech. He suddenly appeared at her side.

Chloe jumped and Arthur swung his gaze to Brandt. 'What do you know of this?' he demanded.

Brandt met his eyes. 'I was there.'

'Precisely where is "there"?'

'Precisely where did Sir Preston say he had compromised Lady Chloe?'

Arthur swung around to face him. 'See here, Salcombe, Lady Kentworth claims—'

Justin, who had been watching in silence, finally spoke. 'I suggest we should discuss this matter in my study. Belle, I would like you there as well.' He looked at Chloe. 'Belle is right, you must change and rest for a short while.'

'But I think I should…'. Chloe began, but the look on his face stopped her. His expression was not unkind, but she knew he had no intention of relenting. 'Very well, your

Grace.' She quickly turned before she humiliated herself further by bursting into stupid tears.

Brandt watched her go, then followed the others into Justin's dark-lined study. Belle sat down on the wing chair near the desk, but the others remained standing. Brandt leaned against the desk. 'What has happened?'

Arthur folded his arms over his chest and glared at him. 'I had barely arrived, hoping to speak to my ward—who, by the way, was nowhere to be found, when that Woman, a term I have grave misgivings about applying in this case, appeared, wishing to speak not only with me, but with the Duke as well. If I do not consent to a match between her son and Chloe, she will spread it about that they were caught in a compromising situation.'

'Oh, dear,' Belle said.

Brandt bit back a curse. 'She's ridiculous.'

Justin spoke. 'Nonetheless, she claims several witnesses noticed Chloe and Kentworth leaving the ballroom together and that they did not return for nearly a half an hour.'

'They were not alone,' Brandt said. 'I followed them.'

Arthur's face turned red. 'What are you saying? Are you telling me Chloe actually left the room with her son? You let her out of your sight?' His voice rose and he turned a furious look on Belle.

Justin fixed him with a cool gaze. 'Might I remind you that you were also at the ball?'

'At any rate, my ward was not properly chaperoned.'

Brandt looked at him. 'They were chaperoned. I was with them.'

'Then why did you not insist they return to the assembly room?' Arthur asked.

'I did.' He decided it was not prudent to talk about the kiss.

'Obviously not soon enough.' Arthur gave him a cold look. 'I've no desire to have that tale put about either. I doubt there's a person in England who would consider you an adequate chaperon. Your reputation is not the most sterling.'

'Arthur!' Belle said.

Justin frowned at Brandt. 'Would you be willing to vouch you were with them if necessary?'

'Of course.'

Justin looked back at Arthur. 'Despite Lady Kentworth's bluster, she will find it difficult to convince anyone that Chloe was compromised, particularly if Brandt vows he was with them the entire time. I will not hesitate to apply more pressure if necessary. A very select dinner party, perhaps. With invitations to those who do not stoop to such vulgar speculation.'

'I will hope that will put that creature's threats to rest,' Arthur said, although he looked far from pleased. 'However, I intend to do one more thing to ensure she will pose no threat to Chloe and to prevent such schemes in the future.' He paced away from them and clasped his hands behind his back. 'Lord Denbigh has offered for Chloe. We intended to wait until we had spent a few days at Denbigh Hall to make the announcement, but in light of this, I feel it is prudent to announce the betrothal now.'

'Lord Denbigh?' Belle's usually calm voice rose. She jumped up, her face ashen. 'No! You cannot have her marry him! He is a…a lecherous old man who would make her miserable!'

'I have already told her where her duty lies. It is quite natural for a young girl to be a little timid around her future husband. As for your other objection, I hardly consider three and forty ancient. She needs a husband and I do not intend to wait any longer. I intend to see her betrothed as quickly as possible.'

'Is tonight soon enough?' Brandt asked.

They all turned to look at him and Arthur shot him a stony glance. 'I trust you are joking, Salcombe. I would never accept Kentworth. Not only is he most unsuitable, I would never risk letting that harpy get a shilling of her dowry.'

'Not Kentworth.' Brandt straightened. 'Myself.'

Arthur's mouth fell open. Belle made a little gasping sound. Only Justin remained impassive.

Arthur spoke first. 'You are offering for Chloe?' His voice was rather strangled.

'Yes. I am making a formal offer.'

'One that I will not accept. I will not see her fortune fall into the hands of a penniless viscount.'

'I would be willing to wager Denbigh has more need of her fortune than I do,' Brandt said coldly. 'You may write a codicil into the settlement that stipulates any money and property she brings to the marriage is hers to do with as she pleases.'

'That is hardly satisfactory. She is an Earl's daughter and can look much higher than a viscount. I cannot possibly consider your offer.'

Brandt folded his arms. 'I suggest you accept my offer. In fact, I insist, unless you want Lady Chloe moving in some of the most unsavoury circles in England. Of course, I will call you out before I would allow that to happen.'

Ralston's mouth tightened. 'Are you threatening me, Salcombe?'

'Yes.'

'I am her guardian.'

Belle stared at Arthur, her face set. 'Chloe will not leave

this house if you persist in this. She will not be forced into marriage with such a man, no matter how high his consequence. I will not allow it.'

'Nor will I,' Justin said. His own expression was cold. 'You will accept my cousin's offer. Chloe will not leave Falconcliff with you unless you decide to abduct her although I doubt you will like the consequences if you decide on that course of action. There are few who would sympathise with your efforts to marry your innocent ward off to a debauched man against her will. I would, of course, be forced to make it known my doors are no longer open to you.'

Arthur cleared his throat. 'I assure you there is no need for such measures. I would not want Chloe to marry someone with such a reputation, of course. Lord Denbigh, however, will not be pleased.' He glanced around at the others as if hoping for sympathy for his plight, but apparently finding none, he relented. 'Very well, Salcombe, I will accept your offer. I will inform Chloe that she is to marry you instead.'

'Let me speak to her first.' The last thing Brandt wanted was to have Ralston coerce her into this. Besides, there were a few points he needed to make clear to her.

'Very well. Although I prefer to inform her first so she will see where her duty lies.'

'I think in this case it would be best if Brandt talks to her before you do,' Justin said. He glanced at Brandt, his expression hard to read. 'In fact, I think you should do so now. I will send for her. You can talk to her here.' He walked to the door. 'Ralston.'

Ralston followed him, his stance showing displeasure. Belle waited until they were gone and then turned to Brandt.

'Why do you want to marry Chloe?'

He shrugged. 'I thought I might be preferable to Denbigh. Or the next unsuitable man Ralston sets his sights on.' His voice sounded too indifferent, but he felt as if he were in some sort of dream.

'Is that the only reason?'

'No. I need a wife.' It did not sound an adequate enough reason at all.

Her eyes searched his face. 'I see,' she said softly. 'I trust you will make her happy, then.'

'I will endeavour to do so.'

She gave him a little smile and then left the room. He watched her go and then moved to the window, too restless to sit. What the hell had possessed him to offer for Chloe?

He must have suffered a moment of temporary insanity. Perhaps he could blame it on Marguerite for her matchmaking. Or on Marguerite and Giles as well as Justin and Belle for being so damnably happy in their marriages. Or the feel of tiny hands against his skin. Or Chloe, herself.

His defences were already shot by the time he'd entered the study, so when Ralston had declared she was to marry Denbigh, he'd lost control of his reason. The thought of Chloe in Denbigh's arms had been so repugnant that he knew he'd do anything to stop such a match.

Including marry her himself.

Chloe stopped in front of the study and took a deep breath. She had no idea why Brandt would want to see her, and the peculiar look on Belle's face had confused her. She had not told Chloe what had happened during the interview and only said that she should see Brandt first.

She knocked and at Brandt's deep 'Come in' stepped into the room. Late afternoon sunlight streamed through the window. He moved and came to stand in front of the desk. Brandt stared at her for a moment before speaking. 'Please sit down.'

She perched on the edge of a hard-back chair and clasped her hands in her lap. 'Belle said you wished to see me about something.'

'Yes.' He leaned back against the desk and almost instantly moved away. He seemed nervous, which was odd because she did not imagine he was often nervous about anything.

He turned to look at her. 'Did she tell you why I wanted to see you?'

'No. She did not say much of anything.' She hardly ever felt annoyed with Belle, but she almost did today. But perhaps it was only because she feared she might cry instead. She raised her chin. 'In fact, I know nothing about what has been said. I suppose Arthur was very angry and demanded to know if it were true that I went off with Sir Preston. Of course, even if I was compromised Arthur would not like that because he wishes me to marry L…someone else instead.' She probably made no sense at all.

'Denbigh?'

Stunned, she stared at him. 'I suppose Arthur told you that. Yes, I am to marry Lord Denbigh. Unless I can think of another way to stop Arthur,' she added bitterly.

Comprehension dawned in his face. 'Is that what you were about with Kentworth? You hoped to compromise him in order to escape marriage with Denbigh?'

Her face flamed. How callous and selfish it sounded, as if she had no thought at all for Sir Preston. She at least owed it to him to try and explain that it was not completely that way. 'Yes, but that was only part of it. I…I thought Sir Preston was exactly the sort of husband I wanted. He is so kind and decent and I wanted to be in love with him.

I suppose I convinced myself that he returned my affections. When Arthur told me I was to marry Lord Denbigh, I decided I would force Sir Preston's hand. I...I realised as soon as he offered me marriage how wicked it was to try and trap him.' She took a deep breath and forced herself to look at him. 'I...I am grateful you followed us. I imagine you told Arthur, and Belle, and Justin that.'

'Only that I was with you in the conservatory. None of the rest.'

'Thank you.' She looked away for a moment. 'Does Arthur wish me to announce my betrothal to Lord Denbigh straight away?'

'No.' He hesitated. 'You are to become engaged to me instead.'

'Engaged to you?' Her head spun for a moment and her voice suddenly seemed far away. 'But why?'

'It was either me or Lord Denbigh. I've no intention of letting you fall into Denbigh's hands, so it was me.'

'You...you offered for me so I would not be forced to marry Lord Denbigh?'

'Yes.' His expression was watchful and she had no idea what he was thinking.

'I still do not understand why. You cannot possibly want to marry me! Is it because of last night? I told you that did not matter.'

'No, it is not because of last night,' he said quietly.

'But why? I still do not understand why. You cannot possibly want to marry me. I don't even think you like me! And I am an heiress! You do not want an heiress!'

A slight smile touched his mouth. 'I have no intention of touching a penny of your money. And you are quite wrong about the other,' he said softly.

A feeling of pure panic washed over her. She had no idea why, but the thought of having him want to marry her scared her. He was not at all the sort of man she wanted. Nor did she want him to...to like her. Not like that.

'No. I cannot!'

'Why not? A few days ago you informed me that Newgate was not a preferable option over wedding me.'

'We...we are not suited. I...I have no idea why you would think so.'

'We agreed earlier that we are both fond of children. You pointed out that you needed a husband to have a family of your own.'

'Yes, but not now!' She hardly knew what she was saying. 'I said I did not want a husband.'

'You are contradicting yourself. You wanted to marry Sir Preston.'

'But that was different!'

'How?'

'He...he would make a comfortable husband.'

'Ah. So you are afraid I will ride roughshod over you and consider you are a mere convenience?'

'Yes, if you must know!'

A little smile touched his mouth. 'I doubt I would ever consider you a mere convenience. Would it help if I promise not to be an overbearing husband? And you would have my house, you know.'

'Your house?'

'Waverly. I believe you told me earlier that you considered it your house and were jealous that I had bought it. It would now be yours as well.'

'It was a most stupid thing to say.' She tore her gaze away and looked down at her lap. 'I...I am much obliged by your offer, but I cannot marry you since—'

In two strides he was in front of her, his eyes blazing with anger. His hands clamped down on either side of her, imprisoning her in the chair. She stared at him and swallowed.

'What you don't understand, my dear Lady Chloe, is that you have no choice. You either accept my offer or you will find yourself betrothed to Denbigh. Or the subject of Lady Kentworth's vicious rumours. Since I will not allow either of those to happen, we will announce your betrothal to me instead. Furthermore, I'm not making you an offer, I am telling you what you are going to do. Do you understand?'

His face was inches from hers. She could see the colour of his eyes, a fascinating mixture of green and brown, and the shadow of beard around his mouth. Her heart was pounding and she felt breathless, and she had no idea if she was afraid or if it was something else altogether. Her gaze went to his mouth and she felt almost dizzy.

'Chloe?'

She blinked to clear her head. 'What?'

'Did you understand what I just said to you?' He pulled away, his voice impatient.

'Yes. I am going to become betrothed to you.' At least that was what she thought he said.

Now he was scowling. 'There is no need to sound so subdued. I am not planning to beat you.'

'I hardly thought that!' She stood and glared back at him. 'But there is no need for you to sacrifice yourself for me. If I hadn't acted so stupidly then there would be no need for you to do this. I think it would be best if I married Lord Denbigh.'

'I'll abduct you before that happens,' he said softly. He took a step towards her and this time she backed up. She could see he was truly angry and it scared her.

He stopped in front of her, but made no move to touch her. 'And you are wrong. I am not sacrificing myself.'

She suddenly felt alone and a little afraid. Everything had spun out of control.

He looked into her face and for a moment she believed he could read her thoughts. The sensation was not welcome. He suddenly stepped back. 'There is no need to look so stricken, I will not force you to the altar. I meant what I said before—I cannot afford a wife and I've no intention of marrying for money. Particularly not you. We will announce our betrothal, but make it clear there will be no wedding in the immediate future. After a suitable time, when all danger of gossip or Lord Denbigh is past, you may cry off. However, I suggest you wait at least two months.'

So, he really did not want her after all. She should feel relieved, but instead she felt as if she wanted to cry. Which made no sense because she did not want to marry him. 'Very well. I agree to your terms.'

'Good.' His voice was neutral. 'Then we should return to the drawing room and tell the others.'

'Yes.' She followed him to the door. He held it open for her and waited for her to pass. In a daze, she went with him to the drawing room. They were all there. She nearly turned tail and ran, but Brandt took her hand and he drew her forward. 'You may congratulate us. Chloe has agreed to accept my hand in marriage.'

None of them looked the least bit surprised, so, she realised, they had known what he planned to do. Justin came forward first. He took Chloe's other hand. 'I am more than pleased with my cousin's choice. Welcome to the family. Again.'

She managed a smile, although she felt as if she were in some sort of strange dream. 'Thank you.'

Belle was next. She planted a soft kiss on Brandt's cheek and enveloped Chloe in a warm embrace. She finally stepped back and Chloe saw she had tears in her eyes. 'Belle?'

'It is just…' Belle stopped. 'Please forgive me.'

Arthur was next. He shook Brandt's hand and then took Chloe's. 'Congratulations. I hope you will be most happy,' he said stiffly. He dropped her hand and looked at Brandt. 'I trust you will announce the betrothal immediately.'

'I will send the notice to the London papers tomorrow.'

'And the marriage? I assume it will take place as soon as the banns are posted.'

'We…' Chloe began.

Brandt glanced at her. 'The marriage will take place after I have finished the major renovations to Waverly. Chloe should at least have a drawing room and a bed-chamber that does not leak.'

'You do have another house,' Arthur said.

'Yes, but Chloe wishes to live at Waverly. It is near her family.'

Arthur looked unconvinced. 'Very well.' He eyed Chloe. 'We will need to inform Maria. I dare say she will be quite disappointed when she learns there will be no visit to Denbigh House, after all, since the purpose was to announce Chloe's betrothal to Lord Denbigh.'

'I am quite certain she will recover from her disappointment when she discovers Chloe is to marry my cousin and live near Belle,' Justin said. 'Of course, Chloe will remain with us until the wedding.'

Arthur cleared his throat. 'Her home is still at Braddon Hall until she marries. I've no doubt Lady Ralston would like her daughter with her.'

'Maria may come here and stay with us,' Belle said. 'I intend to write to her today. Also, of course, she will want to be present for the small party we will hold in honour of the betrothal. You will be invited as well.'

'A party? I would think it more appropriate if such an affair was held at Braddon Hall.'

Everything was going much too fast. 'I would rather there was no party at all.' They all turned to look at her. 'If you will pardon me, I would like to go to my bedchamber.'

Belle instantly looked contrite. 'Oh, Chloe, of course you must. I have no doubt you must be feeling quite confused. Shall I go with you?'

'No. I shall be fine.' She wanted to be by herself.

'I will escort you.' Brandt moved away from the window.

'It is not necessary.'

'But I wish to.'

Out in the hall, she stopped and looked up at him. 'I do not need an escort.'

'Not even your fiancé?'

'You are not really my fiancé.' She started to move away.

He caught her arm. 'But I am.'

'We are only pretending.'

'Not until you officially cast me aside,' he said lightly, but there was something in his eye that made her think he did not find it amusing at all.

Her heart started beating in that odd way again and she felt that peculiar flicker of panic. He dropped her arm. 'I will take you to your room. It would not do if we are seen disagreeing so quickly.'

They did not speak until they reached the door of her bedchamber when she forced herself to meet his eyes. 'Thank you, Lord Salcombe.'

'What happened to my given name? Now that we are betrothed, do you no longer plan to use it?'

'Of course. I…I am just rather confused.'

He looked at her for a moment. 'Quite understandable. In the space of twenty-four hours you have expected to wed three men.'

She felt as if he had struck her. It sounded so callous. She turned away before he could see her expression.

'Damn it, Chloe, that is not what I meant to say.'

'It is quite true.' Her voice wobbled and to her dismay tears suddenly pricked her lids.

'Are you crying?'

'No.' She opened her door. 'G…good day.'

He stepped around so that he was facing her. With gentle fingers he lifted her chin. 'You are crying. I beg your pardon. I did not mean to say something so damnably stupid.' His expression was rueful. 'I only meant to say you have good reason to be confused. I am confused.'

'If you wish to stop this now, I will not mind.'

'No.' He dropped his hand away. 'I do not wish to stop this now. How would that look? Besides, you'd end up with Denbigh again.' He stepped away from her. 'I will see you at dinner.'

'Very well.' She forced herself to meet his eyes. She should not be arguing with someone so determined to save her from a horrible marriage. 'Thank you. You are very kind.'

'I am not kind at all,' he said abruptly. His gaze fell to her mouth and then he jerked it away. 'Good afternoon, Chloe.' He turned on his heel and left.

She watched him, a strange sense of loss creeping over her. Nothing seemed right any longer. She should be grateful to him, but instead she felt horrible that he had felt it necessary to come to her rescue in such a way. All of the things she had thought he was were completely untrue.

Now she had ruined his life as well.

* * *

What the devil had come over her? Brandt had returned to stare at her closed door. He'd fully expected her to take him to task and instead she had looked as if she thought he was about to beat her. The way she said his name.... He'd rather have her call him by his title if she intended to address him in that damnably contrite voice.

Hell. He raised his hand to knock and then dropped it. He could hardly stand here demanding she tell him what was wrong. She would probably retreat even further.

Which was perhaps for the best. He ran a hand through his hair and turned from her door. As much as he might want to tease her, he had no doubt the betrothal would end when the two months had passed. In all truth, despite the attraction he felt for her, she was not precisely the sort of calm, sensible wife he wanted.

Just as he was not the sort of comfortable husband she wanted. He shoved the unwelcome thought aside.

It was perhaps better if they did not appear to be too fond of one another.

Chapter Six

The soft knock startled Chloe from the daze she'd been in ever since Brandt had left her an hour ago. A book lay open on her lap, but reading had proved impossible. She had finally given up and curled up in the chair, staring out of the window at the clouds gathering in the distance over the water.

Belle entered the room and moved to Chloe's side. 'Why did you not tell us that Arthur had plans to marry you to Lord Denbigh? If I had known, if we had known, we would have stopped him.'

'He threatened to cut off my allowance and I did not want that. I have been helping Mama a little, you know she never has any idea of economy and I did not want her to go without. Lord Denbigh showed an interest in London, but then I became ill and I heard no more about him until Arthur wrote that we had been invited to Denbigh Hall. I knew nothing about Lord Denbigh's offer until Arthur arrived.' She avoided Belle's eyes. 'Then I thought that perhaps I might find another husband.'

'Sir Preston?' Belle asked gently.

Chloe drew in a breath. 'It was most ridiculous of me. He was only being kind. Oh, Belle, I was so wicked. I enticed him away to the conservatory and then asked him to kiss me. Then when he offered to marry me I knew it was only because he felt obligated.'

'I see.' Belle was silent for a moment. 'He is very kind and very decent and I've no doubt he considers you a friend. I do not suppose you have had many men that have been your friend. Under the circumstances, I can understand why you thought of him in that way, but I do not think you would have suited.'

'I know that now. Oh, Belle, I have made such a fool of myself.'

'I do not think Sir Preston will say anything. Or Brandt.'

'I cannot marry Brandt, you know.'

'Why not?'

'We are not at all suited either and, besides, I do not think he really wants to marry me. He felt obliged to offer for me so I would not have to marry Lord Denbigh.'

Belle looked at her. 'Then why did you accept his offer?'

'He gave me no choice. He said if I did not he would abduct me.' She was beginning to feel a little annoyed.

Instead of expressing outrage, Belle's lips twitched as if she wanted to laugh. 'Oh, dear. I will own that doesn't sound like a man who feels too obligated. If you really believe you are not suited, then you can change your mind. Justin and I will always help you or Maria if you are in need. But it would be best if you waited before deciding you wish to call off the betrothal. It will look most odd if you cry off right away. And there is Lady Kentworth to consider as well. She has threatened to spread it about you were seen leaving the assembly with Sir Preston. I know you would never want such a malicious thing spread about. At least if that should happen we can put it about that it was Brandt you left with. And that was when he made his offer.' She smiled a little. 'And if you wait, you might find Brandt suits you very well after all.'

'I doubt it.' Chloe plucked at the cover. It all seemed very logical but somehow Belle's assumption was quite irking. 'I doubt he thinks I suit him either. He said I should wait for at least two months before breaking off the betrothal.'

'Did he?' Belle started and then laughed. 'I must say it doesn't sound the most promising way to begin a betrothal with both parties intending to cry off. Oh, dear, what a muddle! At least we will have you with us for another two months and who knows what might happen during that time?' She stood. 'I came to help you dress for dinner.' She looked at Chloe's face. 'Please do not look so disgruntled. It is not a death sentence, you know. Brandt is not so very dreadful. There are any number of women who would envy you.'

Chloe rose. 'Well, I am not one of them. He is not the sort of man I want to marry.'

'But I thought you and Brandt have agreed you won't marry.'

'We did.'

Somehow she did not think Belle was taking her at all seriously, particularly when she cheerfully said, 'Then there is nothing to fret over. And one more thing, which should make you happy. Arthur is to leave Devon tomorrow so you can enjoy the picnic without his disapproving countenance. He is still rather disgruntled that we are not holding the betrothal party at Braddon Hall. However, he has consented to return with Maria in time for your party here.'

Chloe's frowned at the closed door after Belle left. Well, she intended to approach this betrothal in a practical, rational fashion. She certainly did not intend to make sheep's eyes at Brandt or bring his name into every conversation the way some of the young ladies did who had become engaged in the past Seasons. Even Serena had seemed to interject Charles's name a little too often into conversations and now into her letters. No, she would behave with the utmost dignity. She had no intention of making a fool of herself again.

To Chloe's dismay, the next day was perfect for a picnic. Already dressed in her riding habit, she stood at the window, hoping to spot some indication that rain was imminent, but the clouds were fluffy and startlingly white against the cerulean blue sky.

After the events of the past two days she felt little desire to go on a picnic, particularly one that included Sir Preston, Emily and Lady Kentworth. And Brandt.

She closed her eyes for a moment. How had this ever happened? She was betrothed to the arrogant, high-handed Lord Salcombe; a man she had detested the first time she had met him for his cold disdain towards Belle. Even after Belle had told her that in the end he had been responsible for bringing her and Justin together, she could not persuade herself to like him.

Except her dislike was proving more and more difficult to maintain. He and Belle treated each other with the easy familiarity of old friends and Chloe had no doubt he would do everything in his power to protect Belle and Julian if anything should happen to Justin. And how could she detest a man who treated Julian with such gentle care or showed such interest in Will and Caroline? Yesterday, when he apologised, his arrogance gone, she had glimpsed the eager, vulnerable youth he might once have been, and she had known he was someone she could like very, very much.

And for whatever reason, he had offered to marry her in order to save her from Denbigh.

She turned away from the window and wished she did not feel so confused. She would much rather think of him as an enemy, continue to keep him at arm's length. It would be much safer.

Also she did not want to see Waverly, the house he said would be hers if they married. She had no idea why that made her feel so uncomfortable.

Perhaps she could plead a headache. She did have a very slight one that sometimes resulted when she slept poorly, but they generally did not get much worse as long as she was not in the sun for very long. Certainly that would be an understandable excuse to not go to the picnic.

She would write a note now.

A few minutes after sending the note, she heard a knock on her door. She opened it and nearly jumped when she saw Brandt. 'Belle said you had the headache,' he said without preamble. His expression was cool.

'Well, yes. It is just a little one.' Taken aback, she had no time to formulate a more believable response.

'Are you certain? Or do you merely wish to avoid certain persons today?'

She had no doubt the heat flooding her cheeks gave her away. 'That, also.'

'You will need to see Kentworth and the others some time. Preferably today.'

'I would rather not. It is true that I do not feel at all the thing,' she said defensively.

'Then you might consider this.' He rested his forearm against the door jamb. 'Justin has decided it would be wise to informally announce the betrothal before the meal today. It would be best if you were there as well. Unless you would prefer the neighbourhood to speculate that the thought of marriage to me has sent you into a decline. Sir Preston might feel obliged to offer you marriage again in order to save you from my clutches.' There was a slight smile at his mouth that did not quite reach his eyes.

'Do you believe he might do that?' She could not think of anything more horrible at this point.

'Do you wish him to?' His smile suddenly looked rather dangerous.

'No, of…of course not. It would be the most terrible muddle. It would overset Em…everyone.' She took a deep breath. 'If you think it best, then I will go.'

He straightened. 'Are you certain you are well enough to ride today?' he asked abruptly.

'I have the very slightest of headaches, but I will be fine as long as I am not in the sun for very long periods.'

'Then you will ride with Belle and Julian in the barouche. Stay out of the sun and wear your hat. And let me know straight away if you begin to feel unwell. I will see you at the Haversham estate.'

She was too astonished to reply and could only gape as he strode away. Whatever had come over him? First, he had not seemed to believe her at all and then he was suddenly concerned about her health. And then he dictated she was to ride in the carriage.

He was completely incomprehensible. Just because they were betrothed did not mean he could order her about in such a way. Well, she had no intention of riding in the carriage as much as she might like to be with Julian and Belle. She would ride Maisy behind the carriage instead.

But as Chloe approached the edge of Waverly's property, she began to wish she had travelled in the carriage with Belle after all. When she had ridden up to the carriage with Maisy, Justin had told her that with her horse's dawdling pace, they would be fortunate if they arrived at Waverly in time to depart. She had best take the shortcut through the field with Brandt.

She realised Brandt had not informed them that he wanted her to ride in the carriage. She could quite imagine his sardonic expression if she showed up at the stables looking for him now. Instead of going to find Brandt, she dallied around until she was certain he would be gone.

By the time she reached the field at Haversham Hall where they were to meet the others, everyone had gone. Maisy had ambled along on her short legs, and if Chloe attempted to push her at all, she pinned her ears back and wheezed. She finally decided that they must cut through the sunny field rather than follow the path through the shady woods. The bright sun only increased her headache and now that she had finally reached Waverly's property she felt almost dizzy.

She urged Maisy forward, but once in the clearing near the old abbey, she halted again when she saw most of the guests had arrived. More dismaying, she could see no sign of the party from Falconcliff. Whatever would she tell Brandt when he came upon her?

Brandt was nowhere in sight, but she spotted Sir Preston standing with Tom Coltrane and Mr Rushton. Her heart pounded and she berated herself again for coming alone. At least, if she had arrived with Belle and Justin, she would not have drawn nearly as much attention to herself as she would if she rode up by herself.

'Chloe! Chloe!'

Will stood on a section of the old stone wall, waving at her. What if he fell? She urged Maisy into a trot, but before she reached the wall, Will had jumped down. Her heart leapt to her throat when he stumbled, but he recovered and dashed towards her. 'I was waiting for you! Why did you ride poor old Maisy? She can never keep up.' He gave the mare an affectionate pat on the neck.

'Because she wanted an outing. Will, you should not be standing on the wall. It is crumbling and you could be hurt.'

'I won't be! Papa says I climb like a monkey. Look! I lost a tooth last night!' He grinned up at her, the missing tooth making him look even more endearing. 'Come and sit with us! The groom brought Lion and he is sitting with Caroline. And we have a ball so I can help you practise your throws. You are getting much better,' he added encouragingly.

'That would be very kind.' Throwing a ball with Will and sitting with Caroline and their nearly grown puppy appealed to her much more than mingling with the rest of the guests. She must face the others at some point, but perhaps if she put it off a little she would feel better prepared. She slid from Maisy and Jennings, one of the grooms, took the mare's reins.

Will grabbed her hand and led her across the grass and around the east wall of the abbey towards the shade of some tall trees. 'Caroline and Lion are over there.'

As they passed the gate leading to the abbey garden, they nearly collided with Lady Kentworth and her cousin, an elderly lady who acted as her companion. Lady Kentworth stopped and stared at Chloe. 'I wonder that you dare show your face, but then I dare say because you are an Earl's daughter and great friends with a Duchess you think you can be as brazen and bold as you wish!'

The malice in her face made Chloe ill. Before she could say a word, Will marched forward and stared up at her, his face stern. 'You are not to speak to Lady Chloe in such a way! You must apologise immediately.'

Lady Kentworth's mouth fell open. Her cheeks turned

a dull, splotchy red. 'You are impertinent and ill mannered. If you were my son you would be beaten soundly for such manners.'

Chloe found her voice. 'It was wrong of him to speak to you in such a way, but it is just as wrong of you to say such a thing to him.' She looked down at Will. 'You must apologise to Lady Kentworth for speaking to her so rudely.'

'But...' He looked bewildered.

'I know.' She stooped in front of him and looked into his face. 'Please do it.' She feared that, if he did not, Lady Kentworth would take some sort of revenge on him. 'Please, Will.' He stared at her, his mouth stubborn, and then finally looked back up at Lady Kentworth. 'I am sorry that I was impertinent and ill mannered.' His voice was contrite, almost too contrite. Chloe prayed Lady Kentworth would not notice.

The woman stared at him for a moment. 'I trust that in the future you will remember to speak to your elders in a more suitable fashion.' She turned to her companion, who had stood with her eyes down cast the entire time. 'I would like to join the others.' She brushed past Chloe without speaking.

Will stared after her. 'I did not want to apologise,' he said in a low voice. 'She was the one who was impertinent and ill mannered and if she ever says such things to you again I will call her out!'

'You cannot call out a lady,' Chloe said gently. 'I know you did not want to apologise but sometimes it is better to do so even if you feel you are right. I did not want Lady Kentworth to become angry with you because of me.' She looked down at his bowed head. 'It was very gallant of you to stand up for me. I will always remember that.'

He looked up finally. 'I always stand up for my friends.'

'I know.' She smiled at him. 'Shall we find Lion and Caroline, and play a game of catch?' She hoped that would distract him.

He brightened a little. 'All right.'

Caroline sat on a blanket with Lion, a large gangly pup of indeterminate parentage. He bounded up, pulling Caroline with him, and nearly fell himself in his enthusiasm to greet Chloe. Caroline tugged on his lead with all her might in an effort to keep him from leaping on Chloe. 'Sit!' she said.

He sat for an instant and then leapt back up, his eyes intent on Chloe's face. 'Sit, Lion,' she told him in a stern voice. He reluctantly obeyed and she patted his head.

Caroline sighed. 'He never listens to me. I know I should tie him, but he hates it so.'

'Chloe! Here is the ball!' Will called. 'Stand back and I will throw it to you.'

'All right.' Although she really would prefer to sit for a while. She felt tired and the encounter with Lady Kentworth had only increased her headache.

She moved towards the wall and Will tossed the ball. She caught it.

'Very nice.'

She whirled around, the ball falling from her hand. Brandt stood behind her. She stared at him, suddenly breathless. 'What are you doing here?'

'This is my property.'

'I only meant what are you doing behind me. I did not see you.'

He stooped and picked up the ball and then straightened. 'I came over with some intention of greeting you as a proper host should. As well as to inquire why you did not inform me you intended to ride rather than drive. I believe we agreed you were to drive with Belle.'

'No, you told me I was to ride in the carriage and then walked away. I did not have a chance to agree or disagree with you. You merely assumed I agreed with you.'

'I was mistaken. I beg your pardon. Next time I will be certain you agree with me before I walk away.'

'But I might disagree with you.'

'Perhaps, but I will do my utmost to persuade you.' He had a little smile on his mouth.

She had no idea what he was talking about; it was turning into one of those conversations that made her feel out of her depth. She was relieved when Will ran up. 'Uncle Brandt! Have you come to play ball with us? I have been helping Chloe learn to throw and catch. Do you want her to throw the ball to you?'

'Once. Since I am the host, I should not be away too long from my guests.' He glanced at Chloe. 'And Chloe should not overtax herself. She should be sitting, not chasing balls around.'

'I rarely chase balls since I can now catch them quite nicely.'

'Another one of your surprising talents?' He looked amused.

'Yes. So if you will move back I will throw the ball to you.'

He stepped back a few inches. 'Is this too far?'

'No. You may move back.'

He took a few steps back.

'More, if you please.' For some reason, the grin on his face was most annoying. Obviously, he thought she could barely toss a ball. Although her habit was fitted rather tight across the bodice and she could not pull her arm very far back, he did not need to stand so close to her that she could hand the ball to him.

'Is this far enough?'

He'd moved way back now. Too far back. However, she had no intention of standing here all day, directing him to the perfect spot. She drew her arm back and then threw the ball with all her might. As she did so she heard an ominous rip. Brandt ducked as the ball narrowly missed his head and then it fell to the ground and rolled towards the assembled company. Suddenly Lion burst across the grass, his lead trailing behind him. There was a shriek as the ball rolled past Lady Kentworth's feet and Lion scrambled after it. Then Lady Kentworth fell.

Chloe froze, her mouth open in dismayed horror as Lion bounded over to Lady Kentworth and licked her face. The lady shrieked again, this time a much more bloodcurdling scream. Giles grabbed Lion's collar and pulled him away.

Will was jumping up and down. 'That was splendid!'

'But Lion knocked Lady Kentworth down,' Caroline said. She looked as sick as Chloe felt.

'That's why it was splendid!'

'No, it wasn't,' Chloe said. As much as she wanted to run in the opposite direction, Chloe had no choice. She started forward.

'I'd best go fetch Lion. Come with me, Will.' Brandt strode towards the group and Chloe followed.

By this time Lady Kentworth was sitting up and she waved away the vinaigrette Marguerite held under her nose. Giles thrust the lead at Brandt and then turned to Will. 'You will first apologise to Lady Kentworth and then you will come with me.'

Will turned pale. 'I…'

Lady Kentworth stared first at Chloe and then at Will, her eyes narrowed, her face a frightening purplish-red. 'You…!'

'William,' Giles said.

'It was my fault.' Chloe stepped forward and forced

herself to meet Lady Kentworth's eyes. 'I threw the ball. I…I am so very sorry. I did not think it would go so far. Will did nothing wrong.' She was quite aware that everyone looked at her and she felt mortified and foolish beyond belief.

Caroline came up beside Chloe. She bit her lip, but managed to look at Lady Kentworth. 'I was holding Lion. He pulled away from me. I should have tied him but I…I did not. I am very sorry.'

Lady Kentworth stared at them, her mouth thinning. 'Well!'

Brandt moved next to Chloe. 'And I am to blame as well. I stood too far from Lady Chloe so she was obliged to execute a rather forceful throw which undoubtedly accounted for the great distance the ball travelled. In addition, I did not assist in securing Lion and should have known he would most naturally go after a ball. So I must apologise as well.'

Lady Kentworth looked from one to the other, her mouth tight as if she suspected some sort of conspiracy. 'I quite see.'

Giles looked at them, his expression impassive, and then turned to Will. 'I see I erred in judging you without hearing the entire story. However, in the future I expect you to exert more control over your dog otherwise he will be banished from such excursions.'

Will hung his head. 'Yes, sir.'

'And, Caroline, if you cannot control Lion, then you will give him to someone who can.'

'Yes, Papa.' Caroline still looked mortified.

'Perhaps we should secure Lion now,' Brandt said. 'Come with me.'

The two children went with him, undoubtedly happy to get away. Sir Preston helped his mother to her feet while

Chloe made herself move forward. 'There are some chairs. Shall I have—?'

'You have done enough!' Lady Kentworth snapped. 'Do not come near me!'

There was a shocked silence. Chloe dared not meet Sir Preston's eyes, or anyone else's. Her head seemed to spin for a moment. 'If you will pardon me, I will go and see if I am needed…' She started to walk away before she humiliated herself further by bursting into tears.

Chloe found herself in the overgrown garden of the old chapel where she sat on a broken stone bench and prayed she would not weep. She had managed to humiliate herself again in front of most of the neighbourhood.

She had always considered herself practical and never prone to impulsiveness, but since she'd been at Falconcliff she had been nothing but foolish. Everything she did resulted in more disaster. And today appeared to be growing worse. If she had not set out to prove to Brandt that he could not dictate to her, then she would not be on his property with a stupid headache. She probably would not have met Lady Kentworth when she was with Will, so that Will was forced to defend her, thus incurring Lady Kentworth's wrath as well. If she hadn't been so stupidly determined to show Brandt she could throw a ball, Lady Kentworth would not have gone sprawling on the ground. And if she had not been so idiotic to begin with, then she would not be betrothed to Brandt after…

Someone stood in front of her. She slowly looked up into Brandt's face and, to her chagrin, tears pricked her lids.

His face changed. 'You aren't going to cry, are you? Chloe, it wasn't that bad,' he said roughly.

She gulped. 'Y…yes, it was. I knocked Lady Kentworth

down and nearly got Will into trouble again. And made a complete fool of myself.'

He sat down next to her. 'I have no doubt everyone knew it was an accident.'

'I nearly hit you.'

His eyes danced. 'I'm not certain that was an accident.'

'It was. I would never want to hit anyone, not even you.'

This time he laughed. 'I am gratified to hear that. Next time I will show you how to throw a ball properly.'

'I do not think there will be a next time.' She looked away.

'No? Why not?'

'Because it is a completely unladylike thing to do.'

'So?'

'So, I will not do it. I am too old for such things.'

'You will disappoint Will.'

'At least I will not create more trouble for him. He has already incurred Lady Kentworth's wrath twice today because of me.'

'He told me.' His eyes lost their amusement. 'At least come back to the picnic, Chloe.'

She bit her lip. 'I've torn my sleeve as well.'

'It does not matter. Nothing improper shows. And if it worries you I can have my housekeeper repair it for you.'

'Perhaps I should return to Falconcliff.'

'You cannot always run away.'

He undoubtedly referred to the night of the ball. 'Sometimes it is preferable.'

'Sometimes, but most of the time it only puts off what one has to face eventually. You cannot hide away from the neighbourhood. And as much as you might wish to…' his gaze held hers '…you cannot avoid me. We are betrothed.'

The denial she was about to make died on her lips. 'I am sorry,' she whispered.

'You don't need to apologise. I cannot make you like me, but if we hope to convince Lady Kentworth as well as your cousin that we are truly betrothed, it would be best if you could at least hold your dislike in check. And occasionally attempt to appear as if you take some pleasure in my company.'

'Brandt…' she began. 'I am sorry.'

'Don't be.' He rose. 'I think we should return to the others before we cause even more speculation. Belle has probably arrived and will worry if she does not find you.' He held out his hand.

She placed hers in his and stood. His hand, around hers, was warm and strong. She glanced at his face, finding no anger or censure there, something she might have expected after such a conversation. Her actions only seemed more childish.

Marguerite met them as they left the garden. 'There you are! Oh, Chloe, I meant to speak to you immediately but when I turned around you had disappeared. Emily thought you might be here and said she thought Brandt had followed you. Then Lady Kentworth began to fuss about the chair and the lemonade so I was quite occupied trying to mollify her before she ruined everything for everyone else.' She peered at Chloe's face. 'Oh, sweet child, there is no need to look so distraught. You must pay no heed to Lady Kentworth. She is the most unpleasant person and is always exceedingly rude when people displease her and the only reason we put up with her is because everyone is so fond of Sir Preston. I dare say more than one person present wanted to cheer when Lion knocked her down.'

Chloe was mortified all over again. 'I did not mean to do such a thing.'

'No one thinks that at all,' Marguerite said. 'Belle is here and wants to see you. Will gave her a rather confused and quite dramatic version of the event and Belle is now worried. So you must come with me and reassure her.' Her gaze fell to where Brandt still held Chloe's hand. 'Although I can see that perhaps she does not need to worry very much at all.'

Chloe pulled her hand away, self-conscious at the speculative look in Marguerite's eye. Brandt seemed not to notice. 'Then I will send Chloe with you,' he said easily. 'I will see both of you shortly.'

He strode off towards the others while Marguerite turned to her with a little smile. 'Well! I never thought to see you and Brandt walking hand in hand. You must be careful or everyone will start to speculate when the announcement will be made.'

Chloe's cheeks heated. She should say something, but Marguerite was already speaking again. 'I am only teasing you! I know very well Brandt provokes you terribly and is possibly the last man you would ever consider for a husband. However, I hope you will own he is not quite the ogre you thought him to be.'

'I really do not think he is an ogre at all.' She could only imagine the look on Marguerite's face when the betrothal was announced. 'In fact—'

'Chloe! The Duchess is here!' Will dashed up to them. 'Julian has just spat up all over the Duke! Just like Emma does to Papa. And to me,' he added with disgust.

'Oh, dear,' Marguerite said. She met Chloe's eyes over his head, her mouth twitching. 'I fear all babies do that. At least when they are your age, they stop.'

Will made a disbelieving sound. 'I've never spat up on anyone.'

'It is only that you do not remember,' Marguerite said

with maternal fondness. 'Perhaps you can escort Chloe to the Duchess while I see to the food. I am worried some of the hampers have not arrived.'

'Yes, Mama.' He took Chloe's hand. 'Don't worry, I will make sure nothing happens before we reach the Duchess.'

'Thank you.' Chloe hardly knew whether she wanted to laugh or cry at this touching show of male protectiveness. She smiled down at him, a little misty-eyed. 'I will need all the protection you can give me today.'

'Really, Brandt, I do not think you've attended to a word I've said for the last five minutes. If it weren't so impossible, I could almost believe you have developed a *tendre* for Chloe. Particularly after I saw you holding her hand earlier.'

Brandt forced his attention away from where Chloe sat on the quilt with Belle, Julian and Lydia Sutton. He was out of earshot, but it had not prevented him from noticing that her face had grown increasingly paler and her smiles had a strained quality to them. 'What did you say?' he asked Marguerite, who stood next to him.

Her brow arched. 'I said if it were not so impossible, I could think you have developed a *tendre* for Chloe.'

'What makes you say that?'

'You have been watching her for the past quarter of an hour. Although you have been frowning. Did you cross swords again?'

'I meant why would you find my having a *tendre* for her impossible?'

She stared at him. 'Are you saying you do? I cannot think of anyone I would rather have you marry, but I very much doubt Chloe would…that is, I am certain you could persuade her.'

'I merely asked why it seemed impossible.'

'Because...well, it is just that you usually do not like any woman under the age of five and twenty who is not either widowed or married, and you either tease her in a way that sets her back up dreadfully or else seem to be dictating to her in your overbearing fashion.'

His temper was not improved. 'I had no idea you had such a poor opinion of me.'

She laid a hand on his arm. 'Of course I do not. If I weren't so happily married to Giles and far too old for you, I might consider you for myself. You are kind and decent, something you could never quite hide even when you were attempting to be one of London's most notorious rakes. I never thought your heart was quite in it.' She smiled up at him. 'If it is Chloe you want, then I will do everything in my power to help you. However, you had best waste no time for she is to leave tomorrow.'

'Marguerite.' He hesitated. 'There is something you should know.'

Then he bit back a curse when Justin rose from the quilt where he sat with Chloe, Belle and the baby. He held out his hand to Belle and helped her rise. As if sensing something of importance was about to happen, everyone quieted.

Justin still held Belle's hand. 'I am certain all of you were delighted to discover that Waverly, which has stood empty for so long, once again has a master. I've no doubt you will be equally delighted to learn that Waverly will soon have a new mistress as well.'

'Brandt?' Marguerite gasped.

Everyone seemed to be staring at him. He crossed his arms, not daring to look at Chloe.

'Well, Duke, planning to tell us her name or must we guess?' Squire Heyburn boomed.

'That will not be necessary. Lady Chloe Daventry has done Lord Salcombe the honour of accepting his hand in marriage.'

'Chloe?' Lydia Sutton exclaimed.

Marguerite gaped at him. 'When I suggested you waste no time I had not expected…my goodness! Brandt, did you not tell Chloe? She looks as if she is about to swoon.'

Chloe's face was drained of colour. Brandt strode forward and reached her side just in time to catch her before she fainted.

Mrs Cromby, Waverly's kindly housekeeper, chatted away as she arranged cushions under Chloe's head and covered her with a quilt. 'Poor dear, we will have you feeling better in no time. The sun always affects my Molly in exactly the same way. 'Tis fortunate you were so close to the house so that Lord Salcombe could bring you in directly. I fear this sofa is not the most comfortable, but the others are much worse. I doubt old Nate Carington bought a stick of new furniture during his lifetime, the old miser that he was. Of course, in the end he let everything fall to ruin when his health failed him, which was no wonder with all the smuggled rum and whisky and all that climbing about in damp caverns and such. And the draughts in the house caused by all the passages—even one in his bedchamber! I trust his lordship will close that one up straight away!' She finished tucking the quilt around Chloe's shoulders and straightened. 'Now, you are to rest for a while. His lordship gave strict orders you are not to be disturbed.' She glanced at Belle who stood near the sofa. 'I do not think he referred to you, your Grace.'

'You need not worry, I promise I will not disturb Lady Chloe either.' Belle waited until Mrs Cromby had bustled out before turning to Chloe with a rueful smile. 'I dare say your poor head is spinning even more. I know mine is. Mrs Cromby is quite kind and very efficient, but she does tend to talk. I will own I could not follow half of what she said. Except for the secret passages. I must ask Brandt if there really is one in his bedchamber.' She touched Chloe's hand. 'Here I am, talking as much as Mrs Cromby, when you must want to do nothing more than close your eyes.'

'I really feel much better. I am certain I have recovered enough to join the others.'

'And risk Brandt's wrath? I have no doubt he would carry you back in here immediately.' Her eyes held gentle laughter. 'You would do much better to stay here for a little while. Besides, it is your chance to see something of Waverly. Haven't you always wanted to see the house?'

'Not like this.' She hadn't envisioned herself being carried in by the master of the house after nearly fainting in front of a crowd of people. And having the master scowl down at her and demand why hadn't she told him she was ill and why the devil had she insisted on riding instead of driving and then take her to task for running around in the sun after balls.

Never had she thought the master of the house would be her fiancé.

'Perhaps not,' Belle said. 'But Brandt is right, you need to rest. Today has been rather difficult.' She bent down and brushed a light kiss across Chloe's cheek. 'I will be back shortly.'

'Yes.' As Belle left the room in her quiet, graceful way, Chloe nearly called her back, but that was ridiculous. She was twenty, a grown woman, and she should not feel like a small child whose mother had just departed.

Her head still hurt and it was easier to close her eyes. The old library was quiet and in spite of herself, she drifted off.

'Chloe?' Emily Coltrane's soft voice aroused Chloe.

She struggled to sit, still a little dizzy. 'Emily, what are you doing here?'

'I came to see how you were.' Emily moved to the side of the sofa. 'Are you feeling any better?'

'A little.' Her head no longer hurt so much, nor did she feel so sick. 'I usually do not manage to humiliate myself this much in one day.'

'It certainly made the day exciting. Particularly when you fainted just after the Duke announced your betrothal. More than one person wondered whether you were just as surprised as everyone else.'

'It was only because of the sun. If I am in it too long, I sometimes develop the headache. I did not eat much breakfast, which made me feel rather ill as well.'

'I am glad it was not learning you were to marry Lord Salcombe.' She fixed her direct gaze on Chloe's face. 'Are you going to marry him because of what happened at the ball?'

Chloe stared at her. 'Why would you think that?'

'I suppose it is because you have always seemed to hold Lord Salcombe in such dislike. I worried that perhaps Lady…someone tried to cause mischief and you were forced to marry Lord Salcombe because of that.'

Emily was far too astute. 'No, it was not like that.' Chloe made herself look directly at Emily. 'It is true that I did not care for Lord Salcombe at first, but that…that is no longer true. I had no idea that he would even be interested in me and I…' she would undoubtedly sound fickle '…I suppose I was so determined to fall in love with Sir

Preston that I did not realise until I made such a sad mess of everything that I…I cared for Lord Salcombe.'

'I see.' Emily studied her face. If she did not believe Chloe, she gave no indication. 'I just wanted to make certain that neither you nor Lord Salcombe was forced because…'

She suddenly stopped. At the same time Chloe looked up and saw Brandt standing in the doorway. Her heart thudded and she wanted to dive under the quilt. What if he had heard her tell Emily that she cared for him?

Emily rose. 'I wanted to make certain Lady Chloe was better. We were all quite worried when she was so suddenly taken ill.'

He inclined his head. 'Of course.'

'I will not stay much longer.' She looked back at Chloe. 'Perhaps I can visit you.'

'I would like that. Besides, we must plan what you are to wear for the next assembly.'

'But only if you are well enough.'

'I will be.'

Emily hesitated. 'I am glad you will be staying. And I wish you well.'

'Thank you.'

'Then I will see you soon.' She left the room, only pausing to say goodbye to Brandt.

He crossed the room, coming to stand next to the sofa. He looked down at her, his expression quizzical. 'So Miss Coltrane wished to assure herself that we were not forced into an engagement?' he asked.

'Yes.' Chloe plucked at the edge of the quilt. 'I suppose you heard everything.'

'Much of it, including the part where you assured Miss Coltrane you realised you cared for me after all.'

'Oh.' She could not meet his eyes.

'Chloe.' All of a sudden he was sitting next to her on the sofa. He tilted her chin towards him, his fingers gentle. 'Was that a complete falsehood? Or might I hope you do not hold me in complete dislike?'

She found herself staring into his changeable green-brown eyes. 'No. I...I really do not dislike you.'

'I am glad to hear that,' he said softly. 'Particularly since we are betrothed.'

She swallowed. 'But only temporarily.'

'Permanently for the next two months, perhaps longer.'

Her head was starting to spin again, but this time it was not from the sun. His eyes seemed to mesmerise her. Was she starting to sway towards him or was he starting to sway towards her? But it hardly mattered when his lips brushed hers in a kiss as light and gentle as the touch of butterfly wings. He lifted his head for a moment, his hand brushing a strand of hair from her cheek and then he cupped the back of her head, drawing her to him, his mouth returning to hers in gentle possession.

She should pull away, but the feel and taste of him was too intriguing. Her eyes fluttered shut as she gave herself up to his leisurely kiss. Except for the light touch at the back of her head, he made no move to hold her and so she found herself leaning closer to him. Her lips parted under his soft pressure and she hesitantly returned his kiss. The experiment was pleasurable enough that she repeated it with more confidence, this time lightly touching his lips with her tongue. He stilled, almost as if he'd stopped breathing.

'Oh! Oh, my!'

They jumped apart, Brandt uttering a curse. Mrs Cromby stood there, the shock on her face turning to mortification. 'I beg your pardon, my lord. I did not...' She started to back out.

Brandt stood. 'There is no need to leave. In fact, you may congratulate us instead. Lady Chloe has agreed to become my wife.'

Mrs Cromby stared at him and then a smile creased her plump face. 'Your wife? I…I had no idea! Of course, I wish you both much happiness! How delightful—Waverly will have a mistress as well!' She beamed at them and then started. 'Oh, my, I quite forgot. Four of the guests, including the young lady who was here earlier, have arrived and asked if they might see Lady Chloe for a moment if she is well enough to receive them.'

Brandt glanced at Chloe. 'Only if she wishes to.'

'Yes, that would be fine.' Anything to keep from being alone with him, or she might be tempted to ask him to kiss her again. Her cheeks were still heated from the encounter and she did not think she could look at him. It was bad enough she had submitted to his kisses without protest, but to kiss him back in such a brazen fashion…and then to want more.

In a few minutes, Mrs Cromby ushered in Lydia, Emily and Mr Rushton. Lydia stopped on the threshold and looked around the dark, bookshelf-lined room. 'Heavens! This room looks exactly like what one would expect to see in *Udolpho*!'

To Chloe's chagrin, Sir Preston followed. With everything else that had happened, she had nearly forgotten about Lion. Or the kiss in the conservatory.

There was nothing in his face to indicate disgust as he came to her side, however, followed by the others. Lydia swooped down upon her with a warm embrace. 'Oh, you sly thing! I never would have thought! I do hope you are much better. I was so worried when you suddenly fainted although—' she cast Brandt a coy glance '—it was rather romantic when Lord Salcombe carried you to the house!'

Mr Rushton shook her hand. 'You look much better. At least there's some colour in your cheeks. I should have guessed which way the wind was blowing when Salcombe warned me against trifling with your affections.'

'I should hope not,' Lydia said tartly.

Sir Preston also shook her hand. 'Must congratulate you as well. Wondered if something was up after the other night.'

'I am very sorry about knocking Lady Kentworth down. I hope she has recovered.'

'No need to be sorry. The dog knocked her down. Wished to apologise for her taking you to task. Afraid she doesn't hold her tongue when she's overset.'

'I quite understand.' She smiled at him, relieved he still considered her his friend after all that had happened.

'Lady Chloe has not yet recovered,' Brandt said so sharply Chloe looked up. Oh, dear, now what was wrong?

'Which was why I came,' Emily said. 'To make certain no one stayed very long. I did not know you would be here.'

Mr Rushton had strolled over to the mantelpiece. 'Isn't this the room with the entrance to the passage?'

'One of them,' Brandt said. He had his arms folded across his chest, his face impatient.

'There is a passage here?' Lydia skipped over to Mr Rushton's side. 'How exciting? Where?'

'Somewhere near the mantel,' Mr Rushton said. 'Heard a tale where a smuggler actually surprised old Nate when he was dozing in a chair in front of the fire.'

'Tale can't be right,' Sir Preston said.

Mr Rushton raised a brow. 'Why not?'

Sir Preston grinned. 'Entrance is in the fireplace.'

'Sir Preston is correct,' Brandt said.

'Really? Can we see it?' Lydia asked. She was already stooping so she could peer into the fireplace.

'Lydia, Lady Chloe needs to rest,' Emily said.

'I promise we can leave right after that.' Lydia moved closer. 'Nothing looks at all like an entrance! Are you certain it is here?'

'Best show it to her or we'll never drag her out of here,' Mr Rushton told Brandt. 'I'd do so but don't know how to get the thing open. Besides I don't want to cover myself in soot.'

'So you wish someone else to cover themselves instead. Quite understandable.' Brandt strode over to the mantelpiece. Chloe rose and trailed after him, curious about the secret passages she had heard so much about.

Brandt put his hand behind the old clock on the mantel and produced a key. He knelt, reached into the fireplace and inserted the key into the sooty iron grille in the back. With a creaky groan, the door opened to reveal a dark cavernous hole.

'Oh, my!' Lydia exclaimed as the men crowded forward. Even Miss Coltrane looked interested.

'Odd place,' Rushton commented. 'How did you know, Kentworth?'

Sir Preston's smile was sheepish. 'Actually been here years ago. Climbed through the passage with Dick Tenbury and found ourselves in the library. Nearly gave us a fright when the chambermaid came in.'

'Fortunate there was no fire.' Mr Rushton glanced at the company. 'Who wishes to go in first?'

Lydia squealed. 'You can't possibly think of doing that!'

'I will go in,' Emily said.

Sir Preston stepped forward. 'Not a good idea, Miss Coltrane. Dusty, spiders and all that.'

She gave him a cold glance. 'That does not bother me in the least.'

Puzzled by her tone, Chloe glanced at Sir Preston. He appeared taken aback, but said nothing.

'I've no idea what sort of condition the passage is in,' Brandt told them. 'I intend to do what my cousin has done with the passages at Falconcliff, close them.'

'Then I certainly must see it,' Emily said. She rolled her eyes at Lydia. 'Do not worry. I do not intend to do more than look.'

'But, Emily, you will dirty your gown!' Lydia said.

'I won't mind.'

Sir Preston backed out and allowed her to step past him. Chloe suppressed a shiver. She could think of nothing worse than finding one's self in a dark, cold tunnel where there were no exits except at the beginning and the end. She did not realise she was holding her breath until Emily reappeared. 'Well, it certainly is dusty.'

'No mice, spiders or ghosts?' Mr Rushton asked.

'None. The passage does branch off, however.'

'One to old Nate's bedchamber and the other to the cellar,' Sir Preston said.

'Salcombe is probably beginning to wonder if you've engaged in a bit of smuggling yourself,' Mr Rushton told him.

'No, just a bit of exploration.' Sir Preston looked rather guilty.

Brandt bent down and locked the door, then put the key back behind the clock. He rose and his eyes fell on Chloe. 'What are you doing up?'

'I wanted to see the entrance as well.'

He frowned. 'You should be resting.'

'I feel much better.' For some reason, her headache had completely disappeared while he had been…they had been kissing. Her gaze went to his mouth and she felt almost shaky again. She backed away. 'Perhaps I will sit down.'

The others instantly apologised for staying too long and took their leave. Almost as soon as they were through the library door, Belle and Justin entered and announced they had come to take Chloe home in the carriage.

'But Maisy?' She had forgotten all about her little mare.

'She will stay here,' Brandt said. 'The groom noticed she had strained a hock.'

'I did not know that.' Now she had even more reason to regret the day.

'We did not want to distress you further,' Belle said gently. 'At any rate, Brandt will see to it that she is well cared for.'

Chloe looked over at Brandt. 'Thank you.'

'Of course.' He was now polite again as if their encounter earlier had not happened. He was equally polite when he bade her farewell.

But then, she thought later, kisses did not always mean much to men. Lucien and his friends had been prime examples of that. She had been embarrassed to find him locked in an embrace with her governess and then, a few days later, embracing a chambermaid with equal fervour. Both times he had laughed it off and pinched her cheek and told her not to tell. The governess had never treated Chloe quite the same again and had left her position a short time later.

The friends Lucien invited to the house to spend endless hours gambling had been no better; after a while they had forgotten her presence and would speak of women as carelessly as they might their horses. She had not understood half of it, only enough to realise lust and regard did not necessarily go together.

Which was why she could not allow any more kisses, no matter how pleasurable she might find them. Her mother had warned her they could lead to other, more serious things. It did not matter that they were betrothed, for they would not marry, which meant she must do everything she could to keep their betrothal on a cool, distant basis.

Chapter Seven

Brandt followed the path that wound through Falcon-cliff's garden towards the narrow dirt lane that ran along the edge of the cliff. He had no idea why he had even bothered calling at the house—he should have known Chloe would not be there, but would be instead wandering around the property. Her illness yesterday had apparently not acted as a deterrent. Belle had been apologetic as she told him that attempting to keep Chloe inside was like trying to keep a fox in the house, but Belle had made Chloe promise she would sit in the shade.

At least the day was overcast and windy, the clouds a dark grey that hinted of rain. So she wouldn't become overheated again, forcing him to carry her back to Falcon-cliff with her soft curves pressing against his chest. Then he would not be tempted to steal a few more of the innocent provocative kisses that made him want to do much more with her.

The wind had whipped up noticeably by the time he left the stand of trees and started down the path that wound along the cliff. He finally spotted her near a stone bench. She stood facing the sea, her face lifted to the wind. Her bonnet dangled by its ribbons down her back and her hair had fallen from its pins and blew around her face. As he watched, she closed her eyes, held out her arms and twirled in a circle, her skirts flying around her legs. She looked like some sort of pagan worshipping the elements.

He strode forward. 'Your bonnet is off,' he said when he reached her.

She gasped and whirled around, her eyes wide with shock, her hands clasped to her chest. 'Oh! You frightened me!'

'Only because you were preoccupied with your ritual.'

'Ritual?'

'You were worshipping the wind and sea, were you not? Does the vicar know about this?'

The predictable colour rose in her cheeks. 'I loved to dance in the wind when I was a child. I would always feel as if I was part of the earth and the wind. The sea is so wonderful and wild when it is stormy like this—I just wanted to feel part of it.' She looked at him, rather shame-faced. 'I am not behaving as a lady should again. Proper young ladies do not dance in storms. I suppose you wish to scold me.'

No, what he wished to do was pull her into his arms, tangle his hands in her glorious red hair, and kiss her thoroughly while the wind whipped around them.

She watched him with her large eyes, waiting for his answer. 'No, I do not wish to scold you. Although you should wear your bonnet unless you want your skin to become burned from the wind.'

'But you are not wearing a hat. In fact, you do not wear hats very much at all.'

'I prefer to go bare-headed.'

'So do I. I think hats interfere too much with the weather. One cannot properly feel the breeze or... Oh!' A large raindrop had hit her on the nose. Before she could react further, the sky opened.

'In this case, hats would be useful.' He caught her hand and pulled her along the path. By the time they reached the shelter of the trees, they were both breathless, and thoroughly soaked.

He dropped her hand. 'You forgot to put your bonnet on.' It still dangled down her back, now wet and soggy.

'That would have taken too much time. I suppose it is ruined but it might have been ruined even if it were on my head.' She fumbled with the ribbons and then pulled it off.

'You are remarkably matter of fact about it. Many women would be in hysterics over the loss of a bonnet.'

'It is a very old bonnet, which is why I wore it,' she said defensively. 'In fact, Arthur suggested that I should give it away because it is so unfashionable.'

He grinned at her expression. 'I meant to pay you a compliment. I should hate to find myself taking shelter from the rain with a female who was in hysterics over the ruin of a bonnet.'

'Has that ever happened to you before?'

'Not over a bonnet. Over a ruined pair of gloves, however. I once escorted a woman to Vauxhall...' What the devil was he doing? He'd nearly told her about the time he and his then current mistress had been stranded by the rain. 'I should not be telling you these things.'

A little smile touched her mouth. 'I doubt I would be too shocked. Lucien was my half-brother, you know.'

He could not miss the sadness in her voice and she suddenly seemed far older than her twenty years. He'd not given any thought to what it might have been like for her with Lucien. Because Lucien was so much older he had assumed she had been sheltered from him by her parents.

'He spoke of such things around you?' He should not be shocked by anything Milbourne had done, but he was.

'Sometimes.' She avoided looking at him. She moved away and rubbed her arms and shivered. 'I hope the rain will let up soon. Perhaps we should hurry back to the house. I do not think we could get any wetter than we are.'

He followed her. 'Are you cold?'

'A little.'

'Then have my coat. The rain did not soak completely through it.' He shrugged out of it and held it out to her.

She stared at it. 'I cannot do that, then you will be cold.'

'I'm not wearing a thin muslin gown.' He stepped forward and draped it around her shoulders. His fingers brushed the nape of her neck and he had a sudden vision of exploring the soft creamy skin with his lips.

He backed away. Hell. Perhaps he'd best go stand out in the rain for a while and cool down his lust. Or pray the rain would let up and they could get out of here.

She cast a puzzled glance at him and then looked away. She seemed fragile, very young and rather lost in his coat. An uncomfortable silence fell between them as if she had sensed his unspoken thoughts. If anything, the rain seemed to be falling even harder, beating heavily on the canopy of the trees that sheltered them.

He cleared his throat and started to speak. At the same time she said, 'How…?'

He stopped. 'Please go on.'

'I was wondering how Maisy is.'

'She is fine, although my groom told me that she tried to nip Domino today.'

'Oh, dear. I am afraid Maisy does not like strange male horses.'

'Although Domino is not exactly male any more.' He

could have bitten his tongue. Why couldn't he remember she was a proper young lady?

She merely smiled. 'It does not really matter to her. Although she seems to be growing more irritable as she ages.'

'Why did you ride her yesterday? Surely Justin has given you use of a more suitable mount.'

'Because she is still my friend and she looked rather forlorn when I entered the stables. One doesn't desert friends just because they are old and not as useful as they once were. Arthur wanted to put her down because he said she was slow and ill tempered and we had no room, but I would not let him. I wrote to Belle and asked if they would have her and they sent for her straight away.' She gave him a defiant glance. 'I suppose you find that sentimental and ridiculous.'

'No, I find it commendable. You are not afraid to stand up for those you care for. I still recall how you declared you would make Justin very sorry if he hurt Belle, and that if I was not careful I would suffer the same fate.'

'I did mean it. I would not have let either of you hurt her.'

'I know,' he said quietly. 'In fact, that was when I started to change my mind about Belle.' He had come upon Chloe as she backed Justin into a corner at a ball, a young debutante in cream muslin, threatening Justin if he dared to hurt her beloved sister-in-law. When Brandt had made some idiotic remark about how Justin should watch his back, she had glared at him, told him it was rude to listen to private conversations and if she had to, she would spend the rest of her life making anyone who hurt Belle, including him, very sorry. He'd thought her a mouse before then, but her spirited defence had proved otherwise. He'd found himself watching her after that and noticing things about her; the way her face lit up when she smiled, her lack of pretence, her honest gaze. Most of all her belief in Belle's goodness had made him question whether Belle had been an accomplice in Lucien's plan to destroy Justin after all.

'I am glad you did,' she said softly.

'As I am. She has made my cousin very happy.'

Her gaze locked with his. His eyes dropped to her mouth and she swallowed. Almost without thinking he stepped forward and then caught her by the shoulders, drawing her to him. His mouth came down on hers. Her body seemed to meld against his for a moment and then she stiffened and pulled away.

He let her go. 'Chloe,' he began.

She took a step back, pulling his coat more tightly about her as if to protect herself. 'I pray you will not kiss me any more, my lord.' Now she was beginning to look like the old Chloe, the one who made it obvious she held him in complete dislike. The one who roused the devil in him.

He'd been about to apologise but her cool tone set his back up and made him feel as if he'd been slapped. 'Why not? You seemed to enjoy them well enough yesterday.'

She had the grace to colour. 'I do not want a betrothal that includes kisses. I think it would be best if we had a…a practical arrangement.'

'And what precisely is a practical arrangement?'

'An arrangement where both parties enter into a betrothal for purely rational reasons rather like a…a business agreement. They are civil to one another, but there are no other complications beyond that.'

'What sort of complications?'

'Well, kisses for one thing.'

'How would kisses complicate matters?'

She was beginning to look rather angry. 'I would imagine that is rather obvious!'

'Is it? Then why did you ask Sir Preston to kiss you?'

He knew he had gone too far when she took a step back, her cheeks suddenly pale. 'That was unkind,' she whispered.

'It was. I beg your pardon.'

'I…I suppose I deserved it.'

'No.' He now stepped away from her. 'You are right. We had best keep this arrangement on a practical basis. Kisses do make things damnably complicated. We can endeavour to be civil to one another.'

'Yes.' For some reason, she looked less than pleased by his capitulation. Another silence fell between them, this one even more profound. She finally looked away. 'The rain has stopped.'

No wonder it seemed so quiet. 'Then we should return to the house.'

'Very well.' She started to remove his coat. 'I must give this back to you.'

'Keep it on until we reach the house.' He was in no mood to argue the point.

She looked taken aback at his harsh tone, but said nothing. They walked back to the house in silence, both careful to maintain a distance between them. Once inside, she slipped out of his coat. 'Thank you,' she said.

'Of course.'

She searched his face as if trying to read his thoughts, her own expression unhappy. She finally looked away. 'I will see you at dinner.'

'Yes.' He watched her climb the stairs, a strange disappointment enveloping him. What had he hoped? That she might actually come to like him? That someone as decent as Chloe would accept someone as jaded as himself?

He turned away, impatient. Chloe ought to marry the sort of honourable sensible man she had her heart set on. As for himself, he would avoid thoughts of marriage. Particularly marriages that might involve complicated emotions.

He had no idea why the idea suddenly seemed so flat.

Chloe shut her bedchamber door. She leaned against it and wondered why she felt so miserable. She should be pleased with the conversation. She had made it quite clear they were to stay on a practical, impersonal basis with no ridiculous compliments or heady kisses to complicate matters. It was precisely the sort of betrothal she had always imagined.

Telling herself that did nothing to erase the fact that she had wanted nothing more than to melt into his embrace and see if his kisses were as pleasurable as they had been yesterday. It had taken every particle of will she possessed to break away. She had said the words she had so carefully rehearsed in her mind but somehow they did not feel so right when she actually said them to him, as they had when she was alone in her room. For an instant he almost appeared hurt, and then the cool, arrogant mask had slid over his face which had only goaded her more. The camaraderie they had experienced while dashing through the rain had vanished.

Perhaps it was for the best, because if she allowed herself to like him too much, she might make the dangerous mistake of actually falling in love with him, and he would have the power to hurt her much more than Lucien had ever done.

* * *

Chloe stood in the entrance of the assembly hall, her hands clammy. She should not be so nervous, but it was the first time she had been out in public since the picnic four days ago. Nor had she seen much of Brandt since their encounter in the rain. He had risen early to oversee the work at Waverly and returned late, often after dinner. Their exchanges were brief and all that was polite, and strangely unsatisfying.

In fact, although she was loath to admit it, she looked forward to seeing him tonight. He had told Belle he would drive over from Waverly. But she had not yet spotted him.

'I do not think Brandt is here yet,' Belle remarked, reading Chloe's mind. 'I am glad we were able to persuade him to come. He needs a diversion from spending so much time at Waverly. Although Marguerite tells me the rooms on the first floor are nearly finished. She has been trying to persuade him to hold your betrothal party there.'

'Why would she wish to do that?' She could not imagine Brandt allowing such a thing. In fact, she could not imagine he would want a betrothal party at all. She certainly did not. Even the mention of the affair was enough to send a tumult of emotions rushing through her, although desperation seemed to be the presiding one. Marguerite had been over twice to discuss the details with Belle and Chloe, which only increased her anxiety. Perhaps if she said something to Brandt he could talk them out of it. If she ever saw him long enough to do so.

'She seems to think it would be a good way to officially open up Waverly again as well as celebrate your forthcoming marriage, particularly since you are delaying it for so long.' Belle looked at her face and said with a sympathetic smile, 'I know you are not particularly pleased about it, but it is expected. You are the future mistress of Waverly in everyone's eyes.'

'It is just that it seems so deceitful.'

'Perhaps.' Belle turned away to speak to Mrs Sutton who had greeted her.

Mrs Sutton congratulated Chloe warmly on her betrothal. 'We are so pleased! You have become quite one of us and we were loath to have you leave! Now you will—' She broke off. 'Good heavens! Is that Emily Coltrane? Why, she looks quite pretty!'

Chloe spotted Mrs Coltrane and Emily standing near the door with Tom. Emily's dark hair was pulled back in a loose chignon that softened the lines of her square face. The pale peach silk she wore, now devoid of most of its trimming, fell in simple lines becoming to her figure and the vee of its bodice made her shoulders appear less broad. The colour, instead of making her face pale, brought out her creamy complexion. Mrs Coltrane beamed, but Emily's expression was apprehensive as if she had no idea how her startling transformation would be received.

'She looks beautiful,' Belle said.

They were not the only people who stared at Emily, who looked as if she were about to run. Chloe excused herself from Belle and Mrs Sutton and made her way through the crowd to Emily's side.

Emily fidgeted with her fan. 'What do you think?'

'You look lovely. In fact, Belle said you were beautiful.'

A slight flush coloured Emily's cheeks. 'Did she really?'

'That is what I told her,' Mrs Coltrane said with a fond smile, 'but now she refuses to step into the room.'

Tom made an impatient sound. 'Don't know why. For once she's in prime twig and now she doesn't want to go in. I would think you'd want to show off your dress like most girls.'

Emily sniffed. 'I'm not most girls.'

'No, that's for certain.' He grinned at his sister's stormy expression.

'Come with me,' Chloe said. 'We can take a turn around the room.'

'Do go on,' Mrs Coltrane urged when Emily hesitated. 'Now that everyone has seen you it would look quite odd for you to leave now.'

Emily still hesitated. 'Very well,' she finally said. She allowed Chloe to link her arm through hers.

Chloe smiled at her. 'Oh, Emily, I have no doubt some-one will be quite smitten!'

Emily gave her a nervous smile. 'Do you think so?'

'I have no doubt. Shall we find Sir Preston now?'

'In a little bit. I do not want to appear overly eager to see him.'

'I quite understand.' Just as she did not want to appear overly eager to see Brandt, which of course, she wasn't.

Emily paused. 'Lord Salcombe is coming this way.'

'Oh.' Chloe flushed and forced herself not to turn around even when she sensed he stood directly behind her.

'Good evening, Miss Coltrane, Chloe.'

She turned slowly and managed a smile. 'Good evening, Lord Salcombe.'

His gaze sharpened for an instant before he turned his attention to Emily. 'May I tell you how charming you look tonight, Miss Coltrane? I almost did not recognise you.' His tone was polite, but there was no doubting the admiration in his eye. Chloe could have hugged him.

She was even more pleased when Emily, whose gaze had searched his face, smiled. 'You may, Lord Salcombe. And you may tell Chloe as well, for she is the one who wrought the change.'

He glanced at Chloe. 'I really did nothing but advise Emily on her gown,' she said.

'Your advice was sound.' His voice was still polite. 'Lady Chloe, perhaps you would stand up with me for the next set? I would also like to solicit your hand for the following dance, Miss Coltrane.'

'I...' Chloe suddenly saw Sir Preston standing near the wall. Perhaps if Brandt stood up with Emily first she could draw Sir Preston's attention to Emily while she danced with Brandt. 'Would you mind very much if I danced the following set instead? And you and Emily danced now?'

His face was a mask. He turned to Emily. 'Miss Coltrane?'

'I do not object.' She gave Chloe a curious look.

Chloe waited until they had joined one of the sets before heading towards Sir Preston. Halfway there she began to wonder what she was doing. He had congratulated them quite nicely at Waverly but that had been among the others. What if he refused to speak to her? She would not blame him, but to her great relief he did not walk away.

'Good evening, Lady Chloe.' He cleared his throat.

'Have you seen Miss Coltrane tonight?'

'Er, no. That is, haven't really looked.'

'She is dancing with Lord Salcombe at this very moment. She is quite transformed tonight. I scarcely recognised her. See, they are just now passing by.'

He looked. To her dismay, Brandt did as well. The dark expression on his face sent her heart through her throat. Emily did not seem to notice. Her eyes were on Brandt's face and she said something that made him turn from Chloe. Her only gratification was that Sir Preston was staring at the couple with a peculiarly stupefied air. 'Does she not look pretty?' Chloe asked him.

'Pretty? Er, yes. Doesn't look like Em...that is, Miss Coltrane. Never seen her dance quite like that, either.'

'I dare say she will be very much sought after tonight. Particularly since Lord Salcombe has stood up with her.'

'Undoubtedly,' he said absently.

'Perhaps you should ask her for the next dance.'

He tore his gaze away from the dancers. 'Couldn't do that. Can't dance like Salcombe.'

'Oh, that does not matter. I am certain she will be delighted to stand up with you.'

'Do you?' He stared at Emily for a moment longer, his expression bemused. 'Somehow don't think she'll like me stepping on her feet.'

'But you did very well when we were practising with the others.'

'There was just a few of us then.'

She could not persuade him. When the music finally ended, two of Tom's friends were already at Emily's side. Before she could make her way over with Sir Preston, Brandt appeared. He had a slight smile at his mouth, but the expression in his eyes was anything but amused. 'Good evening, Kentworth. I trust you do not mind if I steal my fiancée away for the next dance.'

'Of course.' He still looked rather preoccupied, which Chloe hoped was a good sign. 'Believe I will take myself off to the card room.'

Chloe stared after him and then slowly looked back at Brandt. He still appeared rather grim. 'Did you wish to dance?' she asked him brightly.

'Yes.' He took her arm, a trifle roughly and marched her into the set. He released her, but from his tensed jaw she suspected he was reining in his temper. He looked no less riled as the dance began.

Really! Whatever had put him up in arms? Her speaking with Sir Preston? Just because they were betrothed did not mean he should act so…so possessive.

They came together. 'You should at least make an attempt to appear pleased with my company,' he said.

'Only if you appear pleased with mine!'

'I am.'

'You look as if you are about to have a fit of apoplexy.'

He shot her a stormy look as they parted. At least she had the pleasure of seeing him on the edge of an explosion. Her pleasure was short-lived. The same sense of being trapped washed over her, just as it had with Lucien and her father and finally with Arthur. She was about to be scolded for doing nothing more than attempting to make things right. She had no doubt he intended to ring a peal over her.

Her trepidation increased as the dance drew to a close. And when he said, 'I wish to speak to you,' it was all she could do to keep from shrinking back. She went with him across the floor, her head high and he found a niche behind a large sickly-looking potted plant.

She touched one of its stunted leaves. 'I dare say this poor plant would be much happier if it was moved by a window.'

'I did not bring you here to discuss plants.'

She forced herself to look at him. 'I imagine you wish to give me a dressing-down for speaking to Sir Preston. I would prefer you did it somewhere other than a public assembly, but if you must do it now please begin so I might have it over with.' Her voice shook, but at least no tears threatened to fall as they once had when someone towered over her in a rage. She had learned to keep them at bay.

'Why are you looking at me like that?'

She started. 'Like what?'

'Like you think I am about to rage at you. Or strike you.'

'Aren't you? I mean, are you not about to rage at me?'

'No. Never that.' His mouth twisted as if something pained him and he looked away. Then back at her. 'You do not need to explain why you were with Sir Preston. Or why you did not wish to dance with me,' he said flatly.

She tightened her hands around her fan, not certain why his mood had so abruptly altered. 'I only wished to point out to Sir Preston how pretty Emily looked. I thought if he saw her dancing with you it might make him notice her a little and perhaps he would ask her to dance. But Tom's friends came and then you, and Sir Preston left for the card room. He probably has not even spoken to poor Emily.'

'I am not certain I quite follow this. You thought Sir Preston would ask her to dance after he saw me dancing with Miss Coltrane. Does Miss Coltrane want to dance with him?'

'She is in love with him.'

'Is Sir Preston in love with Miss Coltrane?'

'He could be. In fact, I am certain he will fall in love with her if only he can be persuaded to spend time in her company. I had so hoped he might ask her to dance but he said he did not dance as well as you and did not think she would like it.'

'That is why you were with Sir Preston? Because you wish to play matchmaker?'

'Yes, that is why. I…I was not flirting with him, if that is what you thought.'

'You don't need to tell me that,' he said shortly.

'I don't want you to think that I would be so callous as to do such a thing when I am engaged to you.'

'I know that.' He held her eyes.

She felt breathless and then he pulled his gaze away just as Marguerite appeared around the side of the pot. 'There you two are! Really, Brandt, from the way you dragged poor Chloe away I fully expected to find you quarrelling. Do you wish everyone to speculate that your betrothal is over before it is hardly begun?'

'I doubt that will happen.' Brandt glanced at Chloe. 'We were merely having a conversation.'

'I can see that.' Her fine brow arched. 'I suggest you have these sorts of conversations in private rather than at a public affair. It is not at all the thing to cast such intimate looks at each other in public.'

Chloe's cheeks heated. She didn't dare look at Brandt. 'We were not.'

Marguerite grinned. 'There is no need to look so flustered. I am only teasing you. I came to warn you that Gilbert Rushton and the Squire are demanding you two play cards against each other. They are already taking bets on the winner.'

Brandt looked over at Chloe, a little smile at his mouth. 'Well? Do you wish to play against me?'

She shook her head. 'No. I am certain it was nothing but luck last time.' She did not quite meet his eyes.

'Oh, Chloe! No one thinks it was completely luck!' Marguerite said. 'Just one hand, that is all. It will be fun. Besides, I have already wagered in your favour.' She smiled sheepishly.

Perhaps one game would not hurt, but she would not win. Not only had she scarcely beat Brandt last time, but this time she would play as poorly as she had when Sir Preston had taught her. That would surely discourage anyone else from asking her again. 'Very well. But only one hand.'

'Splendid!' Marguerite grinned at her. 'I am counting on you to increase my pin-money!'

Chloe assuaged her conscience but telling herself that it

was unlikely she would beat Brandt a second time anyway. Brandt said little as they made their way to the card room, but once or twice she felt his gaze on her face. She felt no less apprehensive as they sat down at one of the tables and a small crowd gathered around.

'Whist again? Or something else? Piquet?' He asked.

'Whist will do.' She could not imagine playing piquet with him.

She could almost feel the disappointment when she lost the first round. During the second round, his face held puzzlement and when he finally played the winning hand, there was no triumph in his face.

She hardly heard the good-natured teasing as she rose. She had proved to herself that she did not have to win— she was not Lucien. 'I…I am sorry.' She forced herself to meet Marguerite's eyes.

'Oh, Chloe, it hardly matters so I pray you will not look so stricken,' Marguerite said. 'I certainly will not miss a thing of my wager.'

'Certain you will do better next time,' Mr Rushton said. 'Undoubtedly offputting to play against one's betrothed.'

Other such remarks followed until everyone drifted off. Only Brandt remained silent. She finally excused herself and left the card room. Brandt followed.

Outside, he caught her hand and pulled her around to face him. 'Why did you play so poorly?' he asked quietly. 'And do not tell me it was only luck the last time.'

'It is unlikely I would have beaten you again, anyway.'

'That is hardly an answer.'

'Very well, if you must know, this evening is exactly why. I do not want anyone making a fuss over me or placing wagers on the outcome of games I play.'

'Then why did you agree?'

'I hoped if I played poorly then everyone would see last time was mere luck and not ask me again.'

'But why would you wish that? There is nothing to be ashamed of. In fact, most everyone finds it quite admirable.'

'But I don't! I hate it!' she burst out.

He stared at her. 'Chloe?'

'I pray you will say no more about it!' Ashamed at her show of emotion, she backed away from him, and promptly stepped on someone's foot.

'I beg your pardon.' She turned and found herself face to face with Lady Kentworth.

The woman's mouth curved in a patently false smile. 'Quarrelling again? Every time I have seen you together tonight you seemed to be out of sorts with one another. I would not consider that a promising beginning for a marriage but perhaps, Lady Chloe, that does not matter to you. How pleased you must feel to have captured such a grand prize as a viscount rather than a mere baronet. I am surprised, however, you did not hold out for a much grander title such as an earl or a marquis, but perhaps you had no choice after trying to compromise my son.' She looked at Brandt. 'I do have one piece of advice for you, Lord Salcombe. I would keep a very close eye on your little bride-to-be. She has the unfortunate habit of wandering off and not always alone.'

Brandt stepped towards the woman. 'And I have a piece of advice for you. If you even think of maligning Lady Chloe's character, you will be more than sorry.'

This time her smile faltered. 'Are you threatening me, Lord Salcombe?'

'Precisely.'

The look in her eye was that of pure hatred. 'You shall be quite sorry.' She moved off, a thin, cold figure.

Chloe was sickened by the encounter. Brandt looked down at her face. 'There is nothing she can do. Put her from your mind.'

'She is so very angry.'

He shrugged. 'Only because she wanted you for her son.'

'But I gave her reason to think it might be possible.'

'She would have been disappointed at any rate. I do not think your cousin would have approved the match.' Brandt's voice was impersonal as he took her arm and began to walk towards the assembly room.

'No.' She felt even more wretched. He was right, of course. But she had some sort of naïve idea that once Justin and Belle saw how happy she was they would have used their influence to persuade Arthur.

How ridiculous her plotting seemed in retrospect. It was a wonder Brandt did not completely despise her.

As they approached the corner where Belle stood with Marguerite, he dropped her arm. 'I am going to take my leave of you now. Tomorrow I depart for London. I have some business to attend to there, but I should return in a few days.'

'Oh.' A stab of disappointment pierced her. She managed a smile. 'I will wish you a good journey, then.' She held out her hand.

'Yes.' He took it and looked down at her face. 'Goodbye, Chloe.' He dropped her hand and after speaking a few words to Marguerite and Belle, left the room.

She watched him go and felt almost bereft as though he had taken something she wanted with him. And she had no idea what it was.

Chapter Eight

Brandt left the offices of Blakely, Blakely and Dedham with the solicitor's words still ringing in his ears, 'You are now an extremely wealthy man, my lord. Your investments have paid off nicely.' Edmund Blakely had looked up and said with his dry smile. 'Congratulations.'

He paused in the cool, misty air of a London morning. For the first time in years, he wished he had someone to share such news with immediately. Justin.

Or Chloe.

The desire to see her hit him with such force he was shaken. He wanted to tell her of his good fortune. That he could now do what he wanted.

He could rebuild Waverly from the ground up if he desired. Restore its overgrown gardens, buy back the lands around it.

He could afford a wife, if he so desired.

He could marry Chloe.

Brandt hardly noticed the passers-by as he walked down the street. He must be mad, thinking of Chloe and marriage, when he had hardly considered marriage at all. Although he could not now imagine living at Waverly without her. The house belonged to her as much as it had always belonged to him. He doubted the house would even accept any other mistress.

But would she accept him?

He would have to persuade her. Court her gently so she wouldn't run from him. Convince her that he would make the sensible, comfortable husband she desired. He wanted children, but he would not force her to his bed no matter how much his blood heated at the thought. He would prove to her that her fears were unfounded; not all husbands were overbearing or considered their wives a mere convenience.

He would prove to himself he was not his father's son after all.

Chloe smiled at Will. 'Shall we return to the house? Miss Withers probably thinks I have taken you prisoner.'

A hopeful look appeared on his face. 'Could you? And take me to the secret passage to Waverly? We could hide there for an age.'

She laughed. 'No, I think I should return you to your geography lesson. At any rate, the passage is blocked from the cliffs.'

'There is still an opening. Behind some bushes.' He gave her a sly look. 'I could show you, if you would like.'

'No, thank you. I doubt Lord Salcombe would like it if we invaded his house while he is not home.'

'He would not mind. Now that you are going to marry him.'

'Even then,' she said lightly. With Brandt gone, her betrothal seemed completely unreal. He was to be back late today or tomorrow.

They started up the path and Will took her hand in his. 'I'll help you,' he said. 'It is harder for girls to climb hills because of their skirts.'

'Thank you.' She hid her smile at this piece of male

observation. She supposed she should point out that skirts had never hindered her, but she did not want to crush his obvious desire to play the role of protector. He reminded her of Brandt. They were not related, but she could see the same desire to shield her from harm. So why did Will's efforts fill her with tender amusement while Brandt's made her shy away?

Perhaps it was because Will was so young, or that she knew it was really Will who needed her protection and she was merely indulging him. Or that the role of protector meant having all the power. She could never imagine Brandt in need of protection, or in need of anything, or anyone. Certainly he did not appear to need her.

They continued up the slope and to the top towards the house. Miss Withers, the pleasant-faced, middle-aged governess, waited for them near the garden gate. Chloe bent down and gave Will a hug. He smiled at her. 'When you live at Waverly we can do this every day.'

'Perhaps.'

Chloe watched Miss Withers lead him away and then started back towards Falconcliff, feeling heavy-hearted. Will's words only reinforced how much more of a mistake this betrothal really was. He would be terribly disappointed when she and Brandt parted, as would a good many others.

'Chloe!'

She looked up and saw Emily riding towards her on her grey mare. Chloe waited for Emily to halt beside her.

'I had hoped to see you today,' Emily said. 'Are you on your way back to Falconcliff?'

'Yes.'

'May I join you?' Without waiting for an answer, she slid gracefully from her mare and caught up the reins. 'I have not had the chance to thank you for the assembly. I had the most lovely time!'

'I am so glad, but I really did nothing. You were the one who danced and smiled and completely enthralled everyone.'

'I could not have done so if you had not helped me with my gown and hair and told me I must smile. And, of course, allowed Lord Salcombe to stand up with me for the first dance. I have no doubt that was what made the others take notice and decide I would be worth their while.'

'That sounds so callous! That is not the whole of it, at all.'

Emily merely smiled. 'Perhaps, but is that not how it works in Society? When someone of consequence notices one, others follow suit?'

'Sometimes, but not this time. I think it was because before you looked as if you did not want anyone to notice you. This time you looked much more friendly. As if you would not growl if someone dared to approach you.'

'Is that how I looked before? I suppose that is how I felt. But not any more.'

They walked towards Falconcliff, the mare trailing behind them. Chloe glanced at Emily. 'Did Sir Preston stand up with you?'

Emily gave a little laugh. 'No, but I decided that it did not matter. I am rather tired of waiting for him to notice me.' Nothing in her expression indicated this was not perfectly true.

'He did notice you. When you were dancing with Lord Salcombe, he said he thought you were very pretty and that he did not know you could dance like that. He worried that you would not want to stand up with him since he did not dance very well himself.'

She shrugged. 'If he really felt some sort of attraction to me, then he would have spoken to me. I have no intention of throwing myself his way any more.' She looked straight ahead and then turned to Chloe. 'I would rather hear about your betrothal to Lord Salcombe.'

They had just entered the part of the path on Falconcliff property. Chloe kept her voice light. 'It is not very exciting. An ordinary betrothal, I suppose.'

'Is it? Then why are you not very happy about it?'

'Of course I am. But it is merely a practical arrangement, not a love match.' Her voice came out as matter of fact as Emily's.

'On whose side?'

She glanced at Emily, surprised. 'On both sides, of course. We are both in agreement that marriage should be a practical union of two sensible persons who wish to be comfortable together.'

'That sounds exceedingly dull.'

'I think marriage should be dull.' One where the persons involved did not demand overly much from each other. Certainly no hot passions flaring between them that might lead to heartache and jealousy and who knew what other untidy emotions.

'Is that why you considered Sir Preston? You thought he was dull?' There was a sudden sharpness in Emily's voice.

'No, of course not. I thought him kind and very interesting. I thought we could be comfortable together. But now I see that was quite wrong of me. He needs someone with whom he can be less comfortable. Besides he was never interested in me in that way at all.'

'It is not wrong of you to consider Lord Salcombe because you can be comfortable with him?'

Perhaps it would be better to still be at odds with Emily if she meant to ask such probing questions. 'No, Br…Lord

Salcombe and I are in agreement that this is what we both want. A dull, practical marriage.'

'I cannot imagine Lord Salcombe wanting a dull marriage. His nature seems too passionate.'

Certainly, Emily was blunt. 'I assure you he is not,' Chloe said.

'Has he kissed you?'

Chloe's cheeks heated. 'Kissing is very dull as well.' This was nothing but a lie. She was relieved to see the drive of Falconcliff. 'Can you stay for a bit? The latest *Belle Assemblée* has just arrived and we could look at the gowns. I saw a morning gown that would be perfect for you.'

'The *Belle Assemblée*?' Emily wrinkled her nose. 'It is the dullest...' She stopped. 'I am sorry. Of course I would like to see pages and pages of gowns.'

Chloe laughed, relieved they were off the subject of Brandt. 'Please don't force yourself. We can do something else if you wish such as play billiards,' Chloe suggested. 'Sir...someone said you were a very good player.'

'Hardly, but I do enjoy playing.'

'I'm not very good at all.'

Belle was not at all surprised by their desire to play billiards. 'Please do so. I must own I rather enjoy it. At least now that I can hit the ball most of the time. Occasionally one goes in the right direction,' she said when they asked her for permission to use the table. She was seated in a chair near the long windows of the library.

Justin looked up from the periodical he had been reading in the chair opposite hers. 'I would think that the number of hours I have spent instructing you would have more of an effect.'

'Except that you do not spend much time on instruct—' Belle broke off, her cheeks turning pink.

'Very true.' A look passed between them—one of those looks that filled Chloe with both embarrassment and envy. She looked away, shoving that last thought aside. She certainly did not want anyone looking at her in such a way.

Nor could she imagine what one could possibly do in a billiards room besides play billiards.

Emily was as delighted by the room as she was with the table since it possessed a magnificent view of the sea. Even on overcast days such as today it was possible to see fishing boats and an occasional sailing ship.

While Chloe found the cues, Emily set up the balls with a practised hand.

'Where did you learn to play?' Chloe asked her.

'My aunt and uncle have a table, so when we visit them, Tom asks me to play because he has no one else. When we visited Kentworth Hall...' She stopped and then continued in an off-handed fashion, 'We would play. Of course, I will not be doing that now.' She straightened up. 'Shall we begin?'

Compared to Emily's skill, Chloe's was dismal. Even after Emily's pointers she still hit few balls. Emily finally announced she must leave, but promised she would give Chloe another lesson soon. Belle insisted on sending a groom to accompany Emily home, despite Emily's assurances she always rode alone in the neighbourhood.

Chloe, feeling at a loose end, wandered back to the billiard room and picked up a cue. She had watched Justin and Brandt play and it had looked so effortless. She should be able to do the same. Chloe slammed the ball with her cue and then watched as it rolled off the table and towards the door.

'Drat!' She bent down to retrieve it. A pair of dusty masculine boots suddenly appeared in her vision.

'It might help if you hit the ball with less force.'

Her heart thudded to a halt. She looked up and met Brandt's amused gaze. 'What are you doing here?' she asked.

'That question could be answered in a number of ways.'

She straightened, ball in hand. 'I meant I did not expect to see you. Were you not to be back until tomorrow?'

'I finished my business early.'

'Oh.' She stared at him, unexpectedly glad to see him. He was travel-stained, a slight growth of beard about his mouth, and it occurred to her he had come straight to the billiard room from his journey.

Despite his certain fatigue, he had an air of suppressed excitement about him and a little smile played about his mouth as he looked at her. Again she experienced that odd breathless feeling. His eyes darkened and her heart began to beat most erratically. 'Did you come to play billiards?' she blurted out.

'Not quite.' His eyes were still on her face.

'Oh.'

'I came to see you.'

'Did you?' She resisted the urge to back away.

'Yes.' He took a step towards her. 'I missed you. Did you miss me?'

'Well, yes. A little.'

'Good. That is at least a beginning.'

'Is it?' Chloe had no idea what he was talking about. She bit her lip. 'I...I should put the ball back on the table.' Before she dropped it. Or begged him to kiss her.

Wherever had that thought come from? She scurried to the table and set the ball down. 'Emily, that is, Miss Col-trane, was here earlier. She attempted to instruct me in the finer points of billiards, but I fear it did not help one bit. I came back to practise but I still cannot hit anything.' She was chattering.

He had followed her. 'I would not say you couldn't hit anything. You had just hit the ball when I came in.'

'But it is not supposed to fall on the floor.' At least he had lost that intense look that made her feel so light-headed.

'No. I think you might profit from a few more lessons. We can begin tomorrow.'

'We?'

'Yes. I intend to take over your instruction.'

'I would not think you would have the time.'

He grinned. 'But for you, I do.'

Now she was certain he was teasing her. 'Do you not need to attend to your house?'

'Not every minute. I can find time for more pleasurable pursuits.' He leaned against the table. 'Such as instructing you.'

'I have no doubt you will be wasting your time. I suspect I will be a most disappointing pupil.' Now they were on familiar ground.

'I doubt it.' He still regarded her with that lazy, slightly amused look that had once annoyed her to no end. Now it merely felt familiar, unlike that intense look of earlier. She did not worry about this Brandt.

'We should probably return upstairs.'

'Probably.' He did not move.

'Do you not need to change your clothing?'

A slight smile touched his mouth. 'You are beginning to sound very wifely already.'

'I most certainly am not! If you must know, I do not care a whit about your appearance, I was merely suggesting that you might wish to change before dinner. Not that I care whether you do or not,' she added hastily.

'I am glad to hear that. When we are married, you will

not object if I occasionally come to dinner without changing.'

'We are not going to be married.'

'Aren't we? Then why are we betrothed?'

She gave him an exasperated look. 'Did a carriage accident befall you on your journey back to Devon? If you recall, this is a temporary state of affairs so I do not have to marry Lord Denbigh. You quite clearly told me you do not want to be married until you have amassed enough of a fortune to keep a wife. Not that I think that should matter in the least!'

'It does to me,' he said quietly. He looked at her. 'At any rate, that is no longer a concern.'

Something in his voice gave her pause. 'What is not a concern?'

'My fortune.' He smiled slightly. 'That was what I came to tell you.'

Her stomach lurched and she felt a sudden rush of fear for him. If he had lost everything after working so hard, she did not think she could bear it.

'My solicitor informed me that due to a number of investments I have made, I am now a very wealthy man. I need no longer worry about whether I have the means to do anything I wish.'

It took a moment for his news to sink in. 'Oh! That is absolutely wonderful!' Without thinking she launched herself at him, throwing her arms about his neck. He staggered back a little against the table and then caught her to him, his arms draped loosely about her.

For a moment her cheek pressed against the cloth of his coat and then she suddenly realised what she was doing. She stepped back, completely self-conscious. 'I beg your pardon. It was just I had such a dread that you meant to tell me you had lost everything. I did not mean to throw myself at you in such a way.'

An odd little smile played around his mouth. 'If I had known such news would bring you rushing into my arms, I would have tried harder to gain a fortune.'

'I did not do that because of your fortune.' He couldn't possibly think that it was only his wealth that caused such a reaction. She found herself desperately wanting to explain that. 'It was only because I was so pleased for you. You will have the funds to restore Waverly the way you want and do anything else you want without worry.'

'Yes.' His eyes were on her face. 'And take a wife.'

She forced a smile to her lips. 'That as well.' She looked away.

'I do not suppose you would consider the role.'

Her eyes went to his face. 'What role?'

'The role of my wife. Would you consider marrying me?'

'I…' She felt as if someone had knocked the breath from her. 'Why?'

He moved away from the table. 'Why not? I want a wife, and children. You need a husband. I strongly suspect you want children as well. Since we are already betrothed, it seems a logical conclusion. I've no doubt the arrangement would benefit both of us. There would be no need to go through the inconvenience of finding other suitable prospects.'

His words were rational, his voice calm as if he were proposing a mere business arrangement. Just the sort of arrangement she wanted for her marriage. Why, then, did she feel so panicked, and disappointed, as if it was not what she wanted at all?

'No, I cannot.' She barely whispered the words.

'Why? Did you not tell me you wanted a sensible, practical marriage? That is what I am offering you.'

'Yes.' *But not to you*, she wanted to say. She looked at him, the strong planes of his face, the hair curling at the nape of his neck, the strength of his well-formed physique, but most of all his eyes. Emily was right. He was too passionate. He would not be sensible or practical. The way he looked at her, with that intense dark gaze told her that. He would storm her senses.

And her heart.

'Do you recall I said I wanted a comfortable husband? I do not think you would be very comfortable.'

He turned, his arms folded. 'Are you certain that is what you want? A comfortable husband?'

'Yes.'

'Why do you not think I would be comfortable?'

'You are not dull enough.' The words came before she could think.

His eyes glinted. 'No? I consider that a compliment. I would not want you to think me dull.' He took a step towards her.

'I prefer dull.'

'Do you? What are you afraid of that you need a dull husband?' He took another step.

She backed away, this time finding herself against the billiard table. 'Nothing. I thought we agreed that falling in love was very inconvenient.'

His eyes still had that strange glint, as if he was barely holding back some strong emotion. 'So you fear you will fall in love with me?'

'That is the last thing I would ever do!'

'Is it?' He moved towards her, so she was completely backed up against the table. His body was only inches from her. 'What if I decided to make you fall in love with me?'

'I...I do not think you could do that,' she whispered.

'I consider that a challenge.' He closed the gap between them, his body pressing hers against the table, his hands imprisoning her on either side. Then his mouth found hers, in a hard demanding kiss that left her breathless, demanding her surrender. Her lips parted under his and his tongue slipped inside her mouth, creating sensations that made her head spin. Her legs were trapped between his and she was wholly and completely his prisoner. There was nothing else but him, his mouth moving over hers, his hands, the hardness of his body pressed against hers. Her body seemed to be on fire, a warmth growing in her abdomen making her want more than just kisses. Somehow she was half on the table, and he was leaning over her, her hands clinging to his shoulders, her skirts tangled about her legs. His hand was stroking her, her breasts, her belly and then his hand was beneath her skirts, moving up her leg. She panicked then, a little gasp of fear escaping her.

He released her suddenly as if a bucket of water had been thrown on them. Her eyes flew open in time to watch his expression change to one of pure shock. He backed away from her. 'Chloe,' he whispered.

She straightened, hardly knowing what had happened, as with trembling hands she pulled down her skirt.

His eyes were on her. 'Did I hurt you?' He looked almost sick.

'No.' She turned away. 'Not really.' Except the worn fabric of her gown had torn where the bodice joined the skirt. She was completely confused by her reaction at both wanting and fearing what he had been doing—what they had been doing.

'I did,' he said flatly. 'I beg your pardon. I did not

mean...' He paced away from her. 'I vow I will never touch you again. Not like that.'

She looked up in time to see the anguish on his face. 'You did not hurt me,' she said, not knowing what else to say.

'I could have,' he said in a low voice. 'You are right, we are not suited. I will release you from this betrothal as soon as I can do so without creating more gossip and speculation than necessary.'

He spoke in the same low, impassioned voice. She had never seen him like this, as if all his defences had fallen away. He looked as if he was in the worst agony and she had no idea why.

'What is wrong?' she asked.

'Wrong?' He gave a short laugh. 'Nothing, except that because I was angry I nearly seduced you. It was no better than an act of rape.'

'But you did not seduce me. You stopped.'

'It does not matter. I forced you.'

'You did not. It was not...' *like the other time.* The words stuck in her throat.

She took a step towards him, but he seemed to recoil, his expression now shuttered. 'You ought to return to your room and change,' he said.

'Brandt...'

'I suggest we avoid each other as much as possible.' He did not look at her.

There seemed to be nothing else she could say. 'Very well.' She started towards the door and then stopped and looked back at him. He was staring out of the window at the sea. 'Goodbye.'

She could not tell if he even heard her.

Chloe had wanted to escape to her room, but she met Justin on the stairs. If she had hoped to hide her dishev-

elled state from him, one look at his face told her it was
impossible. His gaze went briefly to where her hand held
her bodice together. 'What happened?'

'I...I had an accident.' She tried to meet his eyes. 'It is
nothing.'

'Your gown is ripped.'

'Yes.' She started to move past him. 'I must change.'

He caught her arm, his touch light, but she had no doubt
he did not mean to let her go until he had an explanation.
'Were you with Brandt?' he asked carefully. 'Belle sent
him to find you in the billiard room.'

She bit her lip. 'Yes, but this has nothing to do with
him.'

She was a miserable liar. Justin's face changed. 'What
did he do?'

'He did nothing. Please, do not ask me any more.'

'He is my cousin, but I consider you my relation as well.
You are a guest under my roof and therefore under my
protection. I will not allow you to be distressed or abused
in any fashion. Go to your chamber. I will send Belle to
speak to you. I am going to seek out my cousin.'

'That is not necessary.' Brandt spoke from below.

Chloe's gaze flew to his face, but he was not looking at
her. He had that same closed expression and nothing about
him told her he knew she was even there.

'I wish to speak to you,' Justin said.

Brandt inclined his head slightly. 'Of course.'

They might have been strangers instead of cousins
closer than brothers. She caught Justin's arm. 'Please. He
did nothing more than...than kiss me.' She had no idea if
Justin had heard. With a sick feeling, she turned, started
up the steps, and prayed things would not get any worse.

* * *

Brandt followed his cousin into his panelled study. He felt curiously numb, as if he were observing himself from outside. When Justin turned and faced him, he waited for the verdict to fall.

'What happened? Chloe assures me nothing, that her ripped gown and dishevelled appearance was an accident, but I find that difficult to believe. She has all the appearance of a woman who has been ravished. Or nearly so.'

Brandt met his cousin's eyes. 'I did not ravish her but I might as well have.' He would never forget the little sound she made and the confused, frightened look on her face when he let her go. It was her bewilderment afterwards, as if she could not comprehend what had happened, which sickened him most.

'Why?'

'Because I forced myself on her. I asked her to marry me and when she turned me down and told me that she would never fall in love with me, I lost my head. I suppose I had some damnable notion of proving her wrong. I kissed her, but it was not a pleasant kiss. Not the sort of kiss you give a young and inexperienced girl.'

'How did her bodice come to be ripped?'

'I backed her against the billiards table,' he said bluntly. 'I suppose it came to be ripped then.' He gave a short laugh. 'I did not tear the cloth deliberately.'

'Did you set out to seduce her?'

'No, but I came damnably close.'

'Why did you stop?' Justin's expression was merely curious.

'Because it penetrated my damnable conscience that I could hurt her, that I was hurting her.'

'She said you did not hurt her. And you did stop.' Justin met his gaze squarely. 'You did not force her.'

'She did not ask for my kiss, I forced it on her because

I was angry and I came close to losing complete control and taking her on the table. I vowed I would never touch a woman in anger. And I did.'

'You are not your father,' Justin said quietly.

'No? I have his blood running in my veins. I have inherited his temper and his lack of control. And his appetites.'

'I have not noticed that. Nor has anyone else.'

'Only because I am careful to keep my passions under control.'

'So you are telling me that underneath your iron control you harbour the desire to seduce virgins for sport and engage in perversions that are best left unspoken of? You'd force yourself on unwilling women?'

'Of course not, dammit.'

'I did not think so. Not even when you were determined to sow as many wild oats as possible did you behave in a less than chivalrous manner.'

Brandt shrugged. 'It does not matter. Chloe has told me that we are not suited. She is right, of course. She wishes for a dull husband. She informed me I am not dull enough. I will, of course, release her from the betrothal as soon as possible.'

'I suggest you wait unless you want Ralston to hurry her off to Denbigh Hall, or Lady Kentworth to spread rumours.'

'I've no doubt you could put a stop to both of those.'

'Perhaps. Or perhaps not.'

'Damn you,' Brandt said softly. 'Do you not see the necessity of my staying away from her?'

'I doubt Chloe is in any danger from any more displays of passion. Quite the contrary, I suspect.' Justin was silent for a moment. 'Do you think I did not feel shame for what

I did to Belle? Forcing her to become my mistress was hardly the act of an honourable man.'

'You thought she had hurt you and your family in the worst possible way.'

'That did not justify my despicable behaviour,' he said. 'I am only grateful that Belle forgave me.'

'She loves you.'

'Yes.' A slight smile touched Justin's mouth. 'Little though I deserve it. I like to think that because of that, I am perhaps a more honourable man that I might have been.'

'You are fortunate.'

'Very.' He looked back at Brandt. 'Chloe could be your redemption as well.'

'She hates me.'

'I doubt it. She seemed more concerned about protecting you than accusing you.'

He shrugged, determined to quell the slight hope that sprang within him. 'She is an innocent. She has no idea what I am.'

Justin merely looked at him. 'I do not think you know either.'

Brandt moved away. 'I must return to Waverly. I trust Belle will understand if I decline her offer for dinner.'

'As you wish. You can dine with us tomorrow.'

'I think not.' He left before his cousin could say anything more.

Chloe stood in front of the window, too numb to move. She supposed she should summon the maid to help her undress, but could not seem to act. She only turned when she heard the door open.

Belle had quietly entered the room. She quickly took in Chloe's appearance. 'Are you all right?'

'Yes.'

Belle came across the room. 'What happened?' she asked quietly.

'Can you first make certain Justin does not call Brandt out?'

Belle stilled. 'Why would Justin wish to do that?'

'I imagine because he thinks Brandt hurt me.'

'Did he?'

'No.' She took a deep breath. 'He…he just kissed me. He did nothing more.'

'And your dress.'

'Somehow it became torn. Brandt did not do it.'

'I see.' Belle looked thoughtful.

'Can you make certain Brandt is safe?'

'I am certain he is.' Belle took her hand. 'Come and sit by me.'

She followed Belle to the bed and sat next to her. 'Do you wish to tell me about it?' Belle asked. 'Only if you wish.'

'He asked me to marry him. He said that we could have a sensible, practical marriage, just as I wished. That because we were already betrothed it would save us the inconvenience of finding other spouses.'

'That is perhaps true. What did you say?'

'I said ''no'' and told him that I did not find him dull enough to be the sort of husband I wanted. Then I told him I would never fall in love with him. And then he…he kissed me.'

'Then what happened?'

She flushed. 'He let me go and then asked if he had hurt me. I said no and he told me he would never touch me again like that. He said I was right, we were not suited and he would release me from this betrothal.' She turned her eyes on Belle. 'He said he...he nearly seduced me. He looked in such anguish—I have never seen anyone so!'

'I imagine he was angry with himself for kissing you in such a way,' Belle said carefully. 'You are young and have not much experience with men or their passions, which, of course, is what is expected of young, unmarried women. It is not acceptable for a man to do more than plant a chaste kiss on the cheek of his affianced bride. He probably feared he had frightened you and was horrified as well at his ungentlemanly behaviour. He has always wanted to protect you, whether you wanted him to or not.'

'Yes.' That was very true.

'There is one more thing.'

Chloe looked up at her, the tone of Belle's voice giving her pause. 'What is it?'

'I do not know what you know of Brandt's father, but he was far from a kind man. He was considered a pious man but he was cruel. Cruel to his wife, and to his son. At the least provocation, real or imagined, his father would strike him. Brandt's mother was a frail invalid and although Brandt loved her, she did not help him. Instead, he bore his father's wrath to stand up for her. He still thinks there was something he should have done or could have done. When Brandt left home after his mother died, he behaved in the worst way possible. Perhaps he wished to punish his father for her death. In the end, he discovered his father did things that were far worse than anything Brandt could ever do. Justin says that Brandt fears he has inherited his father's tendencies.'

'How can he think that?' Tears sprang to Chloe's eyes. Shock and pity mixed with anger towards a father who would abuse his son rushed through her. She could not imagine Giles ever raising a hand to Will in such a way.

Or to Caroline or to his wife. Or Justin striking Belle or little Julian no matter how angry he might be.

'Because despite the fear and the helplessness, one feels such terrible anger. You cannot show that anger and so it is buried along with any other emotion. When you feel again you fear that you will never stop the anger…that you are no better than the person you feared and loathed. You will do anything to prove you are not.'

'Is that how you felt with Lucien?'

Belle hesitated. 'Yes, that is how I felt. After Lucien's death, when Justin returned, determined to make me pay for the terrible wrong Lucien had done to him and to his family, I thought the only way I could atone for Lucien's wrongs and my own was to give him what he wanted. I never thought I would fall in love with Justin or that he would come to love me. So I tried to run from him and from myself. I feared that the happiness I felt with him was only an illusion and I would wake up and find it all gone, that I was not deserving after all. I suspect Brandt feels much the same. He feels he has no right to care for you.'

'But he doesn't. Not in that way.'

'He does.' Belle smiled a little. 'Why else do you think he kissed you with such passion and then instantly regretted it?'

'Do men not do that? Kiss women, whether there is any attachment or not?'

'Sometimes, but I do not think that was what happened today.' Belle hesitated. 'Sometimes when one is first kissed it might not be quite as enjoyable as it will be later. Sometimes it is rather frightening but when you hold someone in regard and they return your affection, it will soon become one of the most pleasurable activities of marriage.'

Chloe's cheeks burned. 'Perhaps. At any rate, I...I am not going to marry Brandt. He does not want me. In fact, he suggested we avoid each other as much as possible.'

'Then you must persuade him otherwise.'

'Why? We are not suited.' But Chloe's words did not quite ring true.

'Oh, but I think you are. As does everyone else.' Belle's face was filled with kindness and understanding. 'He needs you. Sometimes the strongest men are the ones who need the love of a woman the most.'

'I do not want to fall in love with him,' Chloe whispered. 'Or have him in love with me.'

Belle touched her hand. 'Sometimes we do not have a choice about these things.'

Chapter Nine

Chloe did not see Brandt the next day, or the day after. Meanwhile, Belle and Marguerite proceeded with the preparations for the betrothal party as if nothing was amiss. They solicited Chloe's advice at every turn and if they noticed Chloe's lack of enthusiasm, they made no comment. Marguerite cheerily informed her that progress on Waverly was proceeding at a furious pace and she had no doubt it would soon be ready for its new mistress. Chloe tried not to cringe.

Even the news that her mother was coming for the party failed to cheer her. On the third day after the kiss in the billiard room, she accompanied Belle to Haversham Hall. Marguerite shooed her from the drawing room. 'Will and Caroline had been plaguing me for an age to ask if you would take them to the shore. Since I know you love to do so, I think you should go.'

Glad to escape from the betrothal plans which were suddenly turning into a small ball, Chloe left.

Will and Caroline were just as delighted to escape from the house, as was Lion, but rather than stopping to view the sea as they almost always did, they seemed in a hurry to get to the cove. She scrambled down the path after them, almost losing her balance. They ran ahead of her and she followed. Her shoes, adequate for a walk on a tame path, were no match for the sandy beach.

She nearly gave into the urge to pull her stockings and slippers off when they finally rounded the slight promontory and came to the cove. Picking her way over the rocks she did not pay much attention until she heard Lion's excited barks. She looked up to see him dashing towards an all-too familiar male figure.

Her heart leapt to her throat and every instinct told her to flee, but he had already looked up and spotted her. She could almost feel his gaze from across the distance. Will had followed Lion across the sand and now flung himself at Brandt. Caroline stopped and waited for Chloe to catch up.

Her serious eyes searched Chloe's face. 'Mama thought it would be nice if we asked Uncle Brandt as well, but she wanted us to keep it a surprise. I hope you do not mind too much. I will own I do not like surprises very well.'

'It is all right. Sometimes I do not mind a surprise.' But not this one. 'Is this to be a surprise for Uncle Brandt as well?'

'Yes.'

Splendid. She could think of nothing more awkward. Well, she would try to maintain a calm, friendly distance towards him.

At least he seemed to be heading in their direction with Will and Lion. She waited, heart pounding, until he joined her and Caroline. 'Good day, Lady Chloe,' he said.

'Good day.' She was not about to call him Lord Salcombe, but she certainly did not want to use his given name if he intended to be so stupidly formal.

Will beamed. 'Are you not surprised?'

'Very much so,' Brandt said. His gaze was impersonal

as it swept over Chloe. 'Was this a surprise for Lady Chloe as well?'

'Yes, but why are you calling her Lady Chloe? You always call her Chloe.'

'That is the proper way to address her.'

'Only if you aren't her friend. Since you are her friend, then you should call her Chloe.'

Chloe looked at him. 'He is right, of course.' She patted Will's head and smiled at Caroline. 'What shall we do now?'

'Look at the tide pools,' Will said promptly.

'Is that what you wish to do, Caroline?' Chloe asked.

'Oh, yes!' Then, recalling she was trying to behave more as a proper young lady, added, 'But only until the picnic arrives.'

Chloe glanced at Brandt. 'Is that plan agreeable to you?'

'Of course.'

The neutral tone in his voice made her want to hit him. She gave him a determined smile. 'Well, then, shall we go?'

'Yes!' Will dashed ahead and then turned. 'Hurry, Uncle Brandt!'

Caroline and Chloe followed at a more sedate pace. Unfortunately the only access to the tide pools was over a pile of rocks. Caroline was wearing sensible boots, but her own slippers would undoubtedly be cut to shreds if she wore them. Well, she would just have to remove them. At least there was one advantage to always removing shoes whenever possible. She sat down on one of the rocks. 'Please go on with the others. I am going to remove my stockings and slippers.' So what if Brandt thought she was improper? He obviously did not want to marry her anyway. He could think what he liked.

Caroline hesitated. 'Are you certain?'

'Yes.' Chloe shot her a quick smile.

'Very well.' Caroline still looked uncertain. 'Is Uncle Brandt well?'

'Well?'

'It is just he looks rather grim. Like Papa when something is troubling him.'

'Perhaps something is.' She had no idea what to say to this astute child. 'But do not worry about it. I am certain it is nothing very important.'

'I see.'

Just then Will shouted something and Caroline turned and started to climb over the rocks. Chloe bent down to untie the laces of her slippers, her mood growing more foul by the moment. Really, it was one thing for him to look so out of sorts, but another thing altogether if it overset Caroline. If he wished to make it obvious he wanted nothing to do with her, then at least he could do it in private, rather than in front of anyone else.

Not that they would ever be private again. She scowled at the knot she had been attempting to undo and finally pulled the slipper from her foot. After that she rolled down her stockings and climbed up the first rocks. The others were already at the next pile of rocks by the tide pool. She gingerly made her way over the rocky ground. Will looked up from his position on the edge of a pool and waved.

Brandt had removed his coat and laid it across one of the rocks. He knelt next to Will, but she almost saw the muscles tense beneath his shirt at her approach. 'Hello,' she said brightly. 'What have you found?'

Will looked disappointed. 'Only a few anemones. No starfish like last time.'

'Anemones are very interesting,' Chloe said. She moved slightly closer to Brandt. 'So what are your favourite things to look for, Lord Salcombe?'

He started to glance up at her, but his attention was suddenly arrested. He looked slightly stunned before his gaze shifted to her face and narrowed. 'Where are your shoes?'

'That was not my question.'

Caroline looked from one to the other, her expression slightly anxious. 'Chloe often removes her shoes. She says it is much easier to keep her footing. Mama removes her shoes as well and Papa does not mind. At least, not very much.'

'Yes, so there is no need to discuss this now,' Chloe added. She refused to quarrel with him in front of Caroline and Will.

'Very well.' But the look he gave her told her he did not intend to leave the matter alone.

Will jumped up. 'The picnic is here!' He scrambled off the rock with great alacrity. 'Whoever gets there first gets all the tarts.'

'That's hardly fair!' Caroline scrambled after him, her attempts to be lady-like swallowed by the natural competition between siblings.

'Well, I certainly do not intend to go without tarts.' Suddenly shy in Brandt's presence, Chloe jumped off the rock to the one below. She picked up her skirts to better clamber after them, and stumbled on a rock.

Strong arms caught her. She gasped and found herself looking into a cool pair of green eyes. 'What the devil do you think you're doing?'

'Laying claim to my share of tarts,' she replied.

He released her. 'More likely trying to cut yourself or sprain an ankle.'

'I won't. I do this all the time.' She lifted her chin. 'At any rate, since you have made it clear we are no longer to be engaged, you have no business dictating to me.'

'It does not mean that I don't have a responsibility towards you.'

Hurt shot through her. 'No? Well, I don't need your protection!' Chloe stormed away from him and climbed down the last rock. Her slippers and stockings were where she had left them. She had no intention of putting them on with him glaring at her so she picked them up and started across the sand towards the sheltered overhang.

At least he didn't attempt to catch up with her. Will and Caroline were seated on the cloth spread on the ground next to the hampers. The footman had pulled out plates and utensils and she sat down by Caroline. Brandt joined them, carefully sitting as far away from Chloe as possible.

Will chattered most of the time they were eating. Chloe's normally healthy appetite had somehow vanished. She forced a tart down her throat as Will had relented and said everyone should have one since there were too many for him to eat alone.

Afterwards, Will pressed back against Brandt's arm, tart on his face while Caroline sat on his other side. Brandt was smiling at something Will said. Then he looked up and caught her gaze and the smile suddenly shuttered.

Anger shot through her. Did he dislike her so much that every time he saw her he would close up? She hadn't asked him to kiss her in that way! She rose. 'I believe I will walk along the shore.'

'Do you want me to come?' Caroline asked.

'Oh, no. I can take Lion for company.'

But even Lion refused to leave Brandt's side. She walked away, the sand cool between her toes, before anything else could be said. She fought back the tears of anger that threatened to squeeze from her eyelids. Despite Belle's words, she could see no evidence he needed her or even liked her, much less loved her. No more than she loved him. In fact, she was quite certain she disliked him. The romantic picture she had built in her mind of somehow rescuing him from his unhappy life had fled. Not when he made it clear he did not wish to be rescued.

He did not need her. She had always been a failure at that anyway. Her mother had never listened to her advice even when Chloe knew what she was about to do would be a disaster. She had thought that last year she might save Belle from Justin, but instead it had turned out Belle did not need to be rescued, that Justin was her destiny.

Sir Preston hadn't needed her, or wanted her. Her attempts to make that right had failed, too. Emily did not want Sir Preston after all.

Even Caroline and Will did not really need her. They had their parents, and Brandt, whose company they probably preferred anyway.

Feeling sorry for herself, Chloe had hardly noticed she had walked around the small promontory until she felt the water swirling at her ankles. She looked down, vaguely surprised and then realised the tide was coming in. She looked back but could not see the others. The water was starting to lap up over the smaller rocks.

She should undoubtedly return. Not that anyone would miss her.

Which was completely idiotic. Of course they would. At least Belle. And Julian. And Justin. And Marguerite, Giles, her mother, and Will and Caroline, although perhaps not as much as they would Brandt if he was the one walking away to nowhere.

She started back and then halted. Her path was blocked by the incoming tide. She had quite forgotten that the water first surrounded this particular point, turning it into a tiny peninsula before creeping up to cover all but the tallest rocks. She would have to climb over the rocks and make her way to the daunting cliff behind them. She would need to hurry before the water covered the remaining smaller rocks.

Gaining a foothold on the first rock, which came only up to her knee, was not too difficult, but the next circle of rock was much more tricky. She slipped once, scraping her elbow. Her feet were beginning to feel raw and she had to fight the absurd desire to sit down and cry. She reached the end of the rocks and saw the ledge above. She could not imagine how she could climb it.

A shout startled her. She looked up and saw Brandt climbing towards her. She cringed. It was bad enough she was in this predicament—worse that he must come to her rescue again. She made her way over another pile of rocks before he reached the rock ledge directly above her and knelt down.

'Give me your hand.'

She looked up at him, half-expecting to see disdain or impatience, but there was nothing of that in his face, only calm reassurance.

'Chloe, you need to give me your hand so I can help you up. Do you see the rocks to your right? There is a small indent like a foothold.' His voice was firm as it would be if he were encouraging a child.

She found it and placed her foot in the recess. She was able to stand up enough so that he could reach her hand. He pulled her up and she collapsed on the ledge next to him.

He helped her to her feet and then released her hand. For a moment she could not think and then realised he was speaking. 'The water has come in so that we cannot go back to the beach now. We can either wait for the water to fall or climb through the passage in the cave.'

'The cave?' She looked up and saw the dark opening a few feet from them. 'It is Will's cave.'

His mouth curved faintly. 'Actually, it is my cave.'

'I cannot go in there.'

'Why not?'

'I do not like dark places.'

'We have no choice unless we wish to stay here on the rocks until the tide goes out again.'

'I…I would rather do that. You can go without me. Will and Caroline need you.'

'They have gone to Waverly with my groom. Chloe, I will be with you. The cave leads to the grotto in my garden. I've done this trek a number of times, the most recent a few weeks ago with Will. Come with me.' He held out his hand.

The dark opening loomed over her like some sort of cavernous mouth. She shook her head. When she did not take his hand, he took hers. Her gloves were gone so his warm, firm flesh was against hers. She realised it was the first time she had ever held his hand without a glove between them. 'Come, Chloe.' He started to climb and, in a sort of daze, she followed him.

She stepped on a loose rock and flinched. He glanced down. 'Your feet.' He grimaced. 'I would offer you my shoes, but I am not wearing them.' His gaze went back to her face. 'It's not very far. Can you make it?'

'Oh, yes. My feet are perfectly fine.' She would die before admitting they felt as if they'd been cut in a million places.

'I suppose you plan to tell me that you do this all the time?'

'Not exactly this part.'

'I didn't think so.' His hand closed more tightly around hers. 'We can go slowly.'

The cave was dark and damp and smelled of salt water and seaweed. She could barely stand and Brandt was forced to stoop. 'This way.'

She felt the first twinge of panic as they headed into a dark narrow passage. She took a deep breath in an attempt to steady her nerves, but as they advanced further into the tunnel, now completely dark, it was all she could do not to flee. Or scream. She made a little sound.

Brandt turned. 'What is wrong?'

'N…nothing.'

He moved closer to her. 'Are you afraid? Don't be. It's not very far and I am here with you.'

'I…I know,' she whispered.

'I will take your hand again and you can close your eyes and pretend I am leading you through a garden.' His voice was matter of fact and calm, as if he frequently led half-hysterical females through dark, narrow passages.

Somehow that steadied her. 'Yes.' She closed her eyes and gave him her hand.

He started to walk. 'Now we are near a rose bed. There is a particularly red rose just to your right. Further on is a clump of, er…gillyflowers.'

She almost smiled. He kept up a stream of nonsense as they slowly climbed through the narrow tunnel. Time seemed to stand still until a branch brushed against her cheek. Her eyes jerked open. Dazed, she saw they were completely surrounded by shrubbery and tangled over-grown vines, and a tumbling stone wall directly in front of them.

He dropped her hand. 'You are safe.'

She nodded. His clothing was damp and streaked with dirt; a lock of hair had fallen over his forehead giving him a rakish air and his feet were bare and dirty.

She undoubtedly looked worse. From the expression on

his face, she guessed she looked like the survivor of a shipwreck. 'I need to get you back to the house.'

'I should return to Haversham Hall.' She should apologise to him as well for all of his trouble, but she felt too miserable to say anything.

'Not like this.' Before she knew what he was about he had stepped forward and swept her up in his arms.

She gasped. 'I…I can walk.'

'I doubt it.'

'Please put me down. I weigh too much.'

'Not at all.'

'But…'

'Be quiet.'

The deadly calm in his voice quelled her more effectively than if he had shouted at her. She knew then that he was very angry.

Which he had every right to be.

They were met in the hall by Mrs Cromby. 'Oh, my! Whatever has happened? I could not make heads or tails of what the children were saying except you were rescuing Lady Chloe and taking her through the grotto. We have already sent word to Haversham Hall. The children are in the kitchen having gingerbread and milk. You must bring her into the drawing room. I will have a fire set straight away!'

She kept up a stream of chatter as she proceeded Brandt into the drawing room. He set Chloe down on the sofa and Mrs Cromby caught sight of her feet. Her eyes widened in shock and sympathy. 'My poor love!' She turned to the footman standing near the drawing room doors. 'We need a basin of water, rags and bandages. And a blanket. I will get that myself!' She bustled out.

Brandt sat down on the sofa next to her. 'I am going to see to your feet.'

'No!'

He looked up, that same impersonal expression on his face. 'I need to see how badly you are hurt.'

He would not allow her to refuse so she nodded. His touch was gentle as he turned her foot although she could not help flinching when his fingers brushed a particularly sore place. She whimpered a little when he touched her ankle. His hand stilled. He looked up. 'Did you twist your foot?'

'Perhaps a little. I cannot remember.'

'It is bruised and a little swollen, but I do not think it is sprained. You are fortunate that your cuts are small, but you have bruised your feet. Walking will not be particularly comfortable for a few days.'

He sounded exactly like Dr Abbott, the physician who had seen her in London. Brandt stood when Mrs Cromby and the footman returned. The loss of the warmth of his hand made her feel suddenly cold.

He spoke to Mrs Cromby and then turned to Chloe. 'I am going up to change. I'll be back down shortly.'

'Yes.' She should thank him, but the words seemed to stick to her tongue. He had already left the room.

Mrs Cromby set to work washing her tender feet and then bandaging them. After that, she helped Chloe wipe her face and comb her hair and then wrapped her in a quilt. She stood. 'Are you ready for visitors? The young lord and lady are impatient to see you.'

'Of course.'

Will flew into the room with Caroline following close behind. 'Will! Please do not jump on Chloe! You might hurt her,' she called.

Will stopped by the sofa. 'Are you very badly hurt?' he asked.

'No, not much.'

'Oh.' He stared at her. 'Why did you keeping walking? We shouted and shouted at you and you did not stop. Were you running away from us?'

'Oh, no, Will, that was not it at all. I was lost in thought and I did not hear you. Of course, I would never run away from you.'

'I'm glad.'

'So am I,' Caroline said. 'We were so worried when we saw how the water had risen, but Uncle Brandt said he would see no harm came to you.'

'Did you like the cave? Did Uncle Brandt show you where the passage begins that leads to the house?' Will asked.

'No, I fear I had my eyes shut most of the way.' She gave him an apologetic smile. 'I am afraid of dark, tight places.'

'How did you see to get out?'

'Br…Lord Salcombe helped me. He knew the way.'

'So you did not see any of the slimy creatures that live in the cave?' He glanced at his sister, his eyes dancing.

Caroline shuddered. 'Will!'

'None at all,' Brandt said as he came into the room. He was in an immaculate shirt and pantaloons and coat and no one would ever guess that a mere hour earlier he had waded through sea water, crawled over rocks and then crept through a cave.

Although Mrs Cromby had helped wash most of the grime from her face and limbs, Chloe still felt horrid. She pulled the quilt more tightly about her.

Brandt looked down at the children. 'Your papa has sent his carriage for you. Your groom will see Lion safely home.'

'Is Chloe staying here?' Will asked.

He glanced at Chloe. 'Only until I take her home.'

'Can she not come home with us?' Caroline asked.

'Your papa has asked that I escort her back to Falcon-cliff.' Again that polite neutral tone as if they were strangers.

Chloe managed to smile and embrace Caroline and Will before they departed. Brandt escorted them to the waiting carriage and she was left in the silent drawing room. Her chagrin was mixed with anger. She would rather he came out and told her he did not like her than treat her with such icy politeness. It was a wonder he deigned to rescue her. Then why had he been so kind? If he wished to prove they were not suited, he was going about it in the wrong way.

At any rate, she was not staying here like some sort of helpless invalid. She threw off the quilt and stood. She would rather walk home than impose upon him any longer.

Or at least ask that Belle or Justin send a carriage for her. She grimaced. Her feet were sore and the bandages would make walking more than a very short distance difficult. And she had no shoes.

She hobbled to the door only to come face to face with Brandt. 'What are you doing?' he demanded.

'I am going to ask Mrs Cromby to send a message to Falconcliff. I would like a carriage sent.'

'I am going to escort you home in my carriage.'

'I would really prefer that you did not. I have no desire to impose on you any longer.'

'You are not imposing on me.'

'If you must know, I did not purposely go around the promontory so that you would have to rescue me.'

'I never thought you did.'

'There was no need to put yourself out to rescue me. I was perfectly capable of rescuing myself.'

'How?'

'I would have sat on the rock until the tide receded.'

'You are quite mad if you think I intended to let you do that.'

'Why not? You have made it quite obvious you wish to rid yourself of me. I have no idea why you did not finish your picnic and leave.'

'For one thing, Will would have tried to save you himself.'

'I quite understand. The only reason you did so was so that Will would not come to harm.'

'That is not what I said.'

She knew she made no sense, but at least his indifferent politeness had left. 'That is what you implied. So now that Will is gone you can allow me to make my own way home!'

'Did you hit your head?' he demanded.

'No. Did you?'

'You need to sit down.'

'No.'

'This is ridiculous.'

'No, it's not,' she snapped. To her chagrin, she felt tears prick her lids.

'Hell.' He took her arm. 'Come and sit down.'

'I do not wish to.'

'But you will.' He led her to the sofa. 'Sit.'

Chloe sniffed. 'I am not Lion.'

He looked confused. 'No.' He pulled her down on the sofa next to him. 'Don't cry.'

'I'm n…not.' She dashed a tear away. The next thing she knew he was pressing a handkerchief into her hand.

She swiped at her eyes. 'Now…now I have ruined your handkerchief and your clothes. It seems you must go on being kind even though you wish only to…to rid yourself of m…me.'

'I do not wish to rid myself…' Brandt stopped. 'We are not suited. You told me that yourself and I would think that after the other day you would realise I would make a damnable husband.'

'Why?'

'Because…' He turned and looked at her. 'There are things about me you do not know,' he said flatly. 'No gentleman would have kissed you the way I did. Nor would have frightened you as I did.'

'I know about your father. I know you are nothing like him.'

He stilled. 'How do you know that?'

'Belle told me.'

'Did she? Did she also tell you that I frequented some of the worst hells in London? That I had a string of mistresses? That once I fought a duel over another man's wife? Do you know why? Because I wished to prove to myself that I was nothing like my father. In the end, it turned out that my stern, moral parent did all of those things, and he had no compunction in forcing himself upon any woman he desired. Just as I forced myself upon you. Twice, in fact.'

'You merely kissed me. Never once did I think that you intended to hurt me. Or did you?'

'No. I would never hurt you.' He ran a hand through his hair. 'But that does not excuse my behaviour or that I frightened you.'

'It was only that I am not very used to such kisses.' Not his sort of kisses; ones that made her want more, much more.

'I would hope not. Not until you are married and even then I would hope your future husband would exercise more restraint when with a young, innocent wife.'

'What if I hope he doesn't?'

'You've no idea what you are talking about.'

'So men only lose their restraint when they are with their mistresses, but not with their wives?'

To her surprise, a dull patch of colour appeared on his cheek. 'I am beginning to think we have both gone mad. This conversation is exceedingly improper. Most certainly you should not be talking about mistresses.'

'I am not so naïve that I do not know what they are. I heard enough whispers about Lucien's affairs. I am not so stupid or blind that I did not know what Justin intended when Belle left London with him,' she said quietly. 'Nor am I as innocent as you think.'

'Another one of your rhetorical arguments? I suggest we stop this line of conversation before you argue that there is no reason why we would not suit.' His voice was light and mocking. Brandt rose. 'I must take you back to Falconcliff, before my cousin accuses me of abducting you. You have been with me far too long as it is.'

Now he was back to the bored gallant. With sudden insight, Chloe realised that he adopted the role most often when he wanted to hide his true feelings, as he carefully deflected the conversation like a skilled swordsman deflecting an opponent's thrust when the topics were too close to his hurt.

She watched him leave to send for the carriage. He was impossible; arrogant, stubborn, and controlled, but also kind beyond measure. She was beginning to think they were perfectly matched after all.

Brandt handed the butler the bouquet of flowers. 'I will not disturb Lady Chloe while she is receiving other visitors. Please see that she gets the flowers.'

'Of course, my lord.'

He turned away, trying to convince himself that he was

relieved he had a convenient excuse not to deliver the flowers in person. It was best that he not see her nor allow himself to be engaged in any more conversations such as yesterday's. Conversations that might lead him to hope for things he could not have. Such as Chloe.

'Brandt!'

Belle's voice stopped him. He turned. She was coming across the hall towards him, her usual smile of welcome on her face. The longing and envy for the happiness his cousin had found with her hit him with renewed vigour. He forced himself to smile. 'Good day, Belle.'

She seemed to notice nothing amiss. 'Are these for Chloe? How lovely! But you must deliver them to her in person. I know she wishes to see you. She said she never thanked you properly for your gallant rescue yesterday. I believe she would like to do so.'

'Indeed. Yesterday she indicated that there was no need for such a rescue. She told me she had planned to wait on the rocks until the tide receded.'

'I believe she felt extremely foolish to have gone so far in the first place. She has never liked to inconvenience anyone or to feel beholden to them.' She touched his hand. 'So come and see her. Her injuries are much better and she is insisting she should be able to walk about. Perhaps you can convince her to stay down.'

'I doubt it. Does she not have a visitor already?'

'She has had several. Miss Coltrane left a quarter of an hour ago. Miss Sutton arrived shortly after that. And, oh yes, Sir Preston is here.'

Kentworth? What the hell was he doing here? Did he somehow know that their betrothal was only temporary and hoped to stake his claim early? He'd best look elsewhere, for Chloe was still his until the betrothal formally ended.

After that, he still had no intention of allowing Kentworth to have her.

Even as he told himself his speculations were ridiculous, he found himself saying, 'Very well, I'll see her.'

He took the flowers back from the butler and followed Belle through the hall to the staircase. They met Miss Sutton and her mother at the bottom, which meant Kentworth was with Chloe, unchaperoned. To his irritation, the departing guests insisted on exchanging a number of pleasantries, which Belle seemed in no hurry to discourage. He shifted impatiently. At this rate, Kentworth would have time to seduce Chloe if he had a mind to.

He finally broke in. 'I trust you will understand if I take my leave of you and go to see Lady Chloe.'

'Of course,' Mrs Sutton said kindly. 'I have no doubt you are anxious to see how the poor girl is doing for yourself. You must go.'

He started up the stairs, only to hear Mrs Sutton say, 'How nice to see two such suitable young persons in love. Perhaps I am too modern, but I do think love matches are so much nicer than marriages made only for convenience.'

He did not hear Belle's reply. His mind was reeling. In love? Did everyone actually think he and Chloe were in love? He had no idea how they came to such a conclusion when everything in their behaviour should indicate otherwise.

Still unsettled, he stalked into the drawing room just in time to see Kentworth take Chloe's hand and bow over it. 'So I might hope? Never thought to tumble head over ears until…'

It was all he could do to restrain himself from grabbing Kentworth by the throat and backing him up against the wall. 'Is there a reason why you are holding my fiancée's hand?'

They both jumped when Brandt spoke. Kentworth dropping her hand as if burned. Brandt had no idea how to read the emotions that flashed across Chloe's face.

Kentworth straightened. He eyed Brandt with an amazing calm for a man on the verge of being challenged. 'About to take my leave. No need to look like a dog with a bone.' He picked up his gloves and then stopped to face Brandt. 'Hope you know what a right-goer you have, Salcombe.'

Brandt stared at him. 'I do,' he said shortly.

'Good.' Kentworth left.

He turned to Chloe on the sofa. She looked lovely and rather fragile with the quilt over her lap, and completely in need of protection. His protection.

'What the devil was Kentworth saying to you about tumbling head over ears?'

'What lovely flowers! Are they for me?'

He stalked towards her. 'Yes.' He held them out to her and she took them.

'How pretty! Daisies and gillyflowers are my favourites. And there is a rose! Is that from the old shrub that is growing near the south wall? I thought all the roses were spent.'

'I found one. You have not answered my question.'

'Haven't I?'

'Yes. No!' He folded his arms. 'You are still my fiancée, you know.'

The slight smile left her face and he saw she looked rather angry. 'Am I? If you must know, I found your question rather stupid.'

'You think it stupid to question why another man is holding your hand and speaking to you of love?'

'Yes.' She met his gaze.

'Is he in love with you?' Because if he was, he would
be dead.

She took a deep breath. 'No, of course not. He is in love
with Emily. He realised it as soon as she decided not to
be in love with him any more. Except that I think she still
cares for him, but does not want to admit it. Perhaps she
wishes him to suffer the same pain of unrequited love she
did.'

'So he is not in love with you.'

'That is what I said.' Now she sounded exasperated. 'He
was referring to Emily. He wished to know if he had any
hope.'

There was nothing in her clear gaze that belied her
words. He was beginning to feel foolish. 'I see.' He paced
away. 'None the less, I would ask you to refrain from
holding Kentworth's hand in the future or encouraging
such confidences.' He sounded unbelievably pompous
even to his own ears.

'Why?'

'We are betrothed. It is not seemly for you to do such
things with other men.'

'Would it be more seemly if I did such things with you?'
There was a tinge of anger in her voice.

'Yes.'

'Except I can't imagine you would ever need to hold
my hand or confide in me!' Now she sounded truly angry.
'At least Sir Preston makes me feel useful!'

'Does he?' He had no idea what she was talking about,
but the jealousy he had tried to smother burst forth. 'Since
you have nothing but praise for him, then perhaps you
should consider him for your future husband after all.'

Something flashed in her eyes and then she lifted her
chin. 'Perhaps I will, if Emily does not want him.'

'Hell will freeze over before I will allow that to happen!'

'It will be none of your business.'

'It is as long as you are betrothed to me.'

She smiled, a cool little smile that made him gnash his teeth. 'I won't be betrothed to you for ever.'

He stared at her, but before he could say anything, she continued, 'In fact, I think it best if we end this idiotic farce now.'

He took a step towards her, wanting to kiss her until she admitted she was his. Instead, he gritted his teeth. 'I am loath to inform you, that however you might hate it, we will continue this farce until the agreed-upon time. I've no intention of allowing your guardian a reason to cart you off to Denbigh Hall. And you might consider how Belle will feel if you decide to throw me over two days before the party.' He picked up his gloves with a deliberate move-ment. 'I will bid you farewell for now. I will see you the day after next at our betrothal celebration.' He gave the words sardonic emphasis.

He did not give her time to reply, instead he stalked from the room, his temper at breaking point. He ran into his cousin coming from his study. 'In the future I trust you will keep Chloe better chaperoned,' Brandt ground out.

'From you?'

'No, dammit, from Kentworth or any other man who comes to call.'

'I quite see.'

It wasn't until he had swung himself upon his horse that he recalled he had not even inquired after her health. In-stead, he had allowed his own temper and passions to take over.

But then, she did not want him. She had made that very clear today.

Chloe stared at the lovely bouquet of flowers. The gil-lyflowers had already started to wilt. She had been tempted to throw the bouquet at Brandt, but now it only looked sad and forlorn. Just the way she felt. Her temper had cooled almost as soon as he had gone, leaving her with nothing but an overwhelming desire to burst into tears.

Provoking him had given her a great deal of satisfaction at the time, but in the end nothing had been gained. What had she hoped to do? Force him into saying that she could not marry Sir Preston because he loved her? Or he had no intention of letting her go? Instead, he had become more angry by the moment until he had stalked out.

Why he cared whom she married was beyond her. He did not want to worry Belle, he had made that clear.

Chloe clutched the bouquet tighter. The daisy heads had begun to droop as well. She began to cry.

Chapter Ten

Chloe avoided glancing at herself in the looking glass. She did not want to see her undoubtedly pale face or the lovely gown that she had no desire to wear. She picked up her fan and then looked up when the door opened.

'Oh, my love! How beautiful you look!' Her mother entered the bedchamber, a misty smile on her face. 'I still cannot believe that my sweet girl will soon be a married woman!' She traipsed across the room and caught Chloe's hands, her eyes tearing up as they had frequently ever since her arrival yesterday with Arthur. 'You look like an angel. Lord Salcombe will be enchanted, although from all reports he is already quite under your spell.'

There seemed to be no answer other than a sickly smile. Lady Ralston's brow puckered. 'Are you quite well? You have been very quiet since yesterday. I can only imagine how much your feet must hurt! I will not scold you, but I pray you have learned your lesson and will not go about barefooted any longer! I trust your future husband has already persuaded you of that!'

Chloe did not want to discuss Brandt. In fact, she did not even want to think about him. 'Shall we go? I suppose I should not be late.'

'Most certainly not.'

The carriage ride with Arthur and her mother was far too short. For once, Arthur actually attempted to engage her in conversation, but she was too nervous to respond. Thank goodness her mother answered for her. Her stomach churned as they halted in the drive. The house was transformed; lights shone from the windows and the overgrown vines and shrubs had been cleared so the front door and ground-floor windows were visible. Arthur helped Lady Ralston and then Chloe from the carriage. She winced as her tender feet touched the ground.

Chloe entered the hall on Arthur's arm and after Justin and Belle. She had been too preoccupied last time she was here to notice the changes but now, under the gleaming candlelight, she could see the newly polished floor and the gloss of the banister. The footman took her shawl and she, her mother and Arthur were following Justin and Belle up the staircase and to the rooms on the next floor.

Her stomach fluttered as Brandt broke away from the elderly lady at his side to greet them. In his black coat and pantaloons, a diamond gleaming in the folds of his snowy cravat, he was completely elegant, completely male and very disturbing. His eyes met hers and she trembled at the answering surge of awareness she saw in them.

He was not indifferent after all.

He held her gaze as he took her hand. 'You have not met my great-aunt, Lady Farrows. She is anxious to meet you.'

He guided her to the elderly lady and Chloe found herself looking into a pair of intelligent grey eyes in a sharply wrinkled face. She took Chloe's hand. 'So you are the young lady who has finally persuaded my nephew to marry. Certainly you are pretty enough. I trust you have some semblance of intelligence as well.'

Lady Farrows released Chloe's hand. She turned to Brandt. 'Since I did not trust you to remember the necklace and ear-rings I have brought them down myself. She should put them on now. Her gown will do very well with them.' She handed him a jeweller's box.

'I do not think the ballroom is quite the place for Chloe to change her jewellery.'

Lady Farrows waved a hand. 'Then take her to another room. There are certainly enough in this monstrosity. I trust you will find one without plaster raining from the ceiling. While you do that, the Duchess, Lady Ralston and I will greet any guests.'

He glanced at Chloe. 'We have our orders, it seems.' His expression was rueful.

'Yes.' She found herself smiling at him. She had no idea what to think of Lady Farrows who seemed to speak her mind, but it was somehow so artless that she was not certain if she should be offended or not.

His own lips curved in a smile and for a moment they were in perfect accord. She suddenly looked away, remembering they had no business being in such harmony. He took her arm. 'We will return shortly.'

He led her to a small room off the ballroom. 'I have found it best not to argue with my aunt in these matters. She always has her way in the end, it seems.'

He opened the box. 'I had hoped to avoid giving you this set, but I fear I have no choice. It is a family tradition.'

'I promise I will not lose it and, of course, I will return it to you as soon as possible.'

'Actually, it would be a great favour to future wives if you would lose it. The setting is atrocious and will undoubtedly make you look as if you are wearing a harness collar.' He held the necklace up.

Diamonds and emeralds adorned an intricate gold circle,

which was not quite a collar but certainly heavy enough. 'It is not too awful,' Chloe said doubtfully. 'I am certain it must be very valuable.'

'Yes, and it is never to pass out of the family, otherwise I've no doubt it would have been sold long ago or broken up. Do you want me to help you put it on?' His voice was calm and impersonal.

'I might be able to manage.' She undid the clasp to the simple strand of pearls she wore, and set it on the table. Brandt handed her the necklace, but she found the unfamiliar clasp beyond her. She finally gave up. 'I must ask for your help.'

'Of course.' He stepped forward and his fingers brushed her nape as he caught the ends of the necklace. A spark shot through her. He fumbled with the clasp; his light touch was making her knees weak. 'I have it,' he said, but his hand stilled at the nape of her neck. 'Chloe,' he said. 'This is impossible.' His voice was husky.

'What is?'

'All of this. This betrothal. Touching you like this. Having you so close and wanting more than anything to kiss you.'

'Oh.' Her heart started to pound. 'I...I would not mind if you did.'

'Wouldn't you? You told me you did not want my kisses.'

'Perhaps I have changed my mind.'

His hands slid to her shoulders and he slowly turned her to face him. 'I shouldn't do this, you know.'

'Why not? We are betrothed.' She held his gaze.

'Last time I frightened you.'

'No, you did not. Not really.' She hardly thought she could breathe.

He slowly lowered his head. His mouth covered hers in

a kiss that was so gentle she thought she would melt. She found herself pressing closer to him wanting more. He finally lifted his head. 'I forbid you to think about Kentworth.'

'No.'

'Good.' He hesitated. 'Chloe…'

'I trust you intend to show yourselves to your guests at some point.' Justin's voice broke into their reverie.

Chloe jumped back, her cheeks heated. She could hardly meet Justin's gaze, particularly when he said to Brandt, 'You were wrong. It is you who needs to be chaperoned.'

Brandt laughed, but it held genuine amusement. 'I think you are right.' He looked at Chloe. 'I suppose you must put on the equally atrocious ear-rings so at least you have a matching set.'

She nodded, hardly able to speak. She removed her earrings with shaky fingers. What had just happened? There was the kiss, which had been the most breathtaking thing imaginable, but something else had changed as well. The look in his eye, the gentleness of his touch had promised things even more wonderful.

'The ear-rings, Chloe.' He held them out. 'Or should I help you with these as well?'

She coloured. 'No, it is not necessary.'

His smile held a hint of wickedness. 'I agree. It might be dangerous.'

He was flirting with her again, but instead of annoyance, she felt breathless and vulnerable and happy all at once. She managed to put the ear-rings on. They felt as cool and heavy as the necklace but somehow she did not mind. When he held out his arm, she took it, her fingers trembling very slightly, but it was in anticipation.

She hardly noticed the guests they greeted. She was too aware of the man next to her; the strength of his lean hand, the timbre of his voice, the way his chestnut hair curled at the nape of his neck. Not even Lady Kentworth's tight smile and angry eyes burst her happy anticipation.

Gilbert Rushton sauntered in. He took Chloe's hand. 'From the besotted expression on your faces, I am surprised you have not escaped the formalities and gone for a romantic moonlight stroll in the garden.'

Brandt glanced at Chloe who felt as if her cheeks were on fire. 'I've plans for that later,' he said.

'Splendid.' Mr Rushton released her hand and grinned before strolling off.

Chloe did not dare look at Brandt until the musicians struck up the notes of the first set. Belle turned to Chloe. 'Under ordinary circumstances you and Brandt would head the first set, but I do not know if you should dance. Not with your feet still so tender.'

'In fact, I must forbid her to do so.' Brandt smiled down at Chloe. 'Come and talk to me for a moment instead.'

'After that you may stand up with me,' Lady Farrows told him.

Arthur levelled a frown at Brandt. 'I trust you will refrain from doing anything that might cause gossip.'

'I will endeavour to do my best.' He held his hand out to Chloe. She placed hers in his and he led her near a small alcove. He looked down at her. 'I am serious, you know. I want you to meet me in the garden at midnight. By the grotto. Do you recall where it is?' He paused, his expression suddenly less certain. 'Only if you wish to. Perhaps I am being presumptuous.'

'No.' She held his gaze. 'I want to be there. I will be there.'

His eyes darkened in the way she had seen Justin's when he looked at Belle. Instead of wanting to flee, she wanted to go to him, and press her mouth to his.

Was this what it was like to be in love?

The realisation hit her with such force she nearly reeled. She stared at his familiar face, and wondered why she had not known this before. Perhaps she had but had not wanted to admit it, out of a fear that she would be badly beyond her depth.

'What is amiss?' His eyes were watchful.

'Nothing. Everything is quite all right.' She touched his sleeve. 'You must go dance with Lady Farrows.' Everything was suddenly moving too fast and she needed a few moments to sort her tumultuous feelings.

'I will see you at midnight?' It was a question.

'Yes.'

She watched him go and then nearly jumped when Lady Kentworth appeared beside her. 'Another assignation, Lady Chloe? At least this time it is with your fiancé.' She gave Chloe a malicious smile before walking off.

The glow of happiness faded as a feeling of unease stole over her. How much had Lady Kentworth heard? Enough, apparently, to know she planned to meet Brandt alone. Such behaviour was not quite proper even for an engaged couple, but certainly meeting him was nothing Lady Kentworth could turn against them.

Perhaps she should have insisted on meeting somewhere else, or at another time, but she sensed this was too important; that whatever Brandt wanted must not be put off because of propriety or doubts, or anything else. And certainly not because of Lady Kentworth.

If only she could have a few minutes alone to collect her thoughts. First Lydia approached her and after that Belle insisted she must sit so she might watch the dancers. She was never alone after that. Finally Sir Preston stopped to speak to her and she recalled she had promised to help him with Emily. She finally spotted Emily and Mr Rushton near the same alcove where she had stood with Brandt. She rose and asked Sir Preston to escort her to Emily. Emily pasted a strained smile on her face when she saw them. Chloe was too tired to dissemble. 'Sir Preston wishes to dance with you, Emily.'

Sir Preston tugged at his cravat. 'Only if you wish, that is. No obligation to at all, Em…Miss Coltrane.'

'I have promised Mr Rushton…' Emily began.

Chloe cast a meaningful look towards Gilbert. 'I am certain Mr Rushton will understand.'

Gilbert's face was bland. 'Most certainly. Care for a turn about the room, Lady Chloe?'

'I think I would prefer to sit. My feet are rather sore.'

'Of course. I will escort you back to your chair.' He smiled paternally at Sir Preston and Emily. 'Time to take yourselves off to the dance floor.'

Sir Preston held out his arm. 'Miss Coltrane?' Chloe was pleased to see he looked her directly in the eye.

'Yes. I suppose.' Emily placed her gloved hand on his.

Rushton watched him lead Emily to the floor before turning to Chloe. 'Almost as entertaining as watching you and Salcombe dance circles around each other. Glad to see you two have finally come to your senses. Well, let us find your chair and then a glass of lemonade.'

He saw her back to her chair and then left to procure the drink. She quickly spotted Brandt moving through the dance with effortless grace. Had she really fallen in love with him? Was that what this attraction was all about? This half-hope that she would see him, the disappointment when he was not there, the breathlessness when he looked at her? The desire to feel his arms around her, his lips on hers?

It was a much worse feeling than she had ever antici-pated. When she had been with him, everything had seemed to fall into place but suddenly she felt less certain, less happy and much more frightened. If she met him as she had agreed, she would be giving herself to him; perhaps not in the most physical, intimate sense, but in every other way. If she did not go, she would be telling him that she did not want him.

If only she could draw Belle aside and ask her what to do. But this was not something she could discuss with Belle. She must make up her own mind.

She saw Mr Rushton returning with the lemonade. After that, her mother came to sit with her. She scarcely saw Brandt, but when she did she found his eyes on her in a sober, considering way. She was quite aware of passing time and, as half-past eleven approached, she felt as if she was on pins and needles.

It was after eleven thirty that she made up her mind. She was about to excuse herself from Emily and Lydia when a footman appeared next to her. 'I have a message for you. I am to tell you that it is imperative that you read it immediately and then wait for your reply.'

'Thank you.' She took the paper and opened it. It was brief. *Meet me in the west wing chamber. It is important. Salcombe.*

Why would he wish to meet her there? Except for the library, she had never been to the west wing and doubted she could even find her way there. But why else would he send her a message unless he had a reason for changing?

'Is something wrong?' Emily asked.

'Nothing at all.' The footman still waited for a reply. She took a breath. 'Yes, I will be there.'

'I am to escort you.'

At least that would be better than wandering around on her own. She followed the footman from the room and across the hall to the corridor that led to the older wing.

He carried a brace of candles, but they provided little light in the dim passage. He finally stopped in front of a heavy wooden door and waited for her to enter. She stepped inside, grateful to see a burning candle on the heavy table near the door. It took a moment for her eyes to adjust to the dim light. 'Brandt?' she said softly.

She heard footsteps and nearly screamed.

'Lady Chloe? What the devil are you doing here?'

To her astonishment, Sir Preston appeared. He looked as taken aback as she was.

'I was to meet someone here,' she said. 'What are you doing here?'

'I was to meet someone here as well.' He cleared his throat. 'Don't suppose you came to meet Emily, did you?'

'No.'

'Deuced odd. Got a note from Emily saying she needed to see me urgently but shouldn't tell anyone where I was going. Thought it strange but didn't want to not show in case it was important.'

'Yes, I know. My note was very similar.' It must be very close to midnight. Brandt would be waiting for her. 'I must go. There is something I must do.'

'Will accompany you back. Rather dark.'

'I think it would be best if you did not.' She nearly ran to the door, but when she turned the handle it would not budge. She tried again, but still the door would not move. 'Drat!' Growing desperate, she pushed then she turned and found Sir Preston behind her. 'The door will not open!'

'Let me try.' He waited until she stepped aside and then tried the handle, but his efforts were no more successful than hers. He shoved and finally said to her, his face mirroring her own frustration. 'Appears we are locked in.'

'We cannot be!' Brandt would think she had changed her mind. And if she was discovered locked in this ancient bedchamber with Sir Preston... 'There must be some way to force the door. Or another way out!'

'Door is thick oak. Don't think I can break it down.' He looked at her with a doubtful expression. 'Not planning to have hysterics are you?'

'I never have hysterics.' However, if she were going to, this would be the time. She went over to the heavy curtains and pushed them aside; the cloud of dust that rose from them making her sneeze. She tried the window sash, then realised she had forgotten to unlock it. She managed to work the lock only to find the sash would barely move.

'Don't think climbing out is a good idea,' Sir Preston remarked over her shoulder. 'The roof has a devilish pitch. Probably end up in the garden with a broken leg, or worse.'

She whirled around. 'But what should we do then? I cannot stay here. I promised Brandt that I would...would meet him and if I do not...I cannot imagine what he will think!'

'No doubt he'll understand once he sees the note. Kept mine.'

'I kept mine as well.' But it would not be the same. Tears pricked her eyelids. She would not cry because then she would never be able to think, but she was beginning to feel hopeless.

Sir Preston suddenly straightened. 'Thought of something.'

'What?'

'There's a panel in this room. Leads to a passage.'

'A panel? I thought that was in the library.'

'One here as well. Goes to the library.' He strode over to the wall near the cobweb-draped tester bed and she hurried after him. He shoved a small table aside and began to push on the panels then suddenly jumped when the wall opened and Emily stepped through.

Sir Preston goggled. 'Emily? What the devil!'

Dust covered her gown, but she appeared as composed as ever. 'I came to rescue you. Actually, I came to rescue Chloe.'

'How the devil did you know we were here?' Sir Preston demanded. He looked quite stern. 'And what do you mean by coming by yourself?'

'It will take too long to explain.' She looked at Chloe. 'You must hurry, Lord Salcombe is waiting for you. You must go through the passage and continue to your right and then you will come out in the library. Take my candle.'

'Yes.' Chloe took the candle and took a step towards the dark hole and then paused. 'You and Sir Preston are not coming?'

'Not for a while.' Emily's face wore a peculiar little smile. 'I will see you tomorrow and tell you all about it.'

Chloe stepped into the passage and took a deep breath. She would not panic, she would find the library.

And Brandt.

Brandt glanced at his pocket watch but it was not necessary. He knew it was past midnight, nearly twenty minutes past, and there was no Chloe.

She had changed her mind. He was not prepared for the bitter disappointment that washed over him. For a moment in the ballroom, when she had looked up at him, he had hoped that she perhaps wanted him after all, but she had not. For whatever reason, she did not trust him.

He could hear the faint laugher and music issuing from the house. Soon it would be time for Justin to make the formal announcement. His hopes of having her consent to marry him before the announcement were dashed. Instead, he would stand next to Chloe and know that the betrothal was truly a façade.

He must return to his guests, and find Chloe. He left the bench in the grotto and headed towards the terrace and the newly installed French windows that led inside. At the top of the terrace steps he was hailed by Tom. 'Lord Salcombe!'

Brandt turned. 'What is it?' He knew he sounded curt, but he was in no mood for idle talk.

'Have a note from Emily for you. She wanted me to find you and give it to you directly. She said it is imperative that you read it straight away. Had no idea you were in the garden or would have given it to you earlier.'

'At least I have it now. Thank you.' He started to fold it.

'She wanted you to read it as soon as possible,' Tom insisted. 'She looked worried. Can't find her now. Or Lady Chloe, and the Duchess has been asking for her.'

Brandt opened the note. *Lady K. locked Sir P. and Lady C. in west wing chamber. Have gone to rescue them through the passage. I will send Chloe to library through passage. Emily Coltrane.*

She had not changed her mind! His relief was short-lived. He had to find Chloe and then he would deal with Lady Kentworth.

'Something wrong?' Tom asked.

Brandt looked up. 'No. Your sister is fine. I am going to find Lady Chloe. You may tell the Duchess not to worry.'

The best way would be to go through the side entrance, which would allow him to proceed directly to the library. If Chloe had gone through the passage, then he would meet her. Unless she had become confused and taken the wrong turn. He cut around the corner of the terrace and then leapt lightly to the ground. The side entrance was nearly hidden by overgrown ivy, but the door was unlocked. He nearly ran to the library and then realised he had not brought a candle with him.

He prayed Chloe was already there.

The room was empty, but a candle burned in its holder on the mantel. Thank goodness for Miss Coltrane's never-failing efficiency. He took the candle and bent down. The heavy door was unlocked so he pulled it open and climbed through the grate into the dark passage. He would go first to the bedchamber, then, if she was not there, head for the sea. And hope Chloe had not gone very far at all.

Chloe leaned against the wall, hugging herself with her arms, trying to stem the rising tide of panic that threatened to overwhelm her. The passage was completely dark and she was completely lost. Her candle had blown out moments earlier. From the sudden cool breeze that touched her cheeks she knew she was near the sea, far from the passage to the library.

How could she have been so stupid? She should have had Emily repeat the directions, but she had been so determined to reach Brandt she had not waited. She had come to the fork in the passage but could not recall at all what Emily had said. The passage to the right had been narrow and full of cobwebs and the left had been wider. So she had chosen the latter and been completely wrong.

She had realised that when the path suddenly sloped downwards. She panicked then and had stood, immobilized, until she forced herself to turn around. But a few steps later, Chloe saw another fork in the tunnel she had not noticed before. Her mind had gone blank. She had suddenly had no idea where she was or how she had got there. She had forced herself to move and found herself in this gently sloping passage. Then, turning a corner, the candle had slipped from her hand.

Chloe closed her eyes and took a deep breath. She would not panic; she would *not* go mad. She would think of…of gardens. Roses and gillyflowers and daisies.

Then she shrieked as cold water touched her slippers, and her eyes flew open. She looked down and saw the water lapping at her feet. She stared for a moment, wondering how that could be, then her mind began to work again. She was in one of the sea caves. One of the caves that would be submerged with water.

She must move. Chloe forced herself away from the slippery wall and began the slight climb upwards. She must find where the walls and floor became dry. But it seemed to take an age before the surface was no longer slippery. Her feet hurt and her slippers felt as if they were worn to shreds. She slid down the wall and closed her eyes. She was exhausted, the effort to hold her fear at bay taking all her strength. Perhaps if she rested.

'Chloe!' At first she thought she was dreaming, but when she heard her name again she opened her eyes. She could see a faint light down the passage.

She stood. 'Here.' Her voice sounded feeble to her ears.

It must have been enough. 'Stay where you are. Do not move.'

Brandt was coming for her. She waited and then he came into view. He carried a candle. 'Thank God,' he said, and then he was at her side.

'I…I wanted to meet you,' she managed and then burst into tears.

With one arm, he pulled her against him. 'It is all right, Chloe. You are safe.'

She couldn't seem to stop the sobs, so he held her until they finally subsided and she leaned into him, spent. She wanted to stay in the comfort of his embrace for ever, but he finally shifted. 'We must return to the house.'

'Yes.' She stepped away from him and shivered a little.

'You can wear my coat. Can you hold the candle?'

She took it. 'I think so, but I dropped the other one.'

'My poor girl.' His voice was a caress. He shrugged out of his evening coat and draped it around her shoulders, then gently removed the candle from her hand. 'Come with me.'

'I tried to think of gardens.'

'Did it help?'

'A little.' Until the water came. She did not want to think about that. In fact, she did not want to think at all. She followed him up the passage in a daze, aware of nothing but his solid, warm presence. She had no idea how much time had passed when they halted.

'This leads to the library. You will need to bend down a little.' He stepped through and then held out his hand and helped her. In a moment, she was standing in the library with him. Brandt looked down at her. 'You need a change of clothing and a bed. I will send for Mrs Cromby and let Belle know you are safe. But first I need to get you to a more suitable room.'

She nodded. The ball, the guests seemed very far away. He took her hand and led her across the floor to the closed door. He tried it, but it would not open. He stared at it for a moment and then retried the handle again. 'Damn.'

'Is it locked?' Somehow it seemed almost natural for it to be so.

'It appears to be.' He turned and looked at her with the same frustrated expression Sir Preston had worn earlier.

'I suppose we could always go back through the passage to the bedchamber.'

'We cannot,' he said flatly. 'The door is locked from

the bedchamber. I asked Miss Coltrane to lock it. It is doubtful they are still there.'

He tried the door once more, this time pressing his shoulders against the wood, but it did not move.

Her lethargy dissipated. 'Could we call for help? Or climb through a window?'

'The window is impossible. It is a straight drop down to the garden. I can try to call.' He sounded doubtful.

Brandt began to pound on the door and shout. Chloe joined him. After a few tries, he finally turned to her. 'I suspect they cannot hear us. I fear we must manage the best we can until someone comes to look for us. I would hope that would be soon since they should notice that their host and the guest of honour are missing.'

She nodded, suddenly too sleepy to care much. She was cold, tired and exhausted. 'I believe I would like to sit down and wait.'

'Of course.' He ran a hand through his hair. 'There is the sofa, but it is devilishly uncomfortable, you know.'

'I do not mind.' Anything would do.

He took her arm and led her to the heavy, old sofa. She nearly collapsed on it. He stood looking down at her. 'Hell. Your clothing is wet and you must be cold. I would build a fire but there is no wood. Unless I use the furniture.'

'Oh, no, please do not do that. You would need an axe at any rate.' The last thing she wanted was to create more problems than she had already. 'I will be fine.'

'Your gown is soaked.'

'Only the hem.'

'At least I can remove your stockings and slippers.' Before she could protest, he had set the candle down on a side table and knelt down in front of her. He slanted a slight smile at her. 'I have done this before, you know.'

'Yes.' As before his hands were gentle and she closed

her eyes, mesmerized by his soothing touch. When he was done, he straightened. 'You had better lay down. You look as if you are about to fall asleep.' And then he sneezed.

For the first time she noticed how fatigued and cold he looked. The bottoms of his pantaloons were wet and his fine embroidered waistcoat was streaked with mud. Since she was still wearing his coat, he had not had even that extra protection.

'You must be cold as well. You must have your coat.' She started to remove it only to have his hand come down on her shoulder.

'Hardly. I don't need the coat. Lay down, Chloe.'

'I am always much colder when I lay down.'

'You won't be because I intend to lay down with you.' His brow lifted slightly at her expression. 'I am not planning a seduction. I merely intend to keep you warm. This room is damnably cold and the longer we stay here the colder you will feel. I've no intention of allowing you to catch a chill.' He sat down next to her. 'First I'd best remove my own wet stockings and shoes.' He bent and swiftly removed them. After he shrugged out of his damp waistcoat, he turned and held out his arms. 'Come here, Chloe.'

She shifted next to him and his arms came around her, drawing her back against him. He half-reclined against the back of the sofa, legs outstretched in front of him. He moved a little so that he could arrange his coat over her and then settled back against the sofa. His heart beat strong under her ear; his scent was comforting and pleasant, and the feel of his hand on her back made her feel protected and safe. His feet entwined with her colder ones and they, too, soon began to warm. Her eyes drifted shut as a drowsy warmth seeped through her.

She did not even notice when the candle burned its last for she had already drifted off to sleep.

'Brandt!'

His eyes jerked opened. At the same time he realised his cousin was standing over him.

And Chloe was nestled in his arms.

He bit back a curse just as Chloe stirred. She opened her eyes, her face filled with confusion. And then she blanched. 'Oh, no,' she whispered. She tried to push away from him.

He tightened his arm around her and rose to a sitting position with her still cradled against him. 'It is all right, sweetheart,' he said softly. He looked up at Justin. 'What took you so long to find us?'

'We were rather confused about your whereabouts. There seemed to be a number of missing persons including yourselves.' Justin's gaze fell on Chloe. 'Are you all right?' he asked quietly.

'Yes,' she whispered.

'She needs a change of clothing, a warm bath, and a decent bed.'

Justin's gaze raked over him. 'You look as if you need the same. Where were you?'

'In the tunnels. I would prefer to leave the explanations until later.' He rose and gently set her on her feet. 'I am going to carry you to my bedchamber. It is the only one that is truly habitable.'

'I can walk.'

'Your feet are bare.'

'So are yours.'

At least she was showing some spirit. 'Yes, but yours are cut up again. And this is my house.' He swept her into his arms before she could protest and strode with her towards the door.

Justin followed. 'I will at least inform Belle that she is safe. We spent the night here.'

'Please put me down,' Chloe said in a low voice.

'Hush.'

'I am not very light.'

'You are not very heavy.'

'But…'

'Don't argue with me.'

Surprise flashed briefly in her eyes, but she said no more as Brandt carried her into the hall. He nearly cursed when he entered the main part of the house and nearly slammed into his aunt, Lady Ralston and Belle. He did curse when he saw the Earl of Ralston behind them.

Lady Ralston let out a little shriek and dashed forward. 'My poor child! What have you done to her?'

'He has done nothing, Mama,' Chloe said.

'But your feet are bare and your gown is ruined!' She turned accusing eyes on Brandt. 'How could you?'

Belle took her arm. 'Maria, I think it best to wait and hear what has happened.'

'Which can wait until Chloe has been attended to.' Justin had come up behind them.

'So if you will pardon me.' Brandt pushed past the assembled group.

Ralston's face was black. 'I trust you have a rational explanation for this, Salcombe.'

'I've no idea.'

He thought he would be relieved to finally set her gently on his bed, but the sight of her lovely face against his pillows nearly sent him mad. The ache that had consumed him most of the night with the feel of her soft, light body snuggled into his suddenly burst into full, flaming desire.

If it weren't for the fact that Belle and Maria had trailed him upstairs he would have lain beside her and pulled her back into his arms.

He moved away. 'I will send Mrs Cromby to you.' His voice was more curt than he had intended.

Chloe sat up, her face worried. 'But do you not need a change of clothing? And something warm to drink? I fear you are about to catch a chill.'

'I assure you I am not.' Her concern was unnerving. 'I will see you later.' He stalked out and then realised his clothing was in the small room off of his bedchamber. He found Henry, the Crombys' son who had been serving as his valet, and sent him to retrieve a set of clothing and stockings and boots. He pulled them on in one of the empty bedchambers and was about to set off to find Justin when his cousin entered the room. He carried two glasses of brandy and shut the door with his foot. 'Thought it best to corner you here before Ralston tracks you down.' He handed Brandt one of the glasses. 'You look as if you need this.'

'A decanter would be better. Where did you find it?'

'Mrs Cromby. An exceedingly competent housekeeper. I trust you plan to keep her on.'

'With an increase in wages.' He took a sip of the brandy. He'd probably regret it on an empty stomach, but right now it was what he needed. 'How did you come to unlock the library?'

Justin eyed him. 'A short time before that I received a rather mysterious, anonymous note suggesting that we look for you and Lady Chloe in the old library. It also suggested the key might be found in a potted plant.'

Brandt set his glass down on the table nearby. 'There seems to have been an excess of mysterious, anonymous notes circulating last night. Both Chloe and Kentworth received such notes as well. Except it turned out Lady Kentworth was undoubtedly behind those. Chloe's was to arrange an assignation with me in the old master suite and Kentworth's was from Miss Coltrane for the same purpose.'

'So Chloe and Kentworth ended up together?'

'Not only that, but locked in together,' Brandt said.

'Very odd. For when that particular door was forced open at Lady Kentworth's insistence, Kentworth and Miss Coltrane were together. In another rather compromising situation. There will be a wedding shortly.'

'So that was what Miss Coltrane was up to.' Brandt's mouth curved in momentary amusement.

'You do not seem overly surprised. I suppose you know how Miss Coltrane came to be there instead of Chloe.'

'I did not have the time to gather all the facts from Miss Coltrane when I found her in the bedchamber with Sir Preston. She suspected Lady Kentworth might do something to interfere with last night's announcement so she kept an eye on Chloe. After Chloe was handed the note, Miss Coltrane feared something was wrong. She followed Chloe to the old wing where she saw Lady Kentworth close the door and then lock it. I can only surmise she must have stolen the key Mrs Cromby kept in the kitchen. Miss Coltrane asked for pen and paper and then wrote me a note informing me she planned to enter the room through the library passage, and that she would send Chloe to the library.'

'That did not happen?'

His mouth tightened. 'No. Unfortunately, I did not get Miss Coltrane's note until some time after she wrote it. Chloe is afraid of tight, dark places. I did not expect her to even want to enter the tunnels, but when I arrived at the bedchamber she was gone. I feared she had become disorientated and had gone the wrong way.' He looked at his cousin. 'She had. She was nearly at the sea caves. By the time I caught up with her she had started back, but she had lost her candle. She was shaking and terrified.' His blood still ran cold at the memory of her stricken, pale face. 'We managed to get back to the library, but when I tried the door, I found it was locked. The doors in this place should be used in a fortress. No one heard our shouts and we finally sat down to wait. Except it was damnably cold, her gown was wet and her shoes ruined. The only way I could keep her warm enough was to lay down with her.' He gave a short laugh. 'That was all that happened, I swear.'

'You do not need to defend yourself to me.' He looked steadily at Brandt. 'However, Ralston is another matter.'

'That doesn't surprise me.'

'He insists that you and Chloe marry by special licence as soon as possible.'

Brandt stilled. 'Does he? For once he and I are in accord. However, I suspect Chloe will prove less amenable.'

'To what will I prove less amenable?'

They both turned to see Chloe standing in the doorway. She was clothed in a plain, woollen dress that was far too big for her and no doubt belonged to Mrs Cromby. Her hair was caught in a ribbon and hung down her back. Her face was clean but still pale.

Brandt strode to the door. 'What are you doing out of bed?' he demanded roughly.

'I need to speak with you.'

'Where is Belle?'

'With Mama, who is having hysterics. Arthur has convinced her I am now completely ruined. And that we should marry as soon as possible. I told her I would not and she became overset.' She spoke with a sort of calm detachment, but from the way she knotted her hands together he knew she was far from calm.

'The devil take him,' he said softly. More than ever he would enjoy mowing Ralston down, this time for oversetting Chloe and Lady Ralston before anything was decided.

Her eyes were huge in her face. 'I thought you should know before he accuses you of…of ruining me. I tried to tell him that nothing had happened and he was ridiculous but he would not listen.' She took a deep breath. 'And I told him I would not marry you under such circumstances.'

'You've little choice,' he said flatly. '*We've* little choice. The circumstances in which we were discovered were damning to say the least.'

'But you did nothing, and it was not your fault or mine that the door was locked.'

Justin had come up beside them. 'Brandt is right, you have no alternative. Most of the countryside knows you were missing. We came up with some story about lingering effects from the excursion a few days ago and Brandt's desire to see to you, but I doubt few believed the story. Most certainly Lady Kentworth did not, since she knew perfectly well why you were gone. I've no doubt she will not let this ride.'

'But…'

'It is not only your reputation that will suffer—it is Brandt's as well. I do not think you would want him to be accused of seducing you and then abandoning you.'

'No, I would not, but…' She had a hopeless, trapped look on her face that tore at Brandt.

'He will be good to you.' Justin touched her cheek and then looked at Brandt. 'I will let you sort this matter out between yourselves, then I suggest you leave for London as soon as possible.' He quietly left the room.

Chloe's face was pale, the only colour the sprinkling of

freckles across her nose. Brandt wanted to take her in his arms and comfort her but he had no idea what she would do.

'Come in for a moment,' he said.

She hesitated and then stepped inside. He shut the door behind her, not wanting them to be interrupted. She jumped as his hand brushed her arm.

Brandt moved away from her. 'There is no need to look so terrified. It won't be so bad.'

'What won't be?'

'Marriage to me. I will not beat you or lock you up or keep you closeted at Waverly for the rest of your life. You can come and go as you please, you will be able to visit Belle as often as you want and your family. You will have your own money—I have no need of it. I will not interfere with you.'

He hoped his words would bring some sort of relief to her face but instead she looked even more wretched. 'You are very kind.'

'Hardly.' He folded his arms. 'There is one more thing. I will not touch you until you wish me to.'

Colour flooded her cheeks. 'I see.' She looked away for a moment, then back at him. 'This cannot be the sort of marriage you want.'

'Or the marriage you want.' Not when she looked as if she was about to be tortured. He shrugged, not about to let her know he cared. 'If I recall, neither one of us wanted a marriage of passion.'

She looked stricken. 'Yes. But I...' Her voice trailed away.

'I will inform your cousin that we will marry as soon as I procure the special licence.'

'Very well.' She did not quite look at him.

'I will leave today.'

This time she did look up. 'Should you? I have no doubt you are very tired. Perhaps it would be best to wait.'

'So that we might delay the wedding further? I think not,' he said coldly.

She turned away, but not before he saw the swift hurt in her face. 'I had better return to Belle and Mama.' She looked up briefly. 'I wish you a safe journey,' she said before she left the room.

He stared after her, suddenly weary.

Chapter Eleven

Chloe watched the rain pour down in front of the library window at Falconcliff. It had been like this for the past five days ever since Brandt had left for London. Most of the time she liked watching the rain; liked watching the wildness of the sea beating against the rocks while she sat safe and snug in the warm library. But she had felt none of that safeness this time.

Instead she felt restless and waiting. Waiting for Brandt to return.

How had everything become so complicated? Not that her relations with Brandt had ever been simple, but she had never expected their lives to become more and more inextricably intertwined, almost as if fate had decreed it so.

Soon they would be joined together in the most holy and inseparable of bonds until death made its claim.

She rose, too agitated to sit. He was to return today, but she had no idea if the weather would prevent him. She both longed for and dreaded his return. She had not seen him after that last distressing conversation in which they had suddenly become strangers again. Nothing she had said had turned out right. She had been so distressed at

Arthur's accusations that she had fled directly to Brandt. She had meant to warn him, but it had been too late. When he had said that neither one of them had wanted a marriage of passion she had wanted to tell him he was wrong, that she had changed her mind, but somehow, under his cold remote exterior, the words would not come.

She had no idea if the opportunity was now lost for ever.

She shivered, suddenly needing to find Belle and Julian and escape her thoughts. She left the library and came into the hall just as the butler opened the door. 'Lord Salcombe,' he said, his voice surprised.

She stopped and her heart began to pound as a tall, cloaked figure stepped into the hall. He started to speak and was suddenly overcome by a fit of coughing. He straightened and then swayed. The butler grabbed his arm to steady him. 'My lord! You are not well!'

Chloe ran to his side. 'Brandt, what is it?'

He looked down at her. Beneath the dripping brim of his hat, his face was drawn and pale. 'I have the licence,' he said and then promptly collapsed at their feet. Only the fact that Eliot still held his arm as he went down kept him from dashing his head against the floor.

Chloe fell to her knees, fear gripping her. He was breathing, but when she touched his forehead her hand nearly burned.

He groaned a little and she looked quickly up at Eliot. 'You must find Justin or Belle. He needs a bed and a physician.'

'Yes.' He turned. 'Stephens! Find the Duke and tell him Lord Salcombe has taken ill. And send Timmons to help me carry him to bed.'

She hadn't noticed the footman who now scrambled away. She laid her hand on Brandt's burning forehead. 'Can you hear me?'

He turned his head and opened his eyes. 'Chloe? Or are you an angel?'

'Certainly not.' Did he think he was dying? 'We are sending for Justin and a physician. And someone to help you to bed.'

'Not necessary. Apologies for fainting on you. Must get up.' He started to push himself up with his arms.

'No! Just wait for help.'

'Floor is hard.'

'Then put your head in my lap.' She moved so she was sitting in front of him. He obligingly shifted so his head rested in her lap.

A slight smile tilted his mouth. 'Nice. Must do this again.' Then he closed his eyes.

'I pray you will not.' Her voice was sharp with worry. What if he was dying? A sick dread gripped her. She could not bear it if he was gone. A future without him would be a hopeless swirling void. She bent over him and closed her own eyes and whispered a silent prayer.

'Chloe.'

Her eyes flew open. Justin was at her side. 'What happened?' he asked quickly.

'Eliot admitted him and then he fainted. His head is so very hot—he must have a fever.'

'Has he awakened at all?'

'A few moments ago. He spoke, but did not make much sense.'

'The fever, undoubtedly. I've sent for Dr Crowley, but for now we must get him upstairs.' He signalled to Eliot and the young, burly footman who hovered nearby.

Chloe stood aside as the three men lifted and then carried him up the stairs. She trailed them, feeling completely helpless. Belle met them at the top of the stairs. 'Mrs Keith is preparing the blue bedchamber. How is he?' Her face looked as sick as Chloe felt.

'He is alive. He has a fever,' Justin said as they moved past her.

Belle saw Chloe. 'Oh, my poor dear!' She hurried forward and caught Chloe in an embrace. They held each other for a moment and then Belle released her. 'You must go to him. I must tell Lady Farrows and then I will join you as soon as I can.'

They had just laid him on the bed when Chloe entered the room. His eyes were open but unfocused. She stood in the doorway, not certain what to do as Justin's valet set to work removing his muddy boots and stockings. Justin and one of the footmen had already helped him out of his outer coat and were now stripping him of his waistcoat and stock.

Justin looked up. 'You should leave. We need to remove his clothing and put him into a dry nightshirt.'

'I would like to help.'

His face was not unkind. 'For now you should go. He would not like to have you see him like this.'

She backed away, knowing he was right, but wanting something to do, anything to rid herself of this utterly helpless feeling. She felt even more helpless as the servants bustled in and out, and then Lady Farrows, after giving her a brief embrace, joined the others behind the closed door. Dr Crowley arrived just before her mother and Arthur returned from their excursion to the village.

Lady Ralston flew at her. 'I have just heard! My love! How worried you must be!'

Chloe was enveloped in a smothering embrace. 'Mama, please...' She would lose all patience if her mother suddenly had hysterics.

Her mother pulled away. 'My dear, you must come and lay down.'

'No, I must stay and hear what Dr Crowley says.'

'But you are so pale! I fear you are about to become ill as well.'

'I am fine.'

'Chloe… Arthur, you must reason with her.'

Arthur spoke. 'She will undoubtedly be more distressed if forced to rest before she knows the diagnosis.' He took Lady Ralston's arm. 'Come, Aunt. You should change before you catch a chill as well.'

This unexpected support apparently stunned Lady Ralston as much as it did Chloe. Her mouth fell open. She snapped it shut. 'I…I suppose you are right.'

'Good.' Arthur glanced at Chloe. 'I, of course, join you in hoping that Lord Salcombe will soon be fully recovered.'

'Thank you.' She was too taken aback to say any more before he led Lady Ralston away.

Then the door opened and Justin stepped out, followed by the physician.

Her heart slammed to her throat as Justin came over and touched her arm. 'He has the influenza, but his lungs are severely affected.' He paused. 'There is some indication he has developed pneumonia as well.'

'Oh, no,' she whispered. 'What can be done?'

'I have bled him and then administered a dose of laudanum to help him rest more easily. Cool compresses to help lower his fever. In these cases I have found a cool bath to be helpful.' Dr Crowley paused. 'And prayers.'

'Yes.' She caught Justin's arm as soon as the doctor had left. 'I want to see him.'

'It would be best if you waited.'

'No. I will not sit by and do nothing. I cannot bear to do nothing. I can help nurse him.'

'My dear…' Justin began.

'She needs to do this,' Belle said quietly from the doorway. 'She will go quite mad if she doesn't. I know I would.'

Justin looked down at her. 'There is the risk of becoming ill yourself. You are not long recovered from your own illness.'

'I am quite recovered. It does not matter at any rate for this is what I want to do. What I will do.' She walked past him and Belle into the room.

Brandt lay very still on the bed, his chest rising and falling beneath the quilt. The darkness of the stubble around his mouth only emphasised his terrible pallor. She knelt beside him and took his hand. 'Brandt, it is Chloe.' Her voice thickened with unshed tears and she could not say any more. She hardly noticed when Lady Farrows quietly departed and left her holding his hand in silence.

The small sound awakened Chloe from the light sleep into which she had fallen. She opened her eyes, disorientated at first, and then remembered; she was in the dimly lit bedchamber, sitting next to the bed in which Brandt had tossed and turned in feverish delirium for the past four days.

She left the chair and moved to the side of the bed. He slept, one bare arm flung over the quilt covering his chest. She watched him for a moment. His breathing seemed less laboured, nor did he seem quite as restless. She felt his forehead. It no longer felt so hot. Perhaps Lady Farrows had been right in declaring the medicine Dr Crowley had prescribed only contributed to his delirium. She had refused to allow Mrs Keith to give him the last two doses, despite the older woman's great objections. Hope flickered in her.

Where was Mrs Keith? Unable to sleep, Chloe had come to his bedchamber what seemed like hours ago. Mrs Keith, who sat with him, was clearly exhausted, so Chloe had sent her away, promising she would stay with Brandt. Mrs Keith had protested but then said if Chloe did not mind staying she needed to fetch fresh cloths. So Chloe had sat in the wing chair next to the bed, her eyes on Brandt's face, praying his fever would break. She had thought the housekeeper would be gone for only a short while, but the candle on the table by the bed had burnt almost completely. Not that she minded that. She would have sat with him every hour of his illness if they had allowed her. She would return to her chair and stay with him until morning.

Before she could move, his eyes opened. 'An angel,' he murmured.

He had said a number of nonsensical things in the past few days.

'I am Chloe.'

'Then I am in heaven after all.'

'You are at Falconcliff.'

'No.'

So he was still delirious. 'You must rest.'

His hand caught her arm and his grip was surprisingly strong. 'Water, please.'

'You must let go of my arm then.' The hope began to grow. He had not asked for water before. She moved to the bed table and poured him a glass and then returned to the bedside. 'I can help you.' She sat next to him and lifted the glass to his lips. He sipped slowly, but soon finished it. 'Do you want more?'

'Later.'

'I must tell Mrs Keith that you are awake.' She started to rise, only to find her arm again in his grip.

'Later,' he said. 'Stay with me.'

She sank slowly down on the bed next to him. 'Do you know who I am?'

'An angel, and I am in paradise.' His eyes were fixed on her face, but she had no idea if he was truly seeing her.

'No, you are at Falconcliff.'

'Allow me my delusions.' His other hand had come up and caught her other arm. He began to draw her slowly down on his chest. 'Will you kiss me, my angel?'

'You are not well.'

'Perhaps not.' His expression changed and she saw the desire, but even more the longing and vulnerability. 'I need you,' he said simply.

She bent down and kissed him. He lay still under her soft kiss, allowing her to explore his mouth. She touched his face, his hair, his eyelids wanting to feel him, wanting to reassure herself he was alive.

He drew her down to his chest and she found his mouth again. He did not move for a moment and then he groaned. His arms pinned her to him and somehow she was underneath him and he was kissing her with a hot passionate need that swept her away with its force. Her own hands tangled in his hair and she returned his kiss, the horrible worries and fears of the past few days driving her own passion. She wanted to be part of him, to press into him, to reassure herself he was alive, to become part of him. He opened her dressing gown and his hand cupped her breast through the thin linen of her nightrail.

She gasped when he circled the sensitive nipple with a gentle finger. Her stomach contracted and her body arched in an effort to press closer to him. The voluminous folds of the dressing gown suddenly seemed in her way and when he pushed it away she did not object.

There was nothing between them except the thin cotton of her nightrail. His hand stroked her bared leg, moving in sensuous circles upwards until he was stroking the silky soft skin between her thighs. She stiffened at the unfamiliar touch, but then his mouth was on hers and his fingers were inside her, stroking, caressing the most private part of her being.

Waves of tension radiated from where his fingers continued their seductive ministrations. Her legs closed around his hand and she pressed against him, begging for relief from the hot heavy wanting. And then his leg was between her thighs, gently parting them. He removed his hand and she felt the unfamiliar firm, fleshy tip at her opening. He hesitated. 'Chloe?'

'Yes. Please,' she whispered. Her legs seemed to part of their own accord in invitation.

He slowly entered her and then paused and touched her face with his hand. 'My sweet angel,' he murmured and then thrust deeper into her. She bit her lip, startled by the dull pain, and then he was moving in measured, rhythmic strokes inside her. She closed her eyes, and clung to him as his thrusts deepened and quickened. She was a part of him, her own body swept away by his passion as the tension built in her. With a final thrust, his seed spilled into her.

He hovered over her for a moment before withdrawing. He cupped her face, still lying half on her. 'If this is a dream, I pray I will never awaken. You have taken me to paradise.' He kissed her again. And then coughed.

Her eyes jerked opened. The candle had burnt completely, but in the faint moonlight she saw his eyes were glazed. His hair was damp and his forehead wet with perspiration. His hand felt hot against her face and his body heat burned through her nightrail. 'You are feverish,' she whispered. Oh, heavens! What had she done to him.

'Yes, my lovely angel,' he murmured. He closed his eyes, his arm draped over her. She tried to move and he stirred, his eyes opening. 'Don't leave me,' he whispered before his eyes shut again, and she saw he had fallen asleep.

She managed to remove his arm and sat up, her dream-like state rapidly disappearing. *I have been seduced.* No, that was not quite true. If anything she had seduced him, gone to him, wanting to assure herself he was alive, wanting to keep the fears away, and when he had said he needed her, his face vulnerable, she had given herself to him. Somehow, in that peculiar state she had been in, it had seemed only right to surrender to the final, natural conclusion.

She had no idea if he would even remember what had happened. He seemed to think she was an angel. Perhaps he would consider it a dream.

She had no idea whether that would be for the best or not. She rose from the bed on shaky legs and retrieved her dressing gown, which had become tangled under them. The dark stain in its folds seemed to jump out at her; clear evidence that it had not been a dream.

She clutched it to her chest for a moment and took a breath. She could not think about this—she must check on Brandt, for what if she had sent him into a relapse? He was breathing better, but when he coughed again, she jumped. She brushed her hand across his head. He was hot, but not quite as hot as he had been in days past. She straightened the covers around him and prayed she had not harmed him. She looked down at his face, the strong contours of his cheeks, the way his lashes closed over his eyes.

He looked both strong and vulnerable and she wanted nothing more than to lie with him again.

She spun around when the door opened. Mrs Keith bustled in, her face contrite under her ruffled nightcap. 'I am so sorry, Lady Chloe. I meant only to put my feet up for a bit and I fell asleep. I do not know what the Duchess will say as I was not to let you sit with him at night when you so much need your own sleep.'

'There is no need to tell the Duchess, or anyone else. I would not want to be scolded for leaving my bed.' Which had just been long enough for her to seduce Brandt in the midst of his fever.

Mrs Keith looked relieved. 'Then that is all right.' She moved to Brandt's side. 'How is our patient?' She touched his forehead. A little frown crossed her forehead, which only deepened when he coughed. 'His fever has gone up a trifle.'

Chloe felt guilty and sick all at once. 'Is it very bad?'

Mrs Keith glanced at Chloe's face. 'Oh, my dear, 'tis nothing to fret yourself over. Now, you must go to bed— it is nearly dawn. I have no doubt a spoon of Dr Crowley's potent will bring the fever down straight away.'

'Are you certain?' Chloe asked. 'I thought perhaps he seemed a little better without it.'

Mrs Keith moved to the bedside table and picked up the bottle. 'Now, I have no doubt Lady Farrows meant well, for after all he is her great-nephew, but his fever is up again and he is coughing so 'tis best to heed Dr Crowley.' She looked back at Chloe. 'You must go to bed. I promise you I will take the best care of him. He will not want to find you ill when he awakens.'

'No.' There seemed to be nothing else she could do. Her head was reeling and she felt again that she was in some sort of dream.

She was too tired and she must go to her room. Chloe backed away from Mrs Keith and towards the door, not wanting the older woman to see the faint stain on her nightrail. There was no one in the hall as she made her way to her bedchamber. The faint rays of dawn were already creeping across the sky as she climbed into bed.

An enormous fatigue overpowered her almost the moment she hit the pillow, but the last thing she thought of was being in Brandt's arms.

Chapter Twelve

$H$is head hurt and his throat was parched but for the first time in an eternity, the heat that had consumed him was gone. As was the sense of floating in a dream where voices and faces drifted in and out of his consciousness. Except for last night. That dream had been so vivid, so real he had no idea if it had been a dream at all.

He shifted and slowly opened his eyes, half-hoping, half-dreading that she would be there but there was no soft, slender body nor any sign at all in the smooth covers that anyone else had shared the bed with him. He prayed he had only seduced Chloe in his dreams after all.

'Brandt?'

His aunt appeared by his bed. For a moment he had no idea why she would be there and then he recalled the ball. The tunnel. And the licence.

Relief flooded her lined face. 'Oh, my dear boy! Thank God! You are awake. Do you know me?'

'Aunt,' he managed to croak. 'Water, please.'

'Oh, yes.' She bustled over to the night stand and then returned with a glass that she held to his lips. He had a vague memory of Chloe doing the same thing, but perhaps that had only been a dream as well.

'You do not know how we have worried about you!' To his astonishment, he saw her eyes were filled with tears. 'There were times when we did not know if you would live!'

'But I did.' He wanted to close his eyes again, but he needed to know about Chloe. 'Lady Chloe? Is she here?'

'Yes, the poor lamb. She has been at your bedside every day, and sometimes at night, nearly ill with worry.'

Had she been with him last night? 'Must see her.'

'Of course. But first I must tell the Duchess you are finally awake.'

'No, Chloe.'

'I will send her to you as soon as possible. You must rest for now.'

He watched her leave and then tried to sit up, but he was as weak as a newborn. He finally fell back against the pillows. He needed to see Chloe as soon as possible, re-assure himself that nothing had happened between them.

Or find out if it had.

He willed himself to stay awake, but dozed off anyway. He jerked awake when the door softly opened, but it was Belle who entered. She moved to his bed. 'How are you feeling?'

'Weak. Beg pardon for the inconvenience.'

A little smile touched her mouth. 'We are only grateful you managed to make it to Falconcliff in time to incon-venience us. I've sent for Justin. He should be here shortly.'

'Chloe. Need to see her.'

'I know.' She hesitated. 'She is resting now. She has not eaten or slept much in the past few days and Dr Crow-ley felt it best that she stay in bed. He gave her a draught, but I promise that she will see you as soon as she is able. Do not worry, she is not ill, only tired.'

He bit back a curse. 'Should have taken better care of her.'

'Yes, but she insisted she could not stand by and do nothing. She wanted to stay with you.'

He recalled his aunt's words. Day and night. 'Last night? Was she here?'

A puzzled expression crossed her face. 'I do not think so. Mrs Keith was with you and then your aunt.'

'I see.' So she hadn't been there but he still felt uneasy.

'You must rest. I will sit with you until Justin arrives.'

He nodded.

Chloe awoke, her head heavy. She forced her eyes open, disorientated to see the evening shadows on the wall. Why was she in bed at this time? Then she remembered the draught Dr Crowley had administered. She had awoken in the late morning. Dr Crowley had just seen Brandt and Belle had insisted he see her as well. He had proclaimed her fatigued, had prescribed a draught and told Belle she must stay in bed the rest of the day.

She should get up, but she felt too drugged to move. Her head hurt, but more than that was the unfamiliar soreness between her thighs.

A reminder that she had indeed given herself to Brandt. She had allowed a passion she did not know she possessed to overcome her judgement, her morals and her resolution. She was stunned at how swiftly it had happened—had she made a deliberate decision from the moment he had taken her arm and begged her to stay to let matters proceed so far? Or had she allowed herself to be carried away without regard to the costs?

That would be the worse thing of all. A deliberate decision would be one thing, but possessing so little control that she would do something with such grave consequences was much more serious.

She felt as if she did not know herself at all and she had no idea what she would say or do when she saw Brandt.

Brandt shoved aside the thin gruel that his aunt and Mrs Keith had deemed appropriate. It was hardly his choice for his first meal in nearly a week but at least he could keep it down. He had his wits about him enough to refuse the vile potion that he was certain contained laudanum and kept him in a perpetually drugged state.

'Only a few more spoonfuls, my lord,' Mrs Keith said, picking up the spoon. She had taken on the role of nurse with a vengeance and was determined to strong-arm him whenever possible.

'Although it was delicious I do not want to overtax my system.' He gave her his most charming smile. 'I would like you to send for Lady Chloe.'

'Doctor Crowley was quite insistent that you not have too many visitors.'

'Lady Chloe is hardly a visitor. She is my fiancée.'

'Yes, of course, but perhaps I should consult with the Duchess first.'

'Either you inform Lady Chloe I would like to see her or I will inform her myself even if I am forced to crawl down the hall.' He started to throw back the covers.

Alarm crossed her face. 'Of course, my lord.'

'One more question.'

She paused. 'My lord?'

'Did Lady Chloe ever sit with me at night?'

She hesitated and then stiffened. 'The Duchess did not deem it proper for Lady Chloe to sit with you at night.'

He fell back against the pillows after she left. The sun

had set nearly an hour ago. He knew Chloe was up because Mrs Keith had informed him she had come downstairs to dine which had not improved his mood. It would seem she was in no great hurry to see him despite the concern everyone declared she had shown when he was racked with fever.

His mood only darkened when the door opened and Belle entered. 'Where is Chloe?' he demanded.

'Behind me, if you would exercise a bit of patience.'

He saw the figure behind her then. Chloe followed Belle into the room, her hands folded in front of her as if she did not know quite what to do next.

She glanced at Belle, then moved towards the bed and looked down at him with no trembling, no revulsion, no shirking, nothing at all in her quiet countenance to indicate he had done something as vile as taking her virginity while he was half out of his mind. 'How are you feeling?' she asked softly.

'Better.' He saw there were shadows under her eyes and her face was pale. He scowled. 'You look as if you need Dr Crowley's attentions more than I do.'

'It is probably because I slept most of the day. Dr Crowley gave me a draught and I always feel horrid when I wake up.'

She spoke matter-of-factly and Brandt began to relax a little. Surely if he had seduced her there would be something in her manner, some sort of fear or accusation in her face, but he still needed to talk to her alone. He looked at Belle. 'I would like to talk to Chloe a few minutes in private, if you please.'

'I suspect it matters little whether I please or not, so I will not waste my breath. However, I trust you will not scold her for the past few days.'

'No, because I intend to scold you as well as my cousin for allowing her to become this fatigued.'

Belle smiled. 'I will warn Justin,' she said as she left the room.

He fixed his gaze on Chloe's face. 'Sit down. I do not like having you hover.'

She took the chair near the bed. Again, he had the odd sense of having woken up and found her in that exact position. 'Was it true that you insisted on sitting with me?'

'Yes, but we all did. You were so very ill that we did not want to leave you alone for an instant in case you…in case you needed something. Even Justin. He sat up with you one night. Belle is very nearly worn out because Julian is teething and has been fussing most terribly, which is why you should not scold her. I could not sit idly by while they made themselves ill.'

'I am beginning to think that they should ring a peal over my head for running the household ragged.'

'That is not what I meant at all. I only meant that we were so very worried about you that none of us wished to leave you for an instant.'

'Us? Does that mean you worried about me as well?'

'Yes.'

He kept his eyes on her face. 'Then perhaps you no longer hold me in such dislike.'

She flushed a little, but did not look away. 'I do not hold you in dislike.'

'I am glad to hear that.' Then it had been a dream, obviously a vivid one brought on by a combination of fever and drugs and desire, for surely if he had used her so badly she would hate him.

'I should let you rest.' She started to rise and he found his hand clamping around hers. She jumped, her eyes startled, and he had that bizarre sense he had done this before.

Except then he had pulled her down on top of him. He could almost feel the weight of her light, delicate body on top of his. Desire shot through him, hot and immediate.

He released her abruptly. 'I beg your pardon. I had something else to say to you.'

She had frozen at his touch. Now she looked apprehensive. 'What is it?'

He had no idea why she suddenly looked so fearful. 'I want us to marry as soon as possible. Tomorrow, in fact.'

'Tomorrow?' She looked completely uncomprehending as if she had no idea what he referred to.

'Surely you recall I had just returned from London with the special licence when I collapsed at your feet.'

'Oh. Yes.' She flushed. 'But surely you wish to wait until you are well.'

'No. And risk some other damnable thing happening before we are wed?'

'What else would happen?'

'I've no idea.' He only knew that he wanted her safely under the protection of his name and that he did not intend to let her go.

'I do not think...'

'Chloe.' He suddenly felt weary. 'Don't argue with me. I do not have the strength.'

Something changed in her expression. 'I will not argue with you,' she said quietly. 'I will wed you tomorrow if that is what you wish.'

'It is.' He wanted to tell her they would marry only if that was what she wished as well, but it was too late for that. They had no choice. He was not sure if fate had ever given them one.

Chloe sat in the chair by her window, feeling numb. He had not remembered after all. Perhaps last night had seemed part of the restless dreams that had plagued him. For a moment, when he had taken her arm, she had thought he was going to say something about the previous night, but instead he had spoken of the marriage. There had been nothing in his manner to indicate he recalled her even being there.

Perhaps it was for the best to go on as if nothing at all had happened.

But she had agreed to marry him tomorrow. She was hardly aware of what he said at first, and then when it dawned upon her that he wanted to marry tomorrow, she had panicked.

Until she had seen the vulnerability beneath his cool arrogance. The tiredness…the need. And she had responded to it, wanting to erase the weariness from his face.

She knew now why she had gone to him last night.

She loved him.

Chapter Thirteen

Belle sat down on the bed next to Chloe and took her hand. 'It is only natural to be a little afraid before one's wedding. My knees were shaking quite horribly and I scarcely remembered saying the vows.'

'When you married Lucien?'

'Yes, and when I married Justin as well. But particularly with Lucien, I did not know what to expect. I did not know how a wife was supposed to be, and I knew nothing of the intimacies between a man and a woman. Lucien had only kissed me once before we married.' She hesitated. 'Has Maria talked to you at all of this?'

Chloe felt her face grow warm. 'No.' She had no idea what to say.

'I do not want you to go into your marriage as unprepared as I was. The first time a woman is with her husband, she finds the intimacy a little bewildering and perhaps not so pleasurable. But when one is with a man who cares for one and whom one cares for in return, it will soon become one of the most wonderful pleasures of marriage.' Her hand tightened around Chloe's. 'Brandt cares for you. I know he will be patient and kind. He will not hurt you.'

'I...I know.' She wanted to sink through the floor, but

there was nothing she could say. Her unhappiness and self-reproach deepened as Belle gently described the marriage bed. She could only sit, frozen, until Belle finished and then enveloped her in a tight embrace.

Belle released her. 'You must dress. I will send Ellen to you but please, if you need anything, I am here.'

'Yes.' She wanted to cling to Belle, but she could not. 'I know.' She forced a smile to her lips. 'I think I would like to be alone for a little while.'

'Of course.' Belle left the room.

Chloe rose from the bed and went to the window, not really seeing the blue sky or the high fleecy clouds. She felt more and more as if she was about to enter into the worst sort of deception. She was presenting herself as a virginal bride, but she was not.

What would Brandt do when he discovered the truth? If and when he decided to exercise his rights as a husband. She must think of some way of telling him.

She had no idea how.

The short journey to the chapel passed in a sort of dream and then she was stepping down from the carriage into the cool, misty morning. Arthur took her arm and escorted her up the stone steps of the old chapel with her mother trailing behind her. Inside, Caroline and Will waited for her, their faces solemn. Will stepped forward and handed her a bouquet of flowers with a formality so unlike his usual self that she had no idea whether she wanted to smile or weep. Instead, she bent down and hugged him and was rewarded by a fierce hug in return. 'Now, you'll be here for ever with us,' he told her.

'Yes.' She embraced Caroline and then stepped from the vestibule and into the chapel. With some amazement, she saw there were a number of people present. She looked towards the front and her heart leapt to her throat when she saw that Brandt already stood there, elegant in a dark coat and pantaloons, his starched cravat tied in an intricate knot at his neck. His eyes met hers, his gaze dark and intense, and she caught her breath.

Justin came to her side. 'Chloe, are you ready?'

'Y…yes.' To her chagrin, her voice shook.

'Then come. Brandt is waiting for you.'

The ceremony passed in a haze. She hardly heard the vicar's words and barely recalled repeating her vows. She was aware only of Brandt, of his cool but increasingly husky replies, of his body next to hers. Then he was taking her hand and slipping a ring over her third finger and finally tilting her chin towards him. 'Chloe,' he whispered and then his lips brushed over hers in a kiss that made her legs weak. He released her and promptly began to cough.

'You must sit down,' Chloe said, alarmed. His face was white and she feared he would swoon. Justin caught his arm and guided him to a front pew. He sat abruptly, still coughing. Lady Farrows and Marguerite rushed to his side and then the vicar appeared with a glass of water.

Brandt took a few sips and then his coughing subsided. He looked over at Chloe, who had come to stand a little to the side. Chagrin crossed his face. 'I beg your pardon.'

She wanted to brush back the lock of hair that had fallen over his forehead, but she doubted he would welcome it. 'Please do not. One always has such dreadful coughs with influenza.'

'You are too kind,' he said softly.

Giles spoke. 'Perhaps we should congratulate the bride and groom and then see them to Falconcliff before the groom collapses.'

'I've no intention of doing that.' Brandt rose and held out his arm to Chloe. 'Shall we?'

She took it, hoping he would make it to the carriage without another bout of coughing. The others followed them, speaking in quiet voices. The carriage already waited in the small drive in front of the chapel.

'I had better ride with you,' Lady Farrows said. 'Shouldn't want you to collapse on Lady Salcombe.'

Lady Salcombe? Chloe started before she realised Lady Farrows referred to her. But Justin was helping Brandt into the carriage and then Chloe, and finally Lady Farrows who took the place next to Brandt.

Brandt began to cough as soon as the carriage was in motion. Lady Farrows handed him a handkerchief and when he finally stopped, told him to lean back and close his eyes. Chloe watched, feeling useless, for Lady Farrows seemed to have everything well in hand.

She could scarcely fathom she was married and watching Brandt resting against the pillows only increased her sense of unreality. She looked away, fighting the most absurd desire to burst into tears and when she glanced back at him and saw how vulnerable he looked with his eyes closed, she wanted nothing more than to gather him into her arms and comfort him. She could hardly do so with Lady Farrows in the carriage, and even if they were alone, she doubted she would have the courage to do so.

They finally reached Falconcliff. Brandt roused himself when the carriage halted and insisted on stepping down without help. He assisted his aunt down and then held out his hand to Chloe. To her dismay, she stumbled so he was forced to catch her against him. She pulled away. 'I beg your pardon.'

For the first time that day, the familiar smile touched his mouth. 'There is no need to. In fact, I look forward to many such moments in the future.'

'But I might have hurt you.'

'Never.' His arm tightened around her and she caught her breath. His expression changed. 'Chloe.'

For a heart-stopping moment, she thought he was about to kiss her. Lady Farrows voice broke in. 'My dear boy, I suggest you go inside before you catch another chill. I doubt Chloe wishes to nurse you through another illness.'

Brandt's hands fell from her arm. 'Of course.' He escorted Chloe into the hall where Belle, Justin and Marguerite waited. Belle took one look at Brandt's pale face and insisted he go upstairs immediately. 'We can have the wedding breakfast brought upstairs.'

'And crowd into your bedchamber,' Justin added. He grinned at his cousin. 'You may be served in bed if you like.'

'I think not.' Brandt looked at Chloe. 'Unless Chloe wishes to join me.'

She flushed. 'No, I...'.

'Really, Brandt,' Marguerite said. 'You can put her to the blush later. After your guests have gone.'

Chloe looked away, her stomach lurching. In the presence of family and friends, she could easily think nothing had changed, but everything had. Her life was now irrevocably intertwined with his and he had every right to ask anything of her he wished.

She managed to force a few bites of the delicious breakfast down her throat and smile and join in the conversation, all the while aware of Brandt who sat in the wing chair near the fireplace. He ate very little, his pallor only increasing as time went on, his gaze frequently resting on her with a brooding expression she could not interpret.

And finally Belle and Marguerite announced it was time to leave, and that Brandt needed to rest. Marguerite took Chloe's arm. 'The bride needs to rest as well. She is nearly as pale as the groom.'

Brandt rose from his chair. 'I wish to speak to Chloe for a few minutes first.'

Marguerite gave him an arch look. 'Very well, but I hope you remember that you are far from well.'

'I am quite aware of it,' he said drily.

He leaned heavily against the bedpost while the others left. His breathing was more laboured and he was starting to cough again.

The room was quiet at last. Brandt still leaned against the bedpost. He opened his mouth to speak and then coughed.

Chloe poured a glass of water and gave it to him. 'You should be in bed.'

He took a sip. 'I need to talk to you.'

'You can do so in bed.' She took his arm. 'Please.'

He looked down at her, a peculiar light in his eye. 'Will you join me?'

She dropped his arm and froze. 'I...'

His expression changed. 'Chloe, I swear there is no need to look like that. I promised I would not touch you unless you were willing.' His voice was thick. 'Sit down, Marguerite is right, you need a bed as much as I do.'

'I am fine.' But he had already seated her gently on the bed.

He sat down a careful distance from her. 'I beg your pardon for my damnable tongue. I did not mean to frighten you. It was just...' He frowned. 'It will not happen again. This is what I wished to speak to you about. I told you before I would not expect you to share my bed, at least until we are better acquainted. Until you are ready, I will not force myself on you. We will keep our relationship on the businesslike basis we both want.'

She felt as if she were in a waking nightmare. 'Brandt...'

'There is one other thing.' His gaze locked with hers. 'As soon as I am able, I wish to remove to Waverly. Will you come with me?'

She felt a stab of hurt that he would think she might not, as if they were not really married. 'Yes, of course.'

Something like relief flickered in his eyes. 'Good,' he said carefully. 'I will not detain you any further, then.' He started to rise.

She caught his hand. 'You do not need to escort me to the door. I am quite capable of walking myself.'

He had stilled at her touch before he pulled his hand from hers. 'Then I will see you soon.'

'Yes.' She rose and walked to the door and then turned to look back at him. He was watching her, an odd longing on his face. For a moment she wanted to run back to him, but then the longing look vanished.

'Good day, Chloe,' he said and his voice contained nothing but cool dismissal.

Brandt rang for his valet and then fell back against the pillows. He had used all of his strength for the brief ceremony and the breakfast that followed. All he had really wanted to do was be alone with Chloe, take her into his arms and reassure her that she would be safe with him.

She had clearly drifted through the ceremony in a daze as if she wasn't quite sure what was happening. Beneath her smiles he had seen the strain. He wanted to erase that away, but when she took his arm, all control fled and instead he made that damnable remark about joining him in bed.

She had gone so pale he thought she would faint. Was the thought of his making love to her so repulsive she nearly swooned?

Very well, then. He would give her distance to accustom

herself to the fact they were married. He would return to Waverly as soon as possible, but without her. He would use the excuse that the house still was not in order for her.

He would have time to accustom himself as well. And make certain his emotions were completely under control.

Chapter Fourteen

Chloe watched as Betsy unpacked the last of the contents of her trunk. 'Is there anything else, Lady Salcombe? Shall I unpack the smaller trunk for you?'

It took Chloe a moment to realise Betsy addressed her. After nearly five weeks of marriage, she should be accustomed to her new title, but she sometimes forgot. At Falconcliff, most of the servants continued to address her as Lady Chloe so she had nearly forgotten she was married. It had not helped that a week after their wedding, Brandt informed her he would return to Waverly to oversee the remainder of the restoration before her arrival. His manner had been so cool, so final, her pride did not allow her to argue with him. So she had held her tongue and agreed as coolly as he had informed her.

In fact, from his distant manner they might as well not be married at all. Any hope she had that he might change had been dashed in the weeks following the wedding. Not wanting to let him guess her hurt, she in turn, treated him with the same reserved politeness, which was undoubtedly his idea of a businesslike impersonal marriage.

'No, not now. I thought I might do it,' she told Betsy. The girl curtsied and then left the room. Chloe walked to the trunk and felt as if she might cry. The two trunks along with several valises had arrived only today. Her mother had returned to Dutton Cottage two weeks earlier, and had packed the remainder of Chloe's belongings. That they were now in her room at Waverly only emphasised that her home was here.

She had the same lost, sick feeling she had had when she had first gone off to school. In fact, she had not been feeling particularly well for the past few days, but she never felt very well when she was nervous.

She should not feel this way. Although Waverly stood less than two miles from Falconcliff, she felt as if an ocean separated the two estates. It was only that she did not know what she was supposed to do. She wondered if all brides felt so uncertain; Emily, for instance, whose wedding had taken place a few days before her own. She could not imagine Emily with her practical, forthright manner feeling such qualms. Emily had undoubtedly moved into Martin Woods knowing exactly what needed to be done.

She looked around her room. The furnishings were old and the covers faded, but it was clean and neat. The window looked out upon the sea. The garden she had often passed through was below.

She jumped at the light knock on her door. She turned, half-expecting to see one of the servants. Instead Brandt stood in the doorway. Her heart thudded with a mingling of excitement and fear all at once. He stepped into the room. 'I did not mean to startle you.'

'You did not. At least, not very much.' She was babbling to cover her surprise. He had made it quite clear over the past several weeks that their relationship was to remain impersonal. The night she had lain in his arms seemed so long ago that she was beginning to think it had been a dream for her as well. She had managed to put it aside, and as long as he maintained his distance, she could almost pretend it had not happened.

'I trust everything arrived safely,' he said.

'Yes, thank you.' She had no idea why he stood in her bedchamber; but she suddenly wanted his company.

'You would undoubtedly like to rest before dinner. I will let you do so. If you need anything, you have only to ask Mrs Cromby.' His hand was already on the door.

'Wait!'

He turned, his expression polite.

'I really do not want to rest,' she said.

'As you wish. This is your home.'

Did he really care what she did? An anger she was hardly aware of bubbled to the surface. 'I rather think I will walk to the shore.'

The remote politeness was gone in a flash. 'I think not, my dear.'

'You just said that I might do as I wish.'

'That does not include wandering the seashore unaccompanied.'

'I have done it before.'

'Yes,' he said grimly. 'Which is going to change. You are not to go out unaccompanied and without telling me.'

'Why? Does one immediately acquire a keeper as soon as they marry?'

'No, a husband, which means I am responsible for your well-being.'

'I cannot see the difference.' She brushed past him into the hall. 'I am going to the shore. I know the way so there is no need for you to point it out.' She had no doubt she was aggravating him, but anything was better than the polite distance he had been keeping from her.

The hand clamped down around her arm took her by surprise, none the less. He pulled her around to face him.

'You do need a keeper. You will freeze in that thin gown you are wearing, which I've no doubt will be ruined as soon as it is wet. You are not wearing shoes and I doubt very much you intended to retrieve a bonnet.'

His eyes blazed down into hers. Her mouth was dry, but she was determined to not back down. 'Perhaps you should come with me if you are so determined to be my keeper.'

He stared at her and then an odd light appeared in his eyes. 'Perhaps I should.' His eyes strayed to her mouth and for a breathless moment she thought he would kiss her. Instead, he dropped her arm. 'Change into a more suitable gown and put on a pair of boots. You can meet me in the garden in half an hour.'

Her heart thudded as she watched him go. She had the sensation of arousing a sleeping and very dangerous tiger. But then, had that not been her intention all along? To push him out of the cool, passionless marriage of convenience? So what did she want? To lie in his arms as she had that one night?

She only hoped she knew what she was doing.

Brandt stood near the gate that led from the garden to the path down to the sea. He felt on edge, wondering if she would decide not to come. His rational mind told him this would be for the best. Particularly if she was as unpredictable and provoking as she had been earlier.

What the devil had happened? He fully intended to maintain the same cool, impersonal relationship they had agreed upon the day of their wedding. It had been easy enough to do at Falconcliff since he was recovering from his illness. She had seemed no more inclined to seek out his company than he had hers. During the weeks he'd spent alone at Waverly, he had convinced himself that he would have no problem keeping his distance. Except the erotic dreams that plagued him each night left him wanting her with an ache that increased with each passing day.

He had no idea why he had gone to her bedchamber except that, when she stood in the hall with her trunks, he had seen loneliness in her face. He had wanted to reassure himself she was well.

Instead he had lost his damnable temper when she had announced she was going to the shore.

The prickly sensation at the back of his neck told him she was coming. He turned and saw her picking her way through the garden. Her drab gown and old faded bonnet did nothing to stop the unwelcome rush of desire tightening his loins.

'I was beginning to think you had changed your mind after all,' he deliberately drawled, in an attempt to disguise his emotion.

'Of course I did not. It took Betsy a little more time to find my gown and my half-boots.' She met his eyes with that same little defiant look she had in the bedchamber. 'I will take less time on the next occasion since I will know where my possessions are.'

'There will be a next time?'

'Yes, unless you plan to keep me prisoner. I promised Will and Caroline I would take them on picnics quite often.' She gave him a tight little smile. 'Shall we go?' She started down the path.

He easily caught up to her. 'But only with a servant.'

'We shall see.' She walked a little faster.

He gritted his teeth and restrained himself from grabbing her arm. 'You will do as I say.'

They had reached the path that led down the cliff. She stopped and looked up at him. 'I understood I was free to come and go as I pleased.'

'Not if you put yourself in danger.'

'I will hardly be in danger.'

'Perhaps you might recall that last time you were caught on the rocks.'

She lifted her chin. 'That was a special circumstance.'

'Was it?'

'Yes.' She turned and began picking her way down the path.

This time he did catch her arm. 'Perhaps you would allow me to assist you.'

'I think not.' She pulled her arm from his grasp and continued on down.

He stared after her, completely bemused. He had no idea what they were even arguing about. She seemed to be deliberately attempting to provoke him.

Once at the beach she marched over to a rock and sat down, proceeding to untie the laces of her half-boots. He stood in front of her. 'What do you think you are doing?' he asked softly.

She did not look up. 'Taking off my boots and stockings so I might wade.'

'So what is this all about?'

'I wish to wade.' She pulled off one boot.

'I think you are attempting to quarrel with me.'

She looked up then. 'Why would I wish to do that?'

'Perhaps you could tell me.'

'I do not wish for a quarrel. I merely wanted to go to the shore as I always do.' She looked down and pulled off her other boot.

'Chloe.'

She shot him a cool look. 'Perhaps you would look away while I take my stockings off. I do not like to be watched.'

So she was determined to ignore him. In a swift movement he was kneeling in the sand in front of her. 'Perhaps you will allow me to do it for you.' Before she could do more than gape at him, he had her foot cupped between his hands.

She gasped. 'Wh…what are you doing?'

His hand moved up her leg until he found the ribbon holding her stocking in place. He untied it and began unrolling the silky material down her slender limb. If he had hoped to quell his desire, this was hardly the way to go about it. Touching her leg filled him with all sorts of tantalizing images of slowly removing the rest of her clothing.

He finished his task and looked up at her. 'Well?'

Her eyes were wide and she looked as if she had frozen in place. 'I…I can remove my other stocking, if you please.'

'Ah, but perhaps I would like the pleasure.' At that she jerked her leg out of his reach.

'N…no.' At least some of the prickly defiance had left her, although she looked now as if he were about to ravish her.

If she knew how close he was to doing just that, she would probably flee. He rose. 'I believe I will occupy myself with the same task. Then we may both wade.' Not that anything less than a full swim would cool his lust.

She was already in the water when he joined her, the slight breeze moulding her skirts to her slim legs. Her face was lifted to the breeze, her bonnet already dangling by its ribbons down her back.

'You will ruin your skin,' he said. 'Put your bonnet on.'

'I'll only take it off for a little while. One cannot properly feel the breeze in a bonnet. I do not suppose you would understand. Men do not need to worry about such things as a complexion. Or freckles.'

'I believe we discussed this once before. Your skin is too delicate to be exposed to the elements for very long.

I would not want you to become burned, which is quite painful.' He paused. 'Besides, I like your freckles.'

'Do you? I think they are hateful.'

'Not at all. They are charming.'

She smiled, a little shyly. 'Then you will not expect me to continue to use Mrs Butler's Mustard Ointment for banishing freckles?'

'I forbid it,' he said softly. Without realising what he was doing, he had stepped closer. He drew a line across the bridge of her nose and heard her intake of breath, but she remained still. When her lips parted, he was lost.

He grasped her gently by her shoulders and then covered her mouth with his. Her lips tasted as sweet and tantalizing as he remembered, as sweet as in his dream, intoxicating him. She did not protest when he drew her closer, moulding her soft curves to his body. She shyly returned his kiss, pressing herself against him and he thought he would explode.

He pulled away, dazed. 'Chloe.'

Instead of fear, he saw that her eyes were still heavy with passion. In a sort of stupefied amazement, he realised she desired him.

'Chloe,' he said again. He reached for her, wanting to continue what they had started, but she stepped back.

He frowned. 'What is it?'

'Nothing. It is just...' She looked at him helplessly.

'Just what?' he asked softly. 'From your response to our kiss, I would say that you are not indifferent to me.'

'It is not that.' Her expression was unhappy. A wave brushed up against his legs, reminding him they still stood in the water.

'This is not the most suitable place to discuss this.' He took her hand. 'We'll sit on the rocks.'

'Perhaps we should return to the house.'

'No.' He tucked her arm in his and led her across the sand, then drew her down next to him on one of the rocks.

He turned to look at her. 'Why did you back away from me? Are you afraid of me?'

She shook her head. 'No. I do not know.' He sensed she did.

'Don't you?' He touched her cheek with his hand. 'There is nothing wrong with an attraction between husband and wife. In fact, I would say it is preferable to indifference. I am not indifferent to you. I have never been.'

She started, her eyes widening. He held her gaze. 'It is most gratifying to discover you are not indifferent to me.'

'Did…did we not agree to keep our marriage on a passionless basis?' she whispered.

He shifted closer to her. 'We also agreed we would like children. Before she left, my great-aunt again reminded me of my duty to produce an heir. There is no reason why a more intimate relationship cannot be regarded as one of the duties of our arrangement. We can keep it on a passionless basis, of course.'

'I do not think…'

'Don't think. Just regard this as one of the business arrangements.' He pulled her to him, his lips covering hers again. Her lips parted beneath his and she clung to his shoulders. His mouth moved from her lips to her neck and back to her mouth again.

He finally released her, some sort of reason penetrating his brain. Her breath came in short gasps; her expression that of a woman who had been well-kissed. And in the throes of passion whether she wanted to admit it or not.

He would not push her too far, overwhelm her as he did in the billiard room. 'I think that is enough business for now,' he said.

'I…I agree.' She did not quite meet his eyes. 'I would like to return to the house.'

'I will be delighted to escort you to the shore any time you like.'

'Oh.' Delicate colour stained her cheeks as she stood. She still looked dazed as she retrieved her stockings and half-boots.

He watched her, a surge of masculine triumph shooting through him. She was not immune to him and he planned to take full advantage of that. He would give her time, seduce her slowly so that by the time she came to his bed, she would be there willingly. Their love-making would be all the more sweet if he did not rush her too quickly.

There was no need for the marriage bed, even in a marriage of convenience, to be a duty. For either of them.

Chloe's fingers shook as she fastened her ear-ring. In a few minutes, she would descend to the drawing room and then he would escort her to the dining room for their first dinner together at Waverly. And after that…

Her legs felt weak, even thinking about this afternoon. She had no idea how it happened; one moment they were discussing freckles and then she was in his arms. Her body had responded to his and any thoughts of trying to deny her response fled. She had been utterly lost as soon as his lips found hers. Just as she had been that night in his bed.

She must find a way to tell him. Before she went to him again. For he made it very clear that he expected her to be a wife in every sense. After today she could no longer pretend a virginal fear of marriage.

He wanted an heir.

Her stomach lurched. But what was she to say to him? What if he thought she had been unfaithful? How would he ever believe that she had been with him if he had no recollection?

Perhaps, she thought desperately, he would not notice. Or perhaps if she somehow drugged him again?

But then he might not remember again, she thought rather hysterically.

She must find the right words.

Chloe put down her wine glass. She had only taken a few sips just as she had only eaten a few bites of her dinner. Not that Brandt had been anything but the perfect gentleman. He had escorted her into dinner, his touch light and impersonal. His conversation had been on topics of mutual interest, nothing that should fill her with such nervous anticipation. But his fingers brushed hers too frequently and the way he held her gaze rendered her even more uncomfortable and self-conscious than if he had been blatantly flirting with her. He was the sophisticated lover the gossips had whispered about in London. Utterly in control of what he was doing. Perfectly aware of how he affected her.

She was not certain she liked it at all.

'Chloe…' his voice held a hint of amusement '…it is time to withdraw.'

'Oh.' She rose. 'Is it? Then I will go to the drawing room.'

He stood as well. 'I will accompany you.'

'Do you not want your port or brandy or whatever else one drinks?'

'No.' His eyes strayed to her mouth. 'Not tonight.'

Her cheeks heated and she felt rather dizzy. Perhaps it was from the wine. She looked away. 'Should I go to the drawing room?'

'We both can. I rather thought we could play cards.'

Cards sounded quite benign at this moment. 'Very well.' Perhaps he did not intend to make love to her after all.

He held out his arm and she laid her hand on his coat, trying to ignore the little thrill of excitement that raced through her. She was careful to avoid touching more than his arm as they walked the short distance to the drawing room, not wanting him to think she would melt at the slightest contact.

The lamps cast a warm, intimate glow over the room. He led her to a small table near the mantelpiece. 'You can sit here while I fetch the cards.' He brushed her cheek with a careless hand.

She sat down. She was a little angry that he had changed the terms of their agreement without consulting her, but she was even more so at herself for being so weak-willed that she would tremble at his lightest touch. At least that night, he had needed her and she had participated most willingly in her seduction, but tonight, she had no sense he needed her except in the most physical way; he was the skilful predator in pursuit of a wary but naïve prey.

He returned with the cards and took the chair opposite her. He let the cards fall through his fingers. 'Do you play piquet?'

'Yes.'

'You may cut the cards and I'll deal, but first we should decide on the terms.'

'What terms?'

A slight smile touched his mouth. 'The terms. If you are the victor, then what will you claim for your prize? Or if I am, what will I claim?'

She gave him a little frown. 'In general, one plays for money.'

'That is not quite what I had in mind.'

'That is what I had in mind.'

'I would prefer higher stakes. Such as a kiss from you. But only if I win, of course.'

She refused to look away. 'Then I would like to go to the beach tomorrow. Alone.'

His eyes held hers, his expression alert. 'High stakes indeed. I do not intend to allow you to win, you know,' he said softly. 'I want my prize.' He pushed the cards towards her. 'We will play three games. Two out of three will take the prize.'

He did not intend to allow her? She was beginning to feel a little more in control with a deck of cards in her hand. She cut the deck and then passed it to him. 'I do not intend to allow you to win.'

'No?' He smiled. 'We shall see, my lady.'

She looked at her hand. It was not the most favourable, but it was not poor either. He was a formidable player, but then so was she. At least she hoped she would be. She looked up and found his eyes fixed on her face. 'Your play.'

She refused to let him interfere with her concentration, but her hand trembled a little as she declared her first cards. The slight triumph in his expression as he took the point filled her with a desire to toss her cards at him. As the game progressed and she found his eyes on her more often than not, and his hand brushed hers far too often, she suspected he intended to throw her off. She sensed he was not concentrating on the game as much as he was concentrating on her.

It made her angry. She refused to look at him the rest of the game except when necessary and forced herself to concentrate solely on her cards. When she finally reached the winning number of points, she looked up. 'My game, my lord.'

His expression was difficult to interpret. 'So it is.'

'Shall we begin the second game?'

A peculiar light leapt into his eye. 'Yes. By all means.' He cut the cards. 'Your deal.'

She dealt them, glad to see her hand no longer shook. She had removed her gloves and the light caught the sparkle of the ring he had given her. Her heart sank a little when she saw her hand of cards. It was very poor this time.

She played the best she could. This time he no longer stared at her and his focus stayed on the game. He played the winning hand and looked up. 'My game. We are even.'

'We seem to be.'

'But not for long. I intend to win this next hand.'

'So do I.'

He met her challenging gaze. 'Then let us begin.'

This time her hand was good. Very good. She kept her face expressionless, not wanting him to see her excitement. She forced herself to concentrate and this time she forgot everything but the game. As he did. For the first time that evening they were on an equal footing. When she finally but barely won, she had nearly forgotten what was at stake.

'My game.' She gave him a triumphant smile.

He looked rather stunned. 'You still have not told me where you learned to play like that. I doubt there are many men whom you could not best.'

That was a question she preferred not to answer. 'Well, I was only concerned with besting you. Tomorrow I am going to the shore.'

'Yes. You are.' He eyed her, a gleam in his eye. 'I am not finished with this, however. Now that I know what I am up against, I will be better prepared.'

She stood. 'But, please, not tonight. I would like to retire.'

He rose as well. 'Then allow me to escort you to your room.'

'I am certain I can find my way.'

'Undoubtedly, but I am equally certain that I want to escort you. It would hardly be gentlemanly of me to do otherwise.'

This time he did not take her arm. He appeared preoccupied as they climbed the stairs and then went down the hall. He stopped in front of her door. Her heart had started to thud in a most disconcerting fashion, which was ridiculous because he had lost his wager. So there would be no kiss.

He looked down at her. 'Good night, Chloe.'

'Good night.' She started to walk past him into her room, when he caught her shoulders.

'Wait,' he said. Before she could protest he had captured her mouth with his.

This kiss was hard and demanding. And brief. He released her.

She stared up at him. 'That was not fair. You lost.'

His mouth curved. 'The bet was that you would kiss me. There was nothing about me kissing you.'

'You did not specify. So that was an invalid kiss.'

His smile deepened. 'Should I take it back?' He gently brushed his fingers over her mouth in a sensuous caress. 'There. It is gone.'

'You are not playing fair,' she whispered.

His expression was unreadable. 'No. I am not playing fair at all.'

She watched him go in bewilderment. What did he mean by that remark? But she had no idea what he meant by any of it.

Chapter Fifteen

Brandt rose from the cold sea and waded towards the shore. His swim did little to dampen his thoughts or his desire to find Chloe.

Oh, as a gentleman he could not go back on his wager. But as a husband, he had wanted to forbid her to go. Force her to stay where she would be safe. He had sent one of the servants to keep a discreet eye on her and it had been all he could do to keep from following her himself.

It would only convince her that a husband and a keeper were the same. And if he intended to persuade her otherwise, he needed patience.

He looked up and saw Justin waiting for him near the rocks where he had left his clothing. 'I will own I am a trifle surprised,' Justin said as Brandt joined him. 'I would have expected that with a new bride you would find more, er…interesting ways to expend your energies.'

Brandt reached for his breeches. 'We played cards last night.' He pulled his breeches up.

'So?'

'Chloe won. So here I am.' He finished fastening his breeches and reached for his shirt. 'I've no idea why she insists on keeping her talents so well hidden. She could have made a fortune at the tables alone.'

'It is why she does not want to play. She fears she has inherited her brother's bad blood.'

'That is mad!' His hand stilled on the button.

'No more so than the notion you inherited your father's bad blood.'

Brandt's mouth tightened. 'It is not the same.'

'Isn't it?' Justin met Brandt's gaze squarely. 'Both of you fear you will discover you are like your worst relation despite all evidence to the contrary.'

'She is nothing like her brother. She is all that is good and decent...' He stopped. 'What put such a damnable notion into her head? Because she can outwit most men at the tables?'

Justin hesitated. 'There is more. Lucien taught her to play when she was young and then used her most shamefully. I promised Belle I would not betray this confidence. I suggest you ask Chloe.'

'I plan to.' He picked up his stockings and boots. 'In fact, I am going to now.'

Chloe hugged her knees to her chest. She sat on her cloak which she had spread on the sand. Despite the brilliant blue sky and the gulls circling overhead, the day lacked the lustre she had anticipated. Perhaps it was because she was tired and again felt rather unwell.

Or perhaps it was because the day did not feel right without Brandt. Last night she had wanted to prove she would not give in to him, assert her independence, but now her victory seemed rather hollow. She refused to go back to the house until the hour that she had said she would. She had seen the groom lurking about and knew that

Brandt had sent someone to watch her. She supposed she should be angry, but for some reason she felt comforted.

'Chloe.'

He had come up beside her so quietly she had not heard him. A surge of gladness swept through her. She looked up at him and the expression on his face gave her pause. As did his tousled, wet hair and damp shirt. 'Is...is something wrong?'

'You never answered my question last night. About who taught you to play cards like that,' he said quietly.

'You are here to ask me that?'

'Yes.'

She hugged her knees more tightly. 'Lucien taught me,' she said dully.

He knelt down beside her. 'Tell me what happened.'

She looked away. The words seemed to come from someone else. 'I was thirteen. He was bored one day and he thought it would be amusing to teach me some card games. I proved to have a knack for them. He began to play with me, teaching me various tricks and the logic. I suppose I was flattered because he so rarely paid me any attention. Later he had me play against his friends. I was stupid, I did not realise he was only using me. He would place bets on the game and no one thought I could possibly win. At first I enjoyed the attention; everyone was so astonished that a mere girl could play as I did. As time went on, they began to frighten me. They were often drunk and...crude.' She took a breath. 'Papa put a stop to it when Lucien took me to a tavern.'

'What happened at the tavern?'

She could not look at him. No one, not even Belle, knew about this part. 'One of his friends—he caught me in a corner and he k...kissed me. Lucien threatened to kill him.

There was a brawl and the tavern keeper's wife came in and saw me. She took me to her room and sent for Papa.'

He was silent. She tensed, waiting for his condemnation.

'Damn him.' His voice was low and cold.

'I should have known better,' she whispered. 'Papa was furious. He said I should have told him straight away what Lucien was doing. Lucien had told me that my playing would help pay his debts and that Papa should not know and it would overset Mama if she knew he was in debt again. And if Papa had discovered Mama allowed Lucien in the house, he would have been furious with her.'

'You were not to blame,' he said harshly. 'Lucien was twisted. He used anyone and anything to his advantage. My God, any man who could use a child in such a way…' he said savagely. 'To use you… And your father—he was hardly any better.'

'He said I was on my way to becoming a…a fallen woman. And a…a gamester, just like Lucien.' That had hurt most of all.

'Never.' Suddenly he pulled her against his chest, his arms around her, tight and comforting. She could not help the tears that began to fall. He held her until she no longer shook with silent sobs, his hand stroking her hair as if she were a child again.

She had no idea how long he held her; only that she did not want to leave the safety of his embrace. He finally spoke. 'We should return to the house. If you wish to.'

'Yes.' She took a deep shuddering breath.

He slowly released her. 'You will be safe with me.'

She met his eyes for the first time since she had begun her tale. The compassion and caring she saw there made her catch her breath. 'I…I know.'

'Good.' He brushed a gentle kiss across her mouth and then stood. 'Are you ready to go home?' His glance fell to her feet. 'You already have your shoes on. No bare feet today?'

'I really did not feel much like wading.'

'I see.' He helped her to her feet and retrieved her cloak. 'Put your bonnet on, then.'

She tied the ribbons, no longer seeing his admonition as control but rather caring. She felt drained and was glad to go with him in silence. Her fatigue only increased as they started up the path to the top of the cliffs. A bout of dizziness forced her to stop half-way up. She closed her eyes for a moment.

Brandt paused. 'What is wrong?'

'I just felt rather dizzy for a moment. It is nothing.'

'Do you need to sit?'

'No. I will be fine.' The dizziness had passed. She was glad to reach the top without any more bouts, but her fatigue and the heaviness in her stomach had increased.

'You are pale. Are you not well?'

'I am just rather tired, that is all.'

'You have not eaten much since you arrived at Waverly.'

'It is just everything is different. Sometimes I cannot eat when I am in a new place. I remember when I first went off to school, I scarcely ate at all for a fortnight.'

'Perhaps I should send you back to Falconcliff before you fade away.' He was teasing her, but not completely.

'No! That is, this is my home.'

'I am glad you think so,' he said softly. 'However, I am going to carry you the rest of the way.'

This time she did not protest when he scooped her up in his arms. He carried her to the drawing room and put her down on the sofa. 'I will have tea brought in, as well as cake.'

He had an implacable look in his eye that meant he

intended to override her. She was even more stunned when he came in carrying the tea tray himself. He set it down and poured her a cup, then added a small amount of sugar. He handed it to her. 'Drink this while I slice the cheese. Or would you prefer cake?'

'Brandt, you do not need to do this. I can...'

'I intend to see that you eat. Do you want the cheese or cake?'

'Cheese, I think.' Cake did not sound very appetizing.

She did not particularly want the cheese either, but under his watchful eye she managed a few bites along with some bread. The tea was almost too sweet, but she forced most of it down.

She had to admit, however, that having some food in her stomach did help. 'Thank you,' she said. 'I feel much better.'

'I hope so.' He stood looking at her. 'If you continue to feel unwell, I will send for Dr Crowley.'

'Please do not! I am fine.'

'You are to rest for the remainder of the day. Either here or in your bedchamber.'

'Here, if you please.' She did not want to go upstairs to the isolation of her bedchamber.

He hesitated. 'I have some business to attend to in my study. If you need anything, send for me.'

She resisted the urge to beg him to stay with her. 'Thank you.'

'Rest well, then.' He picked up her hand and dropped a brief kiss on her palm.

Brandt shoved the papers aside. Concentration proved impossible when his thoughts were on Chloe. And Lucien. How many other lives had Lucien poisoned with his cruel disregard for everyone in his path? He had nearly suc-

ceeded in killing Justin, and had come close to destroying
Belle. Brandt had wished Lucien to perdition then.

He now wished he had been the one responsible for
sending him there.

No wonder Chloe shied away from him, or from any
man except the comfortable Sir Preston.

He would need to prove to her that not all men were
like Lucien; he would not take advantage of her or destroy
her trust. Or overpower her with his own need. He would
give her time and he prayed that, with time, she would
come to him.

Brandt continued to treat Chloe with the same solici-
tousness he had the day on the beach. Almost as if he
feared she would break. Gone was the remote politeness
that had so irked her, but his kindness was equally bewildering. Had her confession inspired some sort of pity in
him so that he feared he would hurt her? She could think
of no way of asking him.

Three days later Emily came to call. Her face glowed
under a new poke bonnet and stylish spencer trimmed with
braid. Marriage agreed with her.

She pressed a kiss on Chloe's cheek. 'I've wanted to
call for ages, but at first Lord Salcombe was so ill, and
then we went away to Scotland and there was no time. But
I have so wished to speak to you of the night of your
betrothal ball.'

That seemed like centuries ago. 'When I left you with
Sir Preston, I had no idea that you would be locked in as
well and that you would be…be compromised.'

A little smile touched Emily's mouth. 'That was exactly
what I had hoped.'

'You wished to be compromised?'

'Yes. Oh, at first I was furious with Lady Kentworth for

locking you in with Preston and wanted to make certain her plan for discovering you two together would be thwarted. I planned to have the three of us go back through the tunnel and into the library. But then, she would only come up with another scheme to interfere, and so I decided it would be best if she discovered Preston with another woman. Then we would need to be married straight away.'

'I rather thought you had decided against Sir Preston,' Chloe said slowly.

'Oh, no. I merely wanted to teach him a lesson. The only difficult part was keeping him from insisting we follow you through the tunnel. He wished to be the gentleman and protect my reputation.' Again that little smile. 'In the end, I distracted him quite nicely. I had no idea how enjoyable it would be to seduce a man.'

'You seduced Sir Preston?'

'I did not mean to. I merely meant to kiss him, but then other things followed and it seemed quite impossible to stop. And I did not want to.'

Emily laughed at Chloe's expression. 'Are you shocked? I would think after more than a month of marriage you would realise how enjoyable seducing one's husband is. They are so wholly in one's power. But perhaps you have not yet attempted to do so with Lord Salcombe. He seems rather masterful, but I quite imagine he would be completely at your feet if you were to pursue him.'

Chloe should be shocked, but her desire to know more overrode any delicacy of feeling she might display. 'Is it something women do? It is not considered vulgar?'

'By whom? Certainly Preston does not. I doubt if your husband would either. Not the way he looks at you.'

'Emily!' This time her cheeks heated.

'Surely you have noticed! Very well, I will not tease you. There is something else I came to say. I hope you

will forgive me for locking the door to the library after
Lord Salcombe went to find you.' She looked truly contrite.

'Why did you do that?'

'I did not want anyone to discover the door in the fireplace was open and then close it. But more than that I...I
had some thought that if you and Lord Salcombe were
compromised that you would marry sooner and Lady Kentworth would have no more reason to interfere.' She hesitated. 'I had no idea that you would take the wrong path
and become wet and chilled. Or that Lord Salcombe would
dash off to London when he was ill as well. I hope you
will forgive me.'

She looked so uncertain that Chloe did not have the
heart to be angry. If she was. 'I imagine you only wanted
to do what was best. Of course I will forgive you.'

'You are very kind. I am so glad we will be neighbours.'
She gave Chloe an impulsive hug.

She sat back. 'There is one more thing. We are having
a small dinner at Martin Woods. I would like it very much
if you and Lord Salcombe would come. If I am not too
presumptuous now that you are a Vicountess.'

'Of course you are not. I would be more than delighted
to come. I am certain Brandt would as well.'

'I must go.' Emily rose and then hesitated. 'I have one
more thing to tell you. I have not told anyone yet except
for Mama who guessed right away. I...I am increasing.'
She looked shy and pleased all at once.

Chloe fought down the stab of envy that shot through
her. 'How wonderful! But you have not yet told Sir Preston?'

'No, I wished to be certain before I did, but Mama assures me that I show all the signs.'

'I hope you do not feel too horribly unwell. I remember how ill poor Belle was with Julian.'

'No, I do not feel very ill at all. Just sometimes in the morning, but as soon as I eat I am fine. The worst, I suppose, is that I am so horribly fatigued. I wish to lie down and sleep almost all the time which is not like me at all! But Mama assures me that will pass.'

'And it will be worth everything when you have your baby,' Chloe said. She rose and embraced Emily one more time and then Emily was gone.

Chloe sat back down, still stunned by Emily's visit. Most of all, she was shocked that Emily could speak so lightly about seducing Sir Preston. And before they were married.

Perhaps, then, her own lack of control had not been so unnatural; perhaps she was not the fallen woman her father had predicted she would become. And, perhaps, all the power in their marriage did not lie so completely with Brandt after all.

She wondered what he would do if she attempted to seduce him. Or if she told him she wanted a baby. Would his eyes darken in that way they did when he desired her? Or would he back away as if he feared he would hurt her?

She rose. Really, she could not sit here and brood in such a way. Brandt had gone off to look at a fence in need of repair and so she was quite alone except for the servants. Perhaps she should stroll to the garden and see the most recent changes. Even that seemed too much effort. Of late, she hardly felt like doing much but sleep.

Rather like Emily.

Her heart leapt to her throat as a horrid premonition seized her. She could not possibly be with child. Surely not after one night. She was tired, to be sure, and had not felt well, but in the past few days she had been a little

better. She had not had any more bouts of dizziness and
she was eating more. And certainly she was not nearly as
ill as Belle had been.

She should have asked Emily about her other symptoms.
What else did one look for? If only she could ask Belle.
But then Belle would wonder why she asked. What if she
said something to Brandt?

And whatever would she tell him?

No, it was quite impossible.

Chapter Sixteen

Madame Dupont entered the small dressing room just as her assistant finished pinning the hem of Chloe's gown. 'How very charming! The colour, it is complimentary to your complexion.' She straightened the bodice a little. 'Very good, the bodice is not so very tight, which you will find most necessary very soon.' She glanced at Chloe's face, her own sympathetic. 'You must sit for a little while before Ruth helps you change. Always, at first, it is difficult, but it is said to be a most promising sign.'

'What is a good sign?' Chloe had no idea what Madame was talking about. She sank into the chair in one corner of the dressing room. She had begun to feel light-headed and the longer she stood while the little assistant fitted the gown, the more dizzy and sick she felt. The room seemed too hot and she wished she had not let Belle convince her that a new gown was quite necessary for her first public appearance as Lady Salcombe.

'The sickness. It means the child will be healthy.'

Chloe felt the colour drain from her face. She was vaguely aware of the shop bell ringing. 'The child?'

Madame's own face changed. She motioned Ruth to leave the room before kneeling next to Chloe and taking her hand. 'My dear, are you not *enceinte*? Perhaps I should not have said anything but the paleness, the dizziness— how well I remember them from my own confinements.'

'I…I cannot be.' She heard Ruth greet the new customer, vaguely recognising the newcomer's voice.

'I see. You did not suspect. Tell me, when did you last have your courses?'

She could not think for a moment. Not since she had been at Waverly. Or since Brandt's illness. Time had blurred together so much that she had not even considered them. 'I do not know. It has been more than a month. Perhaps nearly two.'

'Then I would suspect you are with child.' Madame squeezed Chloe's hand. 'There is no need to look so. Your husband will be pleased, will he not? He is fond of children. I see him with Lady Haversham's little ones and with his nephew, and I think he must have his own.'

'Yes, he…he will be pleased.' She felt as if someone had dealt her a severe blow. 'I pray you will not say anything to anyone, not even to the Duchess. I wish to tell her…him myself.'

'Of course.' She released Chloe's hand and rose. 'I will send Ruth in now. Do not worry yourself. You are young and strong and you will have a fine, healthy child.'

She was hardly aware of Ruth's helping her change from the gown into her walking dress. Ruth's light chatter fell around her ears and she had no idea what Ruth spoke about, until she said, 'You will not be wanting these corsets soon. They will not be good for the child.'

'No, of…of course.'

She stepped through the curtain, expecting to see Belle Instead, she nearly stumbled over Lady Kentworth, who was thumbing through the pages of a lady's journal. 'I…I beg your pardon.'

'Ah, Lady Salcombe. How delightful to see you.' Her gaze travelled over Chloe's face. 'I understand my daughter-in-law called on you. Such a delightful girl.' She moved a little closer to Chloe. 'And already we have happy news, very happy news. I trust we will soon hear equally happy news from Waverly, will we not?'

'If you will pardon me.' She stepped around Lady Kentworth, wanting to leave her as quickly as possible.

She was shaking as she stepped into the street. What had Lady Kentworth heard? She tried to think when Lady Kentworth had entered. Surely she would not have known Chloe was there. Madame's voice had not been loud, nor had Ruth's. Or had she been merely boasting of her own coming grandchild while at the same time gloating over Chloe's lack of similar news?

She must find Belle and then go home. She needed to be by herself, try to think of what she should do. What she would say to Brandt. Belle was at the milliner's. She would find her there. She started to walk and realised she was going in the wrong direction. She stood there for a moment and then turned. She smashed into a solid, male figure.

'I am sorry.'

'There is no need to apologise. You may throw yourself into my arms any time you want.'

She looked up. Brandt had that slight smile at his mouth. He looked so familiar and welcome and safe. She opened her mouth to greet him and instead burst into tears.

The smile left his face. 'Chloe? What is it?'

'N…nothing. I…I just want to go home.'

He caught her to him. 'Of course. My carriage is just around the corner.' He somehow produced a handkerchief. 'Take this.'

She nodded and sniffed. He gently took her arm and led

her to the carriage. He helped her in and peered in at her, his face still worried. 'Where is Belle? I should send her a message.'

'At the…the milliner's.'

He nodded and disappeared. She sunk back into the cushions. On top of everything else, she had just humiliated herself by bursting into tears in public in front of him. His kindness made her want to weep.

But she wanted to cry even more at the thought of losing him when she told him she was with child.

Brandt watched his wife as she talked to Marguerite on the other side of the Kentworths' drawing room. She looked lovely in the dark green silk, her auburn hair gleaming in the candlelight, but she lacked the quiet animation he had always noticed about her in company. Instead, her smile looked forced.

As it had for days now. Ever since she had burst into tears in the middle of the village, she had become increasingly preoccupied and jumpy. When he had suggested that he send for Dr Crowley, she had looked terrified and then said it was not necessary and she would not see him even if he was sent for. Brandt was no match for such adamant refusal, but when he found her eyes fixed on him with a sort of sadness, he began to think she had contracted a fatal illness and wondered if he should contact Dr Crowley after all.

But it was the kisses that troubled him the most. Determined to be patient and gentle, he had limited himself to nothing more than restrained kisses. Kisses she returned with a fervour bordering on desperation, almost as if she were saying goodbye. When he tried to question her, she assured him it was nothing, and once or twice had looked so much on edge that he had not pushed her further.

He had no idea if she was going mad. Or if he was.

'I doubt if she will disappear if you take your eyes from her,' Justin said sardonically, appearing next to him.

'I am beginning to think she is about to disappear, whether I watch her or not.'

He could feel his cousin's eyes on him. 'What does that mean?'

He shrugged, suddenly too tired to dissemble. 'She has little appetite, droops with fatigue after the least exertion and is so pale at times I fear she is about to swoon. And she bursts into tears at the least provocation. I suggested that perhaps she should return to Falconcliff and she looked as if I had suggested imprisonment. I've not the damnedest idea what to do.'

'Probably not much. I've no doubt the problem will resolve itself.'

He finally looked at his cousin. 'What the devil does that mean?'

'Have you ever considered that she might be pregnant?'

For a moment, he thought he was the one who was about to swoon. 'Impossible.'

'Why not? It is rather to be expected under the circumstances.' Justin eyed him. 'The symptoms sound quite familiar, particularly the tears. In fact, Belle had some idea that might be the case, but did not want to say anything until Chloe did. But perhaps we are more aware of such things since Belle seems to be once again afflicted with the same, er…illness.'

In a sort of daze he found himself congratulating his cousin. He still felt stupefied, as if he had been struck or drugged. He excused himself from Justin. It was impossible; she would not be unfaithful to him; and he had not…for the second time that night he felt almost dizzy.

The dream.

It had not been a dream after all.

'Ah, Lord Salcombe.'

Lady Kentworth stood in front of him. 'You appear nearly as unwell as your wife.'

'I've no idea what you refer to. If you will excuse me,' he said curtly.

She did not move. 'I doubt very much you both are suffering from the same affliction.'

He stared at her. 'I trust you will curtail your speculations.'

Her smile was malicious. 'I fear it is too late since the milliner's assistant has informed half a dozen people already that an interesting event will be occurring at Waverly.'

He took a step towards her, barely containing the urge to mow her down. She backed away.

He found Chloe sitting in a chair in one corner. She was drooping again. Why had he not guessed? He remembered Belle's pregnancy very well—she had had the same pale, wilting look, but he would have considered a pregnancy so improbable he never thought of it.

He wanted to demand why she hadn't told him about that night, upbraid her for lying to him. But when she looked up at him, her eyes filled with weariness and that same sadness, he wanted to take her into his arms. 'We need to leave,' he said.

'Is something wrong?'

He held out his hand and helped her to her feet. 'I need to talk to you, but I do not want to do it here. I will send for the carriage and make your excuses to Emily.'

He saw the apprehension in her eyes. 'There is no need to look like that,' he said roughly. He tightened his grip on her hand.

She nodded. She looked as dazed as he felt as they took

their leave of their host and hostesses. He said nothing on the journey home, but he could not keep his eyes from her face. His thoughts were in turmoil, angry with himself, angry with her, but also the faint beginnings of joy that she possibly carried his child. Their child.

She made no protest as he led her upstairs and then to the small room off his bedchamber that he was using as a study until the downstairs room was repaired. A lamp had been lit on the desk. He closed the door behind them and leaned against it. In the shadows, her face looked drawn and fearful. 'Sit down, Chloe.'

She took the chair he indicated and perched on the edge, her eyes fixed on his face. He took a deep breath. 'Tell me, Chloe, are you with child? My child?'

Chapter Seventeen

The blood pounded in her ears. At the same time she dimly registered he had claimed the child as his. She heard herself whispering, 'Yes. I…I think so.' She forced herself to look at him, waited for the loathing and the fury she knew was to come.

Instead there was silence. His eyes were still on her. 'That night was not a dream, then,' he finally asked.

'No.'

'Why did you not tell me?'

'I did not know how. When you did not say anything, I thought that you did not remember.' She clasped her hands together to keep them from trembling.

'I remembered. I did not know if it was a dream. I tried to ask if you had been there but Mrs Keith said you did not sit with me that night. And when I saw you, you were so calm—' He broke off. 'How could you be after I had seduced you, taken your innocence and used you in the most despicable way and then had not the decency to even recall it?'

'It was not like that. You did not seduce me. You asked me to kiss you and I did. I went to you willingly.'

'You had no idea what you were doing. You were an

innocent. I doubt if even now you realise how mad you drive me, how the lightest touch of your fingers or even the scent of you can make me want to pull you down next to me so I might take you the same way I did that night. How could you know what a kiss would do? Especially to a man who had lost all reason. You were at my mercy.'

'It was not like that.' She could not bear the self-recrimination in his voice. 'You asked me if I wanted to stop but I said no. I…I was not so naïve that I did not know what would happen. I begged you to go on.'

'Why? Why would you allow me to use you in such a way?'

'Because you were alive. And you needed me.'

'I needed you,' he repeated. 'Oh, I needed you, but not to sacrifice your virginity while I was half out of my mind as some sort of reward for living.'

She flinched. 'You do not understand. I needed you as well. I…I wanted you.'

She had no idea if he believed her or not. Or if he even comprehended what she had said. He was silent, staring out of the window at the night. She waited until he finally turned. 'Did I hurt you?'

'No. You did not hurt me.' She asked, hesitatingly, 'Do you remember anything at all?'

'I have no idea if what I remembered was reality. Or what I wished.'

'You were…kind.'

An ironic smile touched his mouth. 'So I should salve my conscience with that? I wonder, however, how you have endured my touch since then.'

She rose and went to his side. 'I bear as much responsibility as you. How could I blame you when I was so certain I was to blame? If you must know, I have considered myself the worst sort of seductress, a wanton creature who would take advantage of a helpless man. The sort of creature my father feared I was. I have felt such a fraud; I did not know what I could possibly say to you. And since I have thought that I might be with child, I have been so terrified. So terrified that you would think I...I was unfaithful.'

'I would never think you unfaithful. Or a fraud,' he said quietly. He looked down at her. 'Perhaps neither one of us is exactly what we thought we were.'

'Or perhaps we have changed.'

'Or perhaps that. I know I have.' He looked away for a moment. 'Do you regret the child?' he asked carefully as if he feared her answer.

'Oh, no, never that!' Without thinking, she caught his hand. 'I want this child so very, very much. You cannot imagine how much. I pray you will never think that!'

'But you have not been happy.'

'Only because I thought you would send me away once I had told you.' She dropped his hand. 'I...I will quite understand if you decide to.'

He stared at her and then with a groan swept her into his arms. 'That is the most damnably irrational thought you have had yet,' he said, his voice thick. His arms tightened around her. 'You are carrying my child, our child, and if you think I mean to let you go, you are mad.'

She wrapped her arms around him, reveling in the comfort of his embrace, wonder and relief flooding her with warmth. They stood together in the moonlight, until he finally slackened his hold. 'You must rest. I will warn you, I intend to play the heavy-handed husband, overseeing every aspect of your confinement.'

'I will try not to protest too much.'

'I am changing the terms of our marriage as well. I no longer wish for an impersonal, passionless marriage. I will do everything in my power to convince you that is what you want as well.'

She looked up at him. 'You do not need to convince me. I…I want the same thing.'

His eyes darkened and then his mouth was on hers in a kiss she returned with equal passion. He finally lifted his head. 'We must stop. Or you will be in my bed.'

'I…I would not mind,' she whispered.

The flare of hot desire made her legs quake. 'But the baby,' he said.

'On our wedding day, Belle spoke to me of the marriage bed.' She could feel the heat rise in her cheeks. 'She said that even when one was in…increasing it was still possible to…to be together with one's husband.'

'But you are not well.'

She rose up on her toes and put her arms around his neck drawing his head towards her. 'I am certain I will feel much better if you will…will make love to me.' Thank goodness for the darkness, for her face must be the colour of her hair.

The flickering flame in his eyes burst into searing fire. His mouth was on hers in a demanding, possessive kiss as if he had thirsted for a long time. She clung to him as he lifted her up and carried her to his bed, his mouth still on hers. He lowered her gently down and then was beside her, touching her, kissing her, murmuring endearments. Her body was on exquisite fire and her last thought before she was completely consumed was that Emily had been right after all.

He stirred, not certain he wanted to awake fully in case last night had only been a dream again, but the soft warmth of her body curled against him was very real. He turned on his side, cradling her against him, his hand clasped over the soft, slightly rounded stomach that would soon be swollen with their child. He closed his eyes, the image making him hard with desire. He was going to have a hell of a time keeping from making love to her a thousand times a day, but until Dr Crowley saw her, he would take no risks.

He could not help brushing his lips over the back of her neck. He would never tire of exploring her, touching her. Or waking with her.

She turned a little and then opened her eyes. They were heavy with sleep, but a soft smile curved her mouth. 'It was not a dream, then,' she murmured.

'No, not a dream. Reality. Our reality.' He stroked her cheek. 'I hope it was much more satisfactory for you than the first time.'

Soft colour stole into her cheeks. 'Yes.'

He looked at her sweet face. 'I still regret that I did not give you all the tenderness and consideration you deserved. I swear I will make it up to you.'

'But you do not need to. I do not regret that night. For there is the baby.' She hesitated and said a little shyly, 'I realised that night that I…I loved you.'

'You love me?'

'I hope you do not mind.' She looked uncertain.

'Mind?' He wanted to fall at her feet. 'Chloe, I…' He stopped and gave a strangled laugh. 'I think I have loved you from the moment I first saw you. When you threatened to run Justin through if he harmed Belle. I had not dared to hope that you might love me in return, but I hoped in time you might need me as much as I need you.' He cupped her face. 'For I need you, not just in my bed, but in every way possible. Your lovely face, your sweet smile, your loyalty to those you love, even such things as your going bare-foot at every possible opportunity. I need all of that.'

The love and wonder in her eyes filled him with gratitude. 'You were always so self-sufficient and always coming to my rescue. I never thought that you might need me. Or...' she hesitated '...that I would need you.'

'We have changed. Both of us.' He brushed a kiss across her forehead and then pulled her more firmly into his arms. 'Right now, I plan to fulfil our most elemental needs. Until Dr Crowley sees you, however, I do not want to take any risks. But there are other ways to fulfil one's needs.' His hand stroked the silky skin of her leg. 'I love you, Chloe.'

'Brandt,' she said, but her eyes were already clouding with desire. She drew him into her embrace and managed to whisper, 'I love you,' before they were lost to everything but each other.

* * * * *

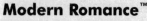

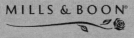

MILLS & BOON®

Live the emotion

Historical Romance™

THE EARL'S INTENDED WIFE
by Louise Allen

Hebe Carlton had no idea of her own charm until
Major Alex Beresford arrived on Malta. His attentions made
her blossom, and her stepmother had hopes of a wedding…
Then a letter arrived – the proposal of marriage Alex had
made to another before ever meeting Hebe had been accepted.
He should be happy…

Regency

A HASTY BETROTHAL by Dorothy Elbury

When Robert, Viscount Sandford, takes Harriet Cordell as his
betrothed it is purely an act of convenience – and most definitely
short term! But a dramatic series of events – including Harriet's
sudden kidnap – force Robert to admit that their hasty betrothal
might need to become much more permanent…

Regency

BORDER BRIDE by Deborah Hale

12th century England

Con ap Ifan had returned – a brave and tested warrior. But
Enid of Glyneira would not let herself be impressed. No
stolen kisses or honeyed promises would tempt her to
abandon hearth, home and betrothed – not even from the
father of her cherished first-born son…

On sale 5th March 2004

*Available at most branches of WHSmith, Tesco, Martins, Borders,
Eason, Sainsbury's and all good paperback bookshops.*

0204/04

2 Books
and a surprise gift!

We would like to take this opportunity to thank you for reading this Mills & Boon® book by offering you the chance to take TWO more specially selected titles from the Historical Romance™ series absolutely FREE! We're also making this offer to introduce you to the benefits of the Reader Service™ —

★ FREE home delivery
★ FREE gifts and competitions
★ FREE monthly Newsletter
★ Books available before they're in the shops
★ Exclusive Reader Service discount

Accepting these FREE books and gift places you under no obligation to buy; you may cancel at any time, even after receiving your free shipment. Simply complete your details below and return the entire page to the address below. **You don't even need a stamp!**

YES! Please send me 2 free Historical Romance books and a surprise gift. I understand that unless you hear from me, I will receive 4 superb new titles every month for just £3.49 each, postage and packing free. I am under no obligation to purchase any books and may cancel my subscription at any time. The free books and gift will be mine to keep in any case.

H4ZEE

Ms/Mrs/Miss/Mr ....Initials.................................
BLOCK CAPITALS PLEASE

Surname..

Address...

....

....Postcode ....

Send this whole page to:
UK: The Reader Service, FREEPOST CN81, Croydon, CR9 3WZ
EIRE: The Reader Service, PO Box 4546, Kilcock, County Kildare (stamp required)